PRAISE FOR *RETURN TO HARDSCRABBLE ROAD*

"George Weinstein is a helluva writer. With dialogue that rings as true as the spoken word and a rugged landscape one can almost taste, he delivers a wild ride through family devotion and a coming-of-age journey. In this sequel, Roger MacLeod and his brothers face a new threat and must become men of integrity and wisdom while doing everything they can to save their family and land. Heart thumping, you will turn the page faster than you can read. Atmospheric, intense and beautiful, the MacLeod legacy flourishes in *Return to Hardscrabble Road*."

—PATTI CALLAHAN HENRY,
New York Times bestselling author of *Surviving Savannah*, *Once Upon a Wardrobe*, and *Becoming Mrs. Lewis*

"Classic Southern Gothic meets classic George Weinstein in this rip-roaring adventure. Buckle up for a wild ride with old friends and hang on tight."

—LYNN CULLEN,
bestselling author of *The Woman with the Cure* and *Mrs. Poe*

"With crackling dialogue, hilarious plot twists, and unforgettable characters, *Return to Hardscrabble Road* is a joy to read. George Weinstein has nailed it again, and his rambunctious crowd entertains with his fine writing and sharp eye for detail. You will love this book."

—Philip Lee Williams,
member, Georgia Writers Hall of Fame

"In *Return to Hardscrabble Road*, Weinstein transports us to another time in a gripping tale of three brothers who return home after WWII to rural Georgia in the wake of their father's murder. It's both a compelling mystery and a heartfelt story about family. Once in a great while a novel grabs you and won't let go long after you turn the last page. This one of those novels."

—Alex Finlay,
bestselling author of *Every Last Fear* and *The Night Shift*

"Fans of George Weinstein have waited, breathlessly, for him to *Return to Hardscrabble Road*. In this unforgettable novel, Weinstein allows us to peer through the rural ramshackle windows of the MacLeod home. Readers have missed these flawed and beautiful souls, folks who make the South sing in all her dysfunctional glory. In *Return to Hardscrabble Road*, Weinstein writes with a steady hand and a keen eye to detail, penning a strong plot with a family of rambunctious rabble-rousers. Weinstein creates characters we long to know more about. This is his talent, his gift to us all. This novel, along with *Hardscrabble Road*, will stay with you a long time."

—Renea Winchester,
internationally acclaimed author of *Outbound Train*
(*De l'autre côté des rails*)

"With *Return to Hardscrabble Road*, bestselling author George Weinstein gives us a brilliantly crafted South Georgia tale of murder, heartbreak, revenge, and redemption—a story that ripples across the pages like a bolt of heat lightning. Weinstein once again displays his gift for creating unforgettable characters, complete with superb dialogue, this time in a 1947 New Year's Day setting amongst a thoroughly dysfunctional backwoods family. Gird yourself, for there's gonna be all sorts of hell to pay."

—Jedwin Smith,
author of *I AM ISRAEL* and
A Marine and a Journalist Walk into a Bar

"Once I left the pages of *Hardscrabble Road* behind, I couldn't wait to get back there. George Weinstein's *Return to Hardscrabble Road* is all I anticipated. And more. It felt good to reconnect with this story of the people and atmosphere of the rural South. Weinstein has created characters that I would know if they passed me on the street. *Return to Hardscrabble Road* reveals the truth that it's only when we leave home do we understand the lessons our childhood taught us."

—Michael Buchanan,
author/screenwriter of the award-winning
The Fat Boy Chronicles and coauthor of *Beneath the Gumbo Limbo Tree* and *Stealing First: The Teddy Kremer Story*

Return to Hardscrabble Road

Share Your Thoughts

Want to help make *Return to Hardscrabble Road* a bestselling novel? Consider leaving an honest review of this book on Goodreads, on your personal author website or blog, and anywhere else readers go for recommendations. It's our priority at SFK Press to publish books for readers to enjoy, and our authors appreciate and value your feedback.

Our Southern Fried Guarantee

If you wouldn't enthusiastically recommend one of our books with a 4- or 5-star rating to a friend, then the next story is on us. We believe that much in the stories we're telling. Simply email us at pr@sfkmultimedia.com.

SFK
PRESS

Romica -
I hope the Return is worth the trip!

RETURN TO HARDSCRABBLE ROAD

A NOVEL

GEORGE WEINSTEIN

Published by

Southern Fried Karma, LLC
Atlanta, GA
sfkpress.com

Books are available in quantity for promotional or premium use.
For information, email southernfriedkarma@gmail.com.

ISBN: 978-1-970137-56-9
eISBN: 978-1-970137-26-2

Library of Congress Control Number available upon request

Line editing, proofreading, book design, and ebook converstion provided by Indigo: Editing, Design, and More:
Line editor: Kristen Hall-Geisler
Proofreader: Bailey Potter
Cover design and interior layout: Olivia M. Hammerman
Ebook conversion: Vinnie Kinsella

Printed in the United States of America

For Kim,

who saved me when I was at my own crossroads and taught me that love is indeed lovelier the second time around.

CHAPTER 1

I FOUND MAMA WAITING FOR ME IN THE KITCHEN. HER BLONDE, shoulder-length hair, always a little wild, seemed neglected instead of carefree, with more silver woven through it than I remembered. Her slim face looked gaunt, dark eyes flinty. The blue-checked gingham apron she always wore while doing chores showed reddish-brown splotches of food, but so did the sleeves of her housedress, which had been stitched from daisy-patterned flour sacks, as if she'd stopped giving a damn about her clothes.

On closer inspection, the stains looked a lot like blood spatter, such as someone might get firing .38 caliber bullets from a Colt revolver into Papa at close range. Six times. And the apron pocket in front sagged as if it might contain that murder weapon, which he used to keep snug in his waistband during my childhood.

"Hey," I said. I draped my greatcoat on the kitchen table and set the Army Air Forces cap atop it. They matched the olive drabs I'd hitchhiked in from the Colquitt, Georgia, bus station. Dropping onto the bench on one side of the splintery table, I realized I'd automatically chosen the spot Papa had assigned me when I was a kid.

Mama sat across from me. "Only two letters since you left?" Her voice hadn't softened a lick.

"You didn't write back after either of them."

"I been busy." She waved a hand in the general direction of the kitchen, which looked and smelled the same, yet different, from almost a year ago.

Everything seemed smaller, but thick cobwebs still coated the rafters, where the latest generation of spiders said grace and devoured whatever flew their way. A bare electric bulb dangled above us now instead of the kerosene lantern that had seemed to create more shadows than light. The same old stove put out welcomed heat on this New Year's Day of 1947, but all I smelled was burning wood without the usual accompanying aroma of cornbread baking in Mama's cast-iron skillet.

My finger traced familiar patterns in the scarred and pitted table with gaps between the slats. As a boy, I once knocked over a glass and sent well water streaming between those spaces and onto Papa's creased slacks. My jaw tightened as I recalled the crack of his backhand that had knocked me to the plank floor. After I had staggered back to the bench, he'd done it again, even harder. Now Papa was dead, shot to pieces, and everybody knew Mama had ended him.

Though desperate to ask her about that—I'd thought of little else during my journey home—her haggard appearance made me hesitate. I didn't want to kick her while she was down.

In one respect, I felt grateful for his murder, because if anyone deserved killing, he did. But I was also horrified by the brutal violence that apparently ran in both sides of the family. I blurted, "How'd it feel, pulling that trigger over and over again?"

"What're you going on about, Bud?"

"I prefer my real name now. Shooting Papa—how'd it make you feel?"

"Well, *Roger*, who said I shot that sonofabitch?"

I snorted. "Everybody."

"You been in San Antone the better part of a year at that Lack of Land place—"

"It's called Lackland."

"That don't make no never mind to me. How can you know what *anybody* round these parts is saying, let alone *everybody*?"

I indicated the port-wine stain that colored the upper quarter of my face like a clock shaded crimson from nine to noon. "With this birthmark, folks recognize me straight off, and they seem to like talking about the MacLeod…history."

"Meaning what?"

"Papa shooting you at the Cottontail Café. Him marrying the Ramsey widow and overseeing her sawmill operations."

She grunted. "Not that he'd bothered to tell me he got a judge to divorce us."

And not that Mama had bothered to let their marriage get in the way of her own countless affairs. Just like him. I'd had it out with her a few years before over her promiscuity—which, among other results, had produced me—and I couldn't stomach another go-round. Instead I said, "They also like talking about his murder in that same sawmill. And your name comes up a lot."

"Aye God, they don't know pea turkey."

Her hands closed into fists on the worn tabletop. Like her face, they also looked thinner. I asked about the other thing heavy on my mind. "Mama, how are you making ends meet?"

"I got my ways. Don't you worry about me none."

The laughter of my two brothers echoed down the hall from the front porch. We had telegrammed each other after my oldest brother, Jay, received news of Papa's death. It provided the perfect excuse for emergency leave so we could reunite here, with the military paying for our travel to the Colquitt bus station and back to our duty stations. I swallowed my reply, swung my legs over the bench, and hurried to greet them.

Twenty-year-old Jay pushed the door open and held out his hand to usher in Chet, eighteen—a year older than me. I hadn't seen either in a long time. Both wore their Army uniforms, military regulations be damned. They must've deduced, as I had, that people were happy to pick up hitchhiking soldiers. With World War II still fresh in everybody's mind, it helped folks show their patriotism.

Jay had made sergeant, while Chet remained a private first class, same as I was in the Army Air Forces. I'd lied about my age to enlist in 1946, and now, for once, he didn't outrank me. We had all traveled light; their green duffels joined my knapsack on the wood plank floor of the front room. It was the same spot where the three of us had been forced to share the one lumpy feather mattress growing up, with them along the edges and me lying in the middle in the opposite direction, keeping their feet company.

They'd put on some much-needed weight in the service. No more having to divide a few wormy tomatoes, a round of fly-specked cornbread, and a handful of butter beans among six people, with Papa getting the lion's share.

Jay had grown tall and become a man after two years in the military, during and after the war. Like many soldiers, he smelled of cigarette smoke; it made him seem even older and more worldly. Chet was a gnat's eyebrow shorter and as handsome as ever, boasting even thicker muscles, as if the Army had decided to make a weapon of him.

Compared with either of them, I still looked like a kid.

Chet gave my uniform a once-over. "I thought you were too good for us Army dogfaces and decided to be a flyboy instead."

"We've got the same outfit as you for just a while longer. Rumor is, they'll create a whole new branch this year called the Air Force and give us nicer duds."

Ever the peacemaker, Jay said, "I wouldn't care if you became a swabbie or a jarhead neither. We're all battling on the same side—"

"Us against the world," Chet and I finished for him.

Jay put his long arms around our shoulders. "Fellas, I wish we'd been born sooner. With all three of us in the fight, we could've ended the war before it really got going. If that ain't the God's honest truth, then grits ain't groceries."

Chet reached behind him and pounded a granite fist between my shoulder blades. "Speaking of the war, we went by the Kraut POW camp, Roger. Looks like you didn't manage to free the entire Afrika Korps."

"Just Hermann. He and Cecilia sent me a sweet Christmas card. She's expecting."

Jay released us and looked at his high-gloss shoes, which he'd somehow managed to keep clean despite the dusty roads. "Um, any word about her big sister?"

"Nothing but sad news. Geneva lost her husband and kids to polio over a year ago. Her parents have been trying to set her up with someone new, but nobody appeals to her."

He nodded. "Maybe she'll give me a shot. What's the latest with you and Rienzi?"

From my breast pocket, I removed the monochrome photo of us arm in arm, posing in front of the Alamo.

Chet glanced at the snapshot before passing it to Jay. "Don't you and Tokyo Rose know we lost that battle?"

"But we won the war. And she's only half-Japanese, on her mother's side."

Jay returned the photo to me. He winked and asked, "Which side is the better smoocher?"

Blushing, I slid the picture back in my pocket while savoring the memory of her goodbye kiss.

Chet said, "I reckon she can still throw you across a room if you get too fresh."

He was right, but I wouldn't give him the satisfaction. Mindful of how quickly I'd lapsed into their slow drawl, the speech patterns of home, I said with my best schoolhouse diction, "Sir, I was raised to be a perfect gentleman."

"By who?" Chet set off down the hall. "Ain't no gentleman or lady did the raising in this hellhole. Hey, Mama!"

"Don't you *hey* me, boy," she said from the kitchen. "You and Roger couldn't be bothered to give me a proper goodbye and don't have the manners for a decent hello."

Jay and I followed him, my oldest brother saying, "That's right, Mama. If the Army catches wind, they might be put in the stockade as a lesson to the other ingrates." He kissed her cheek and hugged her.

She rose onto her shoe tips and glared at me and Chet over his shoulder. "Now this is the way a son's supposed to reunite with his poor old mother."

I couldn't meet the challenge in her eyes. As ever, I envied Jay's ability to always be kind to someone who'd made our lives even worse. If Papa was the tornado that tore through every day of our childhood, Mama had chosen, as often as not, to push us into the path of that twister instead of pulling us to safety. Maybe just to see what would happen.

Still, a boy coming home after so many months away should've greeted his mother properly rather than cross swords with her, as I'd done.

Chet pursed his lips like he wanted to spit. "Now that Papa's out of the way," he said to her, "who's next on your hit list? More important, when's supper?"

She let go of Jay and sidestepped him to face Chet. "I was hoping we'd go to town, seeing as how all y'all is on Uncle Sam's payroll."

"Just like the old days," Chet snapped, giving voice to my thoughts. "Wanting to wring every last cent outta us."

"Aye God, why'd you bother coming back here?"

Outside, somebody stumbled up the back porch steps. The door opened. Our twenty-two-year-old sister, Darlene, back from Atlanta and remarried yet again, shuffled in. The left side of her face was swollen and purplish, the eye there blackened, her blonde hair matted with dirt. Her arms crossed and hovered above her sides as if shielding her ribs while being afraid to touch them.

Jay approached her. She flinched and said through split lips, "No hugs. Please."

She had a gap on the left side of her mouth where two teeth should've been.

CHAPTER 2

I SAID, "I'LL GET SOME ICE," AND HURRIED ONTO THE BACK PORCH. A burlap sack covered what remained of a twenty-five-pound ice block in its battered pine chest. I worked at chipping off a chunk with the rusty pick, calling through the open door, "Your new husband do this?"

Chet snarled, "Mama, if you used up all the bullets on Papa, I'll just have to stomp Wyatt Weaver to death instead."

"Wait," Darlene said. "A woman done it, not Wyatt. In my front yard. Punched and kicked me." She sobbed and then groaned as fresh pain must've seized her. "The man with her just stood by, watching. Never seen either of them before."

Back inside, I accepted a clean hankie from Jay and tied the four corners together to make an ice pack. We led her to a bench at the kitchen table—the spot where she'd always sat as a girl—and eased her onto it.

Mama said, "Put that there ice on your face. I'll send Chet to town for some raw beef for your eye." She cut a glance at him. "And to fetch us some supper."

Jay kissed the top of Darlene's head. "Did either of them say why they did this?"

"No, just sent me here. Said Mama'd know why they done it."

Our mother slumped across from her.

Chet asked, "You know who they are, Mama?"

She nodded. "Your daddy's brother and sister, Harvey and Rutha. Mance pretty much raised them up after their father and uncle had a drunken fight over a shotgun and blew their mother in two."

I stared at the damage done to my sister's pretty face. The bruised skin was nearly as dark as my port-wine birthmark. "Mama," I said, "does this have to do with you? Or with Papa?"

"They think Mance left behind a fortune and that I took it." She snorted and gestured at the worn-out kitchen. "Like I'd be living this way and sitting on a pile of money."

Jay lit a cigarette and shook out the match. "Did they warn you they'd hurt Darlene if you didn't come up with it?"

She shrugged. "Who would've believed them? They're MacLeods. Every one of Mance's people is a born liar."

I shared a look with my brothers. "Seems like we need to start taking them seriously."

Chet crossed his thick arms. "Mama, you know where they're living at?"

"No idea."

"We'll ask around," Chet said. He threw a short, hard jab into the meat of my shoulder, making me stutter-step to keep my balance. "Me and Roger'll go into Colquitt, get their whereabouts, and be back with raw beef, supper, and Harvey and Rutha's heads on sticks."

Darlene cupped the ice pack to her face, looking miserable. Water trickled down her dirt-streaked arm. Mama slouched across from her, and Jay smoked as he stood guard over them at the head of the table, where Papa used to sit at mealtimes.

I followed Chet out the front door and down the porch steps.

The day had warmed—a good thing because I'd left my greatcoat and cap on the kitchen table, and Chet clearly was in no mood to wait. I hustled to the passenger side of Mama's truck, where blooms of patchy rust blended with the marmalade-orange paintjob.

Our mother had left the key in the ignition of the Chevy just as Papa had always done in his Model B Ford. Chet cranked it and pumped the gas pedal until the engine settled into a steady clatter. He said, "Damn sure never thought I'd be here again doing Mama's bidding. The only thing new is that it's Darlene paying for Mama's sins instead of one of us."

"Sins? You get religion in the Army?" Though I made it sound like a joke, I had in fact read the Bible from cover to cover and attended a few services on base. The book raised a lot of questions I hoped he could answer.

"Aw, hell no." He put the truck into gear with a thump and made a wide U-turn over the sandy soil. "But what would you call them? Bad habits?" He drove us down the dirt lane that led to Hardscrabble Road. The county hadn't graded in a while; its washboard earthen surface created a racket that prevented conversation as we bounced along.

I peered out my window in the dimming late afternoon. With no trees nearby, the blue sky scattered with clouds looked as big as it did in Texas—where Rienzi no doubt had her nose in yet another book and was surely not thinking about me as much as I was missing her.

We drove by the spot where Uncle Stan—my real father—had set fire to his house before killing his wife and himself. A new dogtrot homestead stood in place of the wreckage, but the owner had kept the barn where Rienzi and I had hidden after discovering the truth of my parentage.

Fifty yards farther, we passed the small, once-neat home where our old friends and fellow sharecroppers Nat and Leona Blanchard had lived. I'd heard they had both gone to their rewards, and their son Ennis had moved his family up to Detroit, seeking a factory job. Tall weeds had claimed the sandy yard, and two shutters had fallen off their hinges.

Chet paused the truck at the edge of US Highway 27 and bumped us onto an empty blacktop. We puttered to town.

Even if Colquitt had experienced a heyday at some point, it'd never been a big place. Still, I couldn't recall ever seeing it so deserted. A couple walked past the brick-and-glass storefronts, but otherwise we didn't spot another soul.

"I'll be dogged," I said. "So much for asking around about Harvey and Rutha. This feels like we ended up in one of those *Weird Tales* stories I used to read, where spacemen kidnap everybody."

"Just our luck the little green men didn't take Mama too. Unless they did but kicked her out after she tried to seduce one of them bug-eyed monsters. Or shot it."

"Maybe both."

Chet pulled alongside several pre-war cars and trucks and a mule-drawn wagon parked diagonally in front of Dora's, the Negro diner, which seemed to be the only place open for business.

A few years before, to earn money after Papa had been locked up for shooting Mama, Chet had eaten breakfast there every day as part of his payment for helping a man named Jerry Flynn with his early-morning bread deliveries. After Chet had chosen hoboing over living another day under Mama's roof, I inherited the route with Jerry and enjoyed the hot breakfast at Dora's each morning. Too bad Jerry's bread truck wasn't parked out front. I had never gotten the chance to thank him for the trick of faking a family tree in a Bible, which had enabled me to escape underaged into the military and discover a better life in more ways than one.

We followed the aromas of grease and strong coffee into Dora's. The jukebox played Louis Jordan and his Tympany Five doing "Choo Choo Ch'Boogie." A few colored men hunched over their plates at the counter, each with a forearm pointed upward, cigarettes clamped between their fingers. Gray threads drifted from their smokestacks. They didn't turn, but one couple in their Sunday best stared at us from their table. I reckoned we looked as out of place as Martians: a pair of white boys in olive drabs.

Dora's daughter Trudy, who was eighteen, like Chet, drew a wet rag across the countertop. She called over to her mother, who was flipping burgers, "Your pirate's done come back from the sea again. And he brought the typhoon with him."

Chet glanced at me. "She's right—that birthmark sort of looks like a pirate patch."

"And you're a regular typhoon," I replied. "Full of hot air."

Dora waved her spatula at us. "Happy New Year, gents. The usual?" She slapped down another two pink disks of beef without waiting for our reply.

I smacked my forehead. "New Year's—that's why nobody's around."

One of the men at the counter growled, "You calling us nobodies, sonny?"

"No sir," I said. "I misspoke. There aren't many people around, is what I meant to say."

"That's what I thought. Belly up to the bar, soldiers." He gestured with his cigarette at two unoccupied stools nearby. I sat beside him, and Chet took the next seat.

Chet called to Dora, "We need to take some supper home, please: five cheeseburgers plus one raw burger."

"Do what?"

"Our sister's got a black eye. We need raw beef for it."

"Lord have mercy, ground meat would make a frightful mess on her face. Trudy, cut off a bit of that sirloin I set aside and wrap it up for our doughboys."

Trudy folded the meat in waxed paper then conferred with her mother and told us, "The total's a dollar fifty-five."

I pulled change from my pocket and began to sort it on my palm while the King Cole Trio started in on "For Sentimental Reasons." Chet clenched a handful of coins taken from his own pants and said, "Feels like I'm four pennies short." He opened his fist and slid the money onto the counter.

It took a few moments, but I finally saw he was right. I added a dime to his total and told Trudy, "Keep the extra."

She fanned her face and fluttered her long lashes. "Hoo, you MacLeod boys sure do make my knees go weak with your free-spending ways."

The cash register drawer sprang open, pealing a two-tone bell, and struck the hip she'd turned to meet it. She dropped the coins in their slots and bumped the drawer closed. "How'd you do that," she asked Chet, "counting by feel? Are your fingers really that sensitive?"

He looked at her a moment, mouth moving without a sound and then stared at the counter. His face had turned as pink as the burger juice on the plate of the man beside me. I tried not to smile at his perpetual shyness around girls.

Trudy snapped her wrist to flick a paper bag open and pushed the wrapped piece of sirloin and some napkins inside. She said, "C'mon, I wanna know."

Now the men at the counter watched him too. "It's nothing," he murmured. The tendons in his neck looked as rigid as pencils.

"It's not nothing," I said. "He's always known his numbers, especially when it comes to the money in his pocket. But I'll bet he can also tell you how many of your mama's meals he's eaten since Jerry Flynn started bringing him in here."

Trudy smiled. "Is that right? How many?"

"Two hundred and twenty-three," he said in a rush.

"Damn," the man beside us said, drawing out the word. "Brain like that, you can do a helluva lot better than the Army. Head up North and getchu one of them factory jobs."

Chet shrugged and went back to staring at the counter while I savored the smell of sizzling beef and melting cheese from Dora's griddle.

As Dora and Trudy wrapped and bagged our burgers, I asked them, "Do y'all know any of my father's people?"

"No," Dora answered. "Now that he's passed on, Jerry's the only other white soul brave enough to come through my door. 'Cept for you two." She winked at us as she rolled the top edge of the sack closed.

Chet took it and thanked her. Focusing on Dora rather than her daughter, he added, "When Jerry drops by, could you please tell him we're around until Sunday? Then we gotta get back to our duty stations."

"Will do," Trudy answered, finger-combing her black hair. "Meantime, you get hungry again, meal number two hundred and twenty-five is waiting right here."

From the jukebox, Ella Fitzgerald sang "Stone Cold Dead in the Market." The same could've applied to my brother. His skin felt chilly through his sleeve as I led him outside.

CHAPTER 3

THE QUIET OF THE TOWN AT DUSK RELAXED ME AFTER THE clamor of the diner, but it also was a reminder that without more people to talk to, we would have a hard time getting a lead on Papa's brother and sister. "You think of anybody else we can ask about Harvey and Rutha?"

Chet shook my hand off his sleeve. "No, but I need to take a leak before heading home."

"Why didn't you use the washroom in there?" I pointed back with my thumb. "Afraid Trudy would follow you inside and offer to help?"

He sneered at me and raised his fist, but instead of knocking my head off, he stalked down the street to the courthouse, the grandest public building in Colquitt: two-story Greek columns, yellow bricks like slabs of butter, and a copper-domed clock tower with a cupola on top. I followed him at a safe distance to the public lavatory in the building. Even on a holiday, the doors were unlocked, and the bathroom was open—at least for people like us. "Whites Only" signs hung on the men's and women's doors.

The stink of overflowing toilets ambushed us as we entered. Dora kept hers much cleaner.

I accepted the paper food sack from Chet before he walked to the nearest urinal of tall, flat porcelain. Even breathing through my mouth, I felt nauseated. I grabbed the door handle, saying, "I'm going to wait out—"

The door swung into my face, stunning me. Somehow I managed to hold on to our meal and the handle.

Hulking, bearded Hugh Bradley, the oldest brother of my childhood nemesis, glared at me through the gap. "C'mon, numb-nuts, get the hell outta my way."

Still addled, I couldn't make my legs move. He reared back and kicked the door. The wood corner struck my forehead with a bright, hot pain. I didn't remember falling but found myself on my butt. Blood trickled down one side of my nose. My ears rang the way they had done when Papa clobbered me. I was too dazed to be angry or scared.

Hugh loomed over me. He was in his late twenties and at least 250 pounds; he wore stained denims and a greasy, long-sleeved shirt. "You're that MacLeod freak, the one that beat up Buck way back when."

"No," Chet said, zipping up. "Roger only outboxed him. I'm the one who cleaned Buck's plow." At least a foot shorter, a hundred pounds lighter, and ten years Hugh's junior, he peered up at the man. "You want the same?"

Hugh unbuttoned a dirty cuff and rolled the sleeve above his massive forearm. "You little shit. I'm gonna enjoy this."

As the town bully worked on his other sleeve, Chet punched him dead in the Adam's apple. Something cracked inside Hugh's throat. He grasped his neck and fought for breath.

Chet pummeled his exposed gut with rapid jabs. My brother's face was expressionless, eyes distant, like he was daydreaming.

Hugh doubled over, bringing his head to my brother's level. With a blur of overhand lefts and rights, Chet bloodied every inch of his face, each blow sounding like a wet slap.

"Hey," I called, still seated on the dirty floor, mopping at my own face with some of the napkins Trudy had put in the sack. "That'll do him."

Chet continued to strike with a beautiful economy of motion, always in balance. He never exposed himself to a counterattack—not that Hugh could mount one.

The big man collapsed to his knees and then pitched sideways, eyes already swelling to pulpy slits. Chet hadn't broken a sweat and didn't even breathe hard.

As I struggled to push myself upright, Chet strode over to the metal cloth-roll towel dispenser. He grasped its sides as if he meant to tear it off the wall and crush Hugh's skull.

I put my hand on Chet's arm, which now felt like a hot-water pipe. He snapped his head around and stared at me with the same glassy gaze Papa had possessed whenever he beat us—the look that Viking berserkers must've had during a melee.

Dangling the bag between us, I said, "If you hit me, I'll drop our supper on the filthy floor."

He patted the dispenser, as if to reassure it. Ignoring the still-prone Hugh, who wheezed through a pancaked nose and shattered teeth, Chet walked to the sink.

I looked at what was left of the town bully. "Should we find a phone and call somebody to help him?"

Chet washed his hands, tugged down the cloth towel, and dried his fingers with deliberate care, getting under each nail. He exited without a word.

I hurried to catch up.

ON THURSDAY MORNING, MY BROTHERS, sister, and I sat at the kitchen table like in the old days, waiting for Mama to serve breakfast. From the stove, fried ham slices and scrambled eggs scented the air, a reminder that somebody was at least supplying her with food. Maybe she'd hooked a new boyfriend.

Darlene sat across from me, with Jay by her side, and Chet sat next to me. Only Jay had escaped damage on New Year's. Greenish-purple bruises covered the left side of Darlene's face, but the swelling had receded, and her eye had lost its puffiness.

She cupped her hand over the damage, reminding me of how I used to shield my port-wine stain from view. Chet had iced his knuckles after we'd arrived home the evening before. Though battered, his hands looked as hard and lethal as ever.

The vertical red gash had begun to scab over on my forehead where the edge of the lavatory door had caught me. My back bothered me more than the cut, though, aching as it did from sleeping on the floor in the front room atop a pallet of old quilts stitched from flour sacks. The stiffness between my shoulder blades put me in mind of my sawmilling days.

Our sister now wore one of Mama's store-bought dresses, an emerald number with matching shoes and about forty-leven white buttons up the front. My brothers and I had changed into the civvies we'd packed: khaki trousers and denim work shirts. Even out of uniform, we all dressed alike, but Jay's outfit was tailored. As handy as he was, he'd probably done the work himself.

The four of us drank Mama's strong black coffee, which she'd poured into chipped teacups, and Jay savored his first smoke of the day. Still trying to make up for my rude interrogation from the day before, I called out, "Mama, can I help you with anything?"

She turned from the stove with her large cast-iron skillet. "Have you got a thousand dollars to get me by in my old age?" She forked a crisp-edged ham slice and a smattering of eggs onto each of our plates and returned with a pot of steaming grits.

As she plopped down spoonfuls of the thick, boiled cornmeal speckled with pepper, Jay said, "Maybe you can set up some kind of business. Run a café or a dress shop in town. Or I could invent a geegaw you can sell."

"You and your inventions. Why don't you make something useful, like a way to print money?"

Chet cut off a chunk of ham with the side of his fork and chewed it. "Didn't you tell us a story once about your grandfather on his deathbed, him pointing to a tree or rock, a place where he'd hid gold and silver from the Yankees? Y'all ever try digging it up?"

"No, son, me and my sisters decided to leave that treasure in the ground, hoping it'd multiply like rabbits." She bounced the bottom of the pot on his head. "Of course we dug around for it, numbskull. Shoveled up the whole damn yard and then some."

Chet glowered and rubbed his scalp, looking like a kid again.

I said, "Maybe we can tell Harvey and Rutha that story. Keep them busy digging until we figure out what to do about them."

"What we do," Chet said, "is find out where they're staying and then let me at them."

Jay mashed his cigarette in his empty cup. "You'd beat up your aunt?"

"After what she did to our sister?" Chet pointed to Darlene. "You betcha."

Brakes squealed out front. Darlene flinched and said, "Their car made a sound like that."

My brothers and I jumped to our feet. Jay said, "Roger, you go out the back and flank them." He and Chet trotted down the hall, and Mama waited beside Darlene.

I looked at the empty pegs beside the door that once held Papa's old single-shot rifle. Mama had probably sold it. I snatched her ham-flecked carving knife off the counter and eased down the squeaky porch stairs and around the side of the house. The morning was oddly warm, as if Mother Nature had decided to skip ahead to spring—what my people always called tornado weather.

By the time I reached the front corner, Jay and Chet were chatting with a man whose voice sounded familiar, but I couldn't place it. I emerged and saw a shiny car parked in the sandy, weed-infested front yard, a gold star on its door.

The High Sheriff of Miller County had come calling.

CHAPTER 4

Sheriff Pete Reeder was Mama's first cousin and had been reelected every four years since before I was born. A tall man, he still looked plenty fit in his khaki shirt and trousers. A five-pointed gold star enclosed by a circle was pinned to his breast pocket. In his big hands, he held a ranger-style hat. A black revolver was holstered on his right hip.

I flipped the knife behind me into the sandy soil and put on the innocent expression that had helped me survive childhood. Sheriff Reeder glanced my way. "Hey, Bud. Look how you done growed."

"Yes, sir."

"I was just telling your brothers that if all y'all don't reenlist, maybe one of you could be my next deputy. That's assuming Brooks there don't work out." He raised his voice at the last part, gesturing with his head toward the patrol car.

A gangly young man leaned against the passenger door. Brooks looked to be in his early twenties. His trouser cuffs bagged at the ankles, the cuffs of his shirt swallowed part of his hands, and the ranger hat covered his eyebrows. At the sound of his name, he glanced up, then directed his attention toward his scuffed shoe tops again.

"Boy's my grandson," the sheriff confided in a lower voice. "Still learning the ropes, but he can shoot the eye out of a crow at fifty paces."

Chet hung his thumbs on his belt. "There much call for that, sheriff? Meaning, if you deputized me, would I be blinding crows all day?"

Reeder put on his hat, pinched the front brim between the thumb and forefinger of each hand, and resettled it until his eyes were shaded. "Would you rather spend your days beating grown men to death?"

I gulped and stared at Chet, but he continued to look amused. "Don't know, sir, I never done that before. Might take some getting used to."

"Some guys found Hugh Bradley laid out in the courthouse washroom. Hugh told them you and Bud jumped him. The guys thought it was pretty funny, the big man in town getting his ass beat by a couple of teenagers. They spread the word last night. It musta gotten back to Hugh, 'cause he drank battery acid."

I cringed at what had become a common form of suicide among country folk who could afford automobiles. Hugh would've had to feel right poorly about himself to choose such a hard death.

With a shrug, Chet said, "Sounds like he died of shame more than anything."

"Sheriff Reeder," Jay asked, "are Chet and Roger in any trouble?"

"Not necessarily. I drove out here to get y'all's side of things." He turned to me and indicated the gash in my forehead. "Bud—I mean, *Roger*—what was your part in all this?"

I told him about Hugh battering my face with the bathroom door and threatening Chet before adding, "It was David and Goliath, sir. The guy was huge. I'm just glad we didn't get too banged up."

"Your brother don't look any the worse for wear." Reeder turned his head and spit. "You boys come home on leave 'cause of your daddy's death?"

"Yes, sir," Jay said, answering for all of us as he used to do when Papa was around.

"For how much longer?"

"Only until Sunday, sir."

"Just stay out of any more trouble. Everybody knows your mama and me are cousins, but I can't be seen playing favorites, kin or not. Y'all got it?"

"Yes, sir," Jay and I replied. Chet only mouthed the words as he smiled.

The front door opened, and Mama walked onto the porch. She'd draped my greatcoat over her shoulders like a cape despite the balmy temperature. Darlene shuffled after in the emerald dress, looking as if every step pained her.

"Hey, Petey," Mama said. "You come for breakfast?"

"Only to talk to your boys, Reva. If you had a danged phone, I would've called to tell you I was on my way. What happened to your girl there?"

"You know Mance's brother and sister, Harvey and Rutha?"

The sheriff lifted the brim of his hat with a forefinger and narrowed his eyes. "This have to do with Mance getting shot?"

"Only 'cause they think he left behind money, and they're fixing to try and get it. Why don't you go after them for what they did to Darlene instead of hassling my poor boys?"

"I think they live somewheres in Seminole County. That's out of my jurisdiction."

"But they did this," she jerked her thumb at Darlene, making her recoil, "just up the road from here, in Miller County. I reckon your juris-*dick*-shun don't extend far at all."

"Dammit, Reva, you'd try the patience of a saint."

"If that saint was wasting his time on pretty young things instead of doing what he was paid to do. You any closer to catching the man that shot Mance?"

He turned his reddening face and spit again. "I don't rightly know that any *man* done it."

"Seems to me you got plenty on your plate for a Thursday morning. We don't wanna keep you from it. C'mon, kids, breakfast's getting cold." She turned on her heels, swirling my coat behind her, and marched back inside, followed by Darlene.

Reeder grumbled and headed toward his patrol car.

Chet called out, "Hey, Sheriff? You know if our daddy's buried nearby?"

"I heard they laid him to rest in Decatur County, around Eldorendo. Why?"

"We ain't paid a visit to his grave yet."

He eyed each of us in turn. "If you're up to something, just keep it out of my backyard, you hear?"

We promised to do so, and he and Brooks departed with a fantail of sandy dirt.

Jay said, "Let's bring shovels to the old home place and dig around for the family fortune Mama and the other Elrods somehow overlooked."

"Sure," Chet replied, "but I wanna see the grave first."

Following in birth order as usual, I retrieved the knife and took up the rear, thinking probably the same thing as my brothers: the other reason for the shovels was to make sure the sonofabitch was really dead.

CHAPTER 5

AFTER BREAKFAST, WE TRIED TO CONVINCE OUR SISTER THAT she'd be safer with Mama, but Darlene insisted she needed to clean house before her husband returned for supper. "Wyatt likes everything just so," she explained, exposing the gap where Aunt Rutha had knocked out two teeth.

Nobody wanted to stay around Mama, so my brothers and I all volunteered to take Darlene home. As kids, the four of us could jam into the truck cab, but now we'd grown too big, so I volunteered to keep company with the shovels we'd loaded in the rusty bed.

The warm wind felt good as the Chevy jounced over rutted dirt roads and cow paths. A rangy black-and-white mutt ran alongside the truck for a while, barking. It put me in mind of our old hunting dogs, Sport and Dixie. Given away by Mama when she did the same with me and my brothers, they were probably long gone by now. So much from my childhood was like that, with precious little to mark its passing—just memories.

Darlene's little homestead was a duplicate of Mama's dogtrot house, as if our sister wanted to escape back into her past. Or maybe she just couldn't escape from it. Beset by stiffness now as well as pain, she needed our help to climb from the truck and shuffle inside.

Shutters covered the windows. There was no glass, but the indoors still felt stuffy. While Chet opened the shutters to get some air circulating, Jay and I settled her in a nearby ladderback chair over her protests that her housekeeping couldn't wait. She told us Wyatt was rotating off guard duty at the German POW camp near Colquitt later that day. The Afrika Korps troops were to be sent home as soon as Germany was rebuilt enough to accommodate their captured soldiers' return. When that happened, Wyatt would probably be posted elsewhere and take Darlene with him.

Growing up, I used to resent her because she hadn't been forced to do chores or labor in the fields. Now I saw that we boys had so many more options than she did. It made me feel doubly sorry for her. I kissed her undamaged cheek and promised to stop by later. Without so much as a thank you, she shooed us out the door.

Jay, Chet, and I clambered back into Mama's pickup. It felt as stuffy as Darlene's house, so we rolled down the windows. But the heat in my cheeks came from guilt over abandoning Darlene more than from the truck's interior.

Behind the wheel, Jay lit a cigarette, blew out a plume of smoke, and sighed. "I sure hate leaving her in that state, but I 'spect she was about to get after us with a broom. Next stop, I reckon, is Papa's grave."

"Good," Chet said. "I need to take another leak."

I replied, "Last time you did it in public, a man died."

"No chance of that happening where we're going, unless some mourner gets a look at my tallywhacker and kills hisself out of jealousy."

Laughing, Jay put the truck in gear. "Anybody know where exactly he's supposed to be buried at?"

"On one of his whiskey drop-offs," I said, "I remember us passing a cemetery near Eldorendo and him telling me and Lonnie that his family had a plot there. It was that time the Ashers made him swig their hooch before he bought it. He was drunk and a lot more talkative than usual."

Jay sighed. "I hope ole Lonnie is staying out of trouble in Alabama. I miss him. Nat, too. We wouldn't have survived without them."

The colored sharecroppers had been better fathers to us than Papa had ever tried to be. We should've been more appreciative back then—we should've told them how much we loved them. But it was far too late for that and much else.

Feeling hollowed out, I said, "When Mama and the rest are gone, I wonder if this will all seem like it never happened. We might be riding here fifty years from now, asking each other if it really did."

Chet grumbled, "If I end up back here in fifty years, I want y'all to put a large-caliber bullet in my head. Please and thank you."

Jay returned us to US Highway 27, going south. On both sides of the road were flat, empty stretches of green grass and weeds to the tree-lined horizons, with sandy dirt alongside the pavement. Kneading the steering wheel, he said, "I'm wondering if Harvey and Rutha are each as bad as Papa was—double trouble."

"So," Chet said, "we should kill them if we have the chance, right?"

"There's already one person dead," I said.

He replied, "I didn't murder him. What's your point?"

"We're three kids—"

"Speak for yourself."

"Roger's right," Jay said. "We're not in the killing business. We'll find a way to buy them off and make them go away. Our dear, sweet aunt and uncle." He flicked the butt of his cigarette out his window. "It's a helluva family tree we fell out of, fellas. Every day I wake up telling myself not to be like the people I came from but the person I wanna be."

"You're the best of us," Chet said. "Papa always hit you the most, but you're still the sunniest."

"Naw, I had it easy compared to Roger." My oldest brother looked past Chet and gave me a nod before returning his attention to the road. "With your birthmark and the way you used to stutter, and Papa always knowing deep down you weren't his? He might've punished me the most, but he beat you the worst."

Chet snorted. "Now I'm feeling sort of left out. My backside still recalls all the times he walloped *me*."

"He was afraid of you," Jay and I said together. We both laughed, and I added, "You were always the one most likely to murder him in his sleep."

Chet shook his head. "That ain't so. If I had done it to him, I would've made sure his eyes were wide open so he'd know it was me sticking the knife in."

We were silent for an uncomfortable moment. The blacktop scrolled under the truck as we cruised through Boykin, which was just a wide place in the road. Finally I asked, "Why a knife instead of a gun?"

"'Cause a knife is personal. You gotta get up close."

Jay said, "So why'd Mama use a gun on him?"

"Maybe she stabbed him first and then emptied the Colt into his body to make sure he was deader than a hammer."

We traveled through a few more miles of green and brown emptiness, and then I called Jay's attention to a crossroad we were approaching. "Hang a left there. That time he was drunk, he got all teary-eyed as he described burying his mama at the Eldorendo Baptist Church. Then he bragged about burning up his daddy's body and then his uncle's out of spite when each of them finally passed. He scattered their bones in the woods, so we won't see headstones for those two."

Past the red-brick, white-steepled church, we rolled to a stop. Unfenced burial plots spread out on a green lawn along the right side of the building.

We emerged from the truck and walked among the graves. Dry grass crunched under our shoes like slivers of bone.

Chet pointed ahead. "I see a few with our last name."

A dozen or so headstones memorialized MacLeods, our father's people. Among them, a temporary marker made from yellow pine faced the blue sky alongside a coffin-sized hole and uneven mounds of brown and red dirt.

"What the hell…?" Jay breathed.

My brothers stared down into the pit while I read the simple writing etched into the wooden rectangle. "It's Papa's—got his name and birth and death dates but no epitaph."

"Step aside," Chet said, unzipping his fly. "I got his epitaph right here." He commenced to urinate downwind on the board, splashing across it and gradually filling in the grooves. "Served him right, getting shot at his sawmill. It was Christmas week, that goddamned Scrooge."

Jay still gazed at the hole. "Wasn't he buried already?"

I said, "He was. See how the dirt's flung every which way? Somebody dug him up."

CHAPTER 6

CHET SHOOK HIMSELF OFF AND INVITED US TO ADD OUR parting salvos, but Jay and I declined. Our oldest brother led the way back to the truck. Chet and I fell in step behind. I asked, "You reckon it was Harvey and Rutha?"

Jay said, "That's my guess, but why?"

"Maybe they thought his money was buried with him," Chet said, sliding onto the middle of the bench seat.

I climbed in beside him and pulled the door shut. "Or, like us, they wanted to be sure he was dead."

Jay went to work on another smoke and cranked the engine. "Naw, I got a funny feeling he was good to them—good to everybody but us. You remember that time you were with him in Bainbridge and got in a fight with that boy Papa gave a Popsicle to?"

I said, "Tommy Rush, the one Papa had with the waitress at the café there."

"Little bastard," Chet muttered.

"Hey, I am too."

"Maybe so, but you're like family." He grinned at me. "Jay's point is that Papa treated Tommy and his mother right nice, same as he always treated Darlene. He only had it in for the three of us."

"Mama, too," I reminded him. "Y'all see how thin she is? I'm worried about her. We should do something, set her up somehow."

Jay said, "Yeah, it'd be a way to thank her for doing what she did to Papa. For avenging us."

Chet shook his head. "You two can take that combat assignment. I can't bring myself to thank her for nothing." He cracked his knuckles. "Where to now?"

"Bainbridge?" I asked. "I don't know Seminole County, other than riding with Papa through there on bootlegging runs. But maybe we can get a line on where Harvey and Rutha have been at least, if not where they're at."

Back onto the southbound highway, we swapped stories about our military experiences and our plans for the future. Like me, they didn't want a career in the service, not when the GI Bill gave us a shot at attending college and an even better life outside the armed forces.

When we reached the Bainbridge town square, I looked at the shop windows still decorated for Christmas and thought about the thin fold of dollar bills in my pocket. Much of my childhood had been spent daydreaming about what I would do in Bainbridge if I had a little spending money. Get a blue Western Flyer bike from the Western Auto down the block. Gobble up every kind of penny candy in the Grimsley Pharmacy. Go to each showing at the nearby Roxie Theater, from the matinee to the late show.

Instead I'd once ridden around Bainbridge on the handlebars of our friend Fleming's cheaper American Flyer while he, Jay, Chet, and Darlene clustered on every other available surface of the bike. Long ago, I had mastered the self-control needed to make a single black licorice whip last me all day, so I could get full value for my penny and then some. And the only picture shows I'd seen at the Roxie were the cheap matinees.

In spite of it being my favorite destination as a kid, Bainbridge had also been the scene of some of my worst memories. Discovering our half-brother Tommy Rush. Spilling the beans about this to Mama after she'd threatened to slap the truth out of me outside the Roxie. Saving her life in the Cottontail Café when she confronted Papa over his affair, and he tried to do to her what she eventually did to him—with the same revolver.

The waitress and Tommy had packed up and left while the café manager was still mopping up Mama's blood. Poor Tommy was still out there somewhere, a bastard like me but without the support of older brothers whose motto was "Us against the world." Despite everything, I realized how lucky I was.

"Now," Jay said, "don't that bring back memories." He pointed a freshly lit Lucky Strike across the little town square toward the café, where a familiar Sunbeam truck was parked. Its side panel showed a girl with ribbons in her hair chomping into a buttered slice of bread. "Jerry must have a new route."

Jay backed out of the parking space, drove us halfway around the square, and stopped in the diagonal slot beside Jerry Flynn's truck.

We spotted our old friend in his deliveryman uniform—dark slacks with a collared shirt and a tie—inside checking off items on a clipboard and getting the manager to sign for them. Jerry's hair was still a thicket of black curls beneath a peaked cap, and long eyelashes like a deer's softened his broad, ruddy face. He'd rolled up his sleeves; one of his hairy forearms sported a blue-green tattoo of an anchor, just like Popeye's.

The manager wore a paper hat folded to a point in the front and the back like my military cap. He glanced over as we strode in and did a double take in my direction. "I remember that face. You're Mance MacLeod's kid."

Jerry turned and grinned. Reaching out, he shook our hands, saying, "Hey, boys! Did all y'all get kicked out of the service already, or did you just go AWOL?"

"That one's bad luck," the manager barked. He pointed at me. "Go on and git."

"Bad luck nuthin'," Jerry said. "I don't remember you saving Reva's life. Roger is the bravest person I know."

I blushed and stared at my shoes.

Jay said, "You hear about Papa getting shot to death before Christmas?"

"See?" The manager scurried behind the wood counter. "Another shooting. Their whole family's cursed. Take it outside before somebody else gets pumped full of lead, will ya?"

Jerry tilted his head toward the door and led us out to his truck. He tossed his clipboard onto the driver's seat.

I said, "Thanks for your tip about faking our family tree in a Bible."

"It's like a country birth certificate. Works every time with military recruiters."

"Well, the Navy recruiter didn't go for it, but an Army officer let me slide."

He looked at the three of us. "If y'all came back for yer daddy's funeral, you're a little late."

"No," Chet said. "We just wanted a reunion—him dying was a great excuse. The military even paid our bus fare, round trip."

Jay tossed his spent butt into the street. "The only bad thing is, his brother and sister threatened Mama, and they beat up Darlene pretty bad to drive their point home. You know Harvey and Rutha?"

"Never met 'em, but I heard they're a rough pair of cobs. What's all this about?"

I said, "They think Papa left money behind and Mama took it after she killed him."

Jerry shook his head. "If anybody has Mance's money, wouldn't it be his widow, the one that owns the Ramsey sawmill?" We all shrugged in response. He said, "Before Thanksgiving, she bought O'Neil Gowdy's store across from the mill. She was in there running things when I made my delivery earlier today—must get lonely clattering around in her big ole house with only her son to keep her company, so she got herself a place to work in."

Jay said, "We'll drive over and see if she's heard from them."

I looked back at the café, thinking about meeting Jerry right after I'd saved Mama's life and how he had come by every day to check on us and mind her recovery. Maybe he was the key to setting her up with a solid situation—and I couldn't have asked for a better stepfather. "Jerry, you like Mama pretty well, right? Do you think you two could—"

He shook his head. "No, son. We're the same age, but that's all we have in common. We'd be fighting like cats and dogs in no time flat."

"You reckon there's anybody who might take her?"

He laughed. "Trying to marry her off before yer time is up here?"

"I'm just worried about her prospects."

Chet snorted. "With her reputation, she'll never be lonely for long."

"Go easy on her," our old friend said. "Hard times can make for hard people, and she's had it tougher than most."

Jay nodded, a calculating look in his eyes. "Maybe the sawmill heiress will give her a job. Only one way to find out."

CHAPTER 7

JERRY HAD TO CONTINUE WITH HIS DELIVERIES, SO WE DROVE to the Ramsey Lumber Company back in Miller County. Each of us had worked there at some point in the past few years. The place had left our hands bristling with splinters and sticky with turpentine, our backs perpetually aching, and our pockets full of loose bills and change from the forty-cents-an-hour wage.

"Surprised Papa didn't rename it after hisself," Chet said as we stared through the windshield at the company signage.

"Maybe he did, right after I quit," I said, "but his widow put the old sign back up."

Jay chuckled, a new cigarette bobbing in the corner of his mouth. "Yeah, probably to get rid of his haint."

Beyond the stockade-like wooden wall that surrounded the property, familiar fifteen-foot-high towers of sawed boards cured in the outdoors, looking like temples built to honor a sun god. I rolled down my window to better hear the steady thud of wood being stacked in the yard and the screech of timber running through massive cutting and planing machines.

Inhaling the sweet scent of fresh-cut wood, I said, "Another thing the military saved us from. Just thinking about working here again makes my back hurt."

"C'mon," Chet said. "Let's see if the lady who took a fancy to Papa is in her store."

Jay drove us across the road and parked beside the grocery. New pine benches sat near the plate glass window in front with a shiny brass spittoon between them. The cinderblock wall had been whitewashed, covering "Gowdy," the name that had been stenciled there since the turn of the century. In its place, cornflower-blue cursive letters spelled out "Bonny's."

"Who's that?" Chet asked.

"The one we're looking for," I said. "Everybody called her 'Mrs. Ramsey' and then 'the Widow Ramsey'—and I reckon 'Mrs. MacLeod' for a time—but that's her first name."

Jay led us inside. The store had never been much to look at in Old Man Gowdy's day: a scarred counter with a tin cashbox, some shelves with canned goods and jars, bins of candy, and a cold drinks box near the door with a wooden rack to hold empties returned for the deposit.

Now the walls and ceiling gleamed with a fresh coat of white paint, new pine planks glowed butter yellow underfoot, and the careworn counter had been replaced with stained oak. In the center, a cast-iron stove with a steaming kettle atop it perfumed the air with woodsmoke. The shelves held the usual assortment of basic goods—the grocery still catered to the sawmill workers—but I was willing to bet even that would change in time.

"Howdy, can I help y'all?" A woman of forty or so stepped from behind an engraved bronze cash register and strode around the counter, heels clicking. Her blonde hair was done up in waves and curls, and teardrop pearl pendants dangled from her ears. She wore a striped dress that was nicer than anything Mama had ever bought in town. Betty Grable might've been as pretty, but only at her best and not on any old Thursday.

Chet looked like he'd stopped breathing.

Jay coughed once around his cigarette. "Ma'am, we're Mance's sons."

"Oh my! He told me all about the three of you." Her voice was warm and friendly, her accent not local but somehow familiar.

I stepped forward and smelled gardenias, a perfume that put me in mind of Mrs. Gladney, my favorite teacher and first crush. "Are you from Texas, ma'am?"

"Houston, born and raised. I'm Bonny Peterson."

I offered a handshake. "I'm Roger—but Papa might've referred to me as Bud." She took my hand in both of hers. Her fingers felt warm and smooth, and I noticed she still wore a wedding band even though she gave what I assumed was her maiden name. No way she could have gotten remarried so fast after Papa's death. "I'm stationed in San Antonio, ma'am, so I hear a lot of Texas accents."

"You're just how he described you."

Out of habit, I tilted my face away to shield some of the birthmark.

"Oh, I don't mean that." She patted my arm. "Your father called you a fine young man."

"He did?" I straightened and found myself standing at attention. Even his secondhand praise made me puff up with pride despite him putting me and my family through hell. His continued hold on me made my stomach lurch.

"Yes indeed-y. And you must be Jay and Chet." She shook their hands, using both of hers again. "I'm so pleased y'all dropped by. I just wish your daddy could've been here with us."

Chet said, "If he was, then we wouldn't be." He seemed to be talking to a spot above her left shoulder.

"I know, hon. He told me how you didn't always see eye to eye. But you're here now, so what can I do for you?"

Jay said, "Have his brother and sister come by, ma'am?"

"I heard tell of them from Mance, but they weren't at the funeral and haven't paid their respects."

"If they visit," I said, "it probably won't be a social call."

After we took turns describing what they'd done, she hefted a cut-down shotgun from beneath the counter. "I'd like to see them try any of that with me. I've got a son about Jay's age from my first marriage who's my pride and joy—he taught me how to use this but good."

I wondered whether my brothers and I should combine our cash and buy the weapon for Darlene. Instead I said, "Ma'am, I know it's not polite to ask about money, but do you know if Papa left behind anything from his bootlegging days?"

She returned the shotgun to its hiding place and shook her head. "When I met your daddy, he wasn't long out of the penitentiary. Didn't have two nickels to rub together, bless his heart. All he had to his good name was a Bible some prison chaplain had given him and the love of Our Lord and Savior. Of course, I only knew him after he got saved, but based on the stories I've heard, I can assure you he was a changed man."

I remembered different. The man who'd installed himself as the overseer of her sawmill had struck me as a spruced-up version of the bully who'd ruined my childhood, someone who used religion as a Get Out of Hell Free card. But Papa was a chameleon, changing as needed based on the company he kept. Had we seen the actual version, or had Bonny Peterson, or our half-brother Tommy Rush and his mother at the café, or the Ashers, who made the bootleg whiskey Papa had wholesaled? Were Harvey and Rutha the only ones to really know him?

This was getting us nowhere, so we thanked her for her time and promised to drop by again before we all had to head to our duty stations. Back inside the truck, Jay finished his smoke and said, "Papa sure had an eye for pretty ladies. I guess I gotta thank him for passing that along anyway."

"She wasn't as ugly as a mud fence," Chet allowed.

I sighed. "Reckon she can probably take care of herself too, but I can't see Mama working there, what with her having killed the same man Miss Bonny is still over the moon about. And we're no closer to finding Harvey and Rutha. So, now what?"

Chet leaned forward to peer up at the sun through the windshield. "Dinner. Looks like it's almost noon, and I'm starving."

"Not the Cottontail," Jay said with a grin. "I hear Roger's not welcome."

We ate at a nearby joint that happened to be whites-only. Neither the food nor the atmosphere was any match for Dora's—folks didn't know what they were missing.

By the time we finished our meal, the day had warmed to the point where I had to roll up my sleeves. Still thinking about Darlene's situation, we went to a pawn shop in Colquitt and split the cost of a used Smith & Wesson .38 Special and a box of bullets for her. Then we decided to treat ourselves to a furlough from our concerns about our sister and Mama.

Acting like the three soldiers on leave that we were, we ambled around town. We were too young to legally drink, not that any of us craved alcohol anyway—we'd seen the ruin it could bring. Instead we bought penny candy and RCs, which we doctored with salted peanuts to make the cola foam up. Gulping down the explosion of bubbles made us burp like bullfrogs.

Jay chatted up every group of teenage girls who crossed our path. Chet always looked like he wanted to join in, but by the time he opened his mouth, the girls were on their way and the opportunity had passed. The only feeling they stirred in me was the desire to get back to Rienzi in San Antonio.

Whenever we happened upon an adult, we asked if they knew either of Papa's siblings, but we didn't have any luck. In the late afternoon, we decided to call it quits and return home.

Back on US 27, Jay unwrapped a fresh pack of Lucky Strikes, steering with the heels of his hands. "Maybe they'll hear we're asking about them and show up."

Chet grunted. "No, they're gonna hide until we've went, scared they'll get what-for if they poke their heads out."

"If they lay low until then," I said, "how can we protect Darlene and Mama?"

"Dunno. Maybe we gotta hope Sheriff Reeder does his damn job."

Shifting into small talk, we reminisced about happier times: sliding off the barn roof into Nat and Lonnie's arms, whiling away Sundays at our favorite fishing spots, and eating second-table at the old home place with Mama's kin and then seeing who dared to stand the closest to the train tracks when the Seaboard Railroad thundered past. At last, Jay steered onto Hardscrabble Road and then the lane leading us home.

When we were in sight of Mama's house, Chet barked, "Stop." He pointed at the oxblood 1942 Chrysler Royal sedan parked in front. "I know that car."

I recognized it too. "It's Papa's."

CHAPTER 8

As I stared at Papa's car, my chest tightened. Rienzi would've told me to be logical and scientific, but I couldn't help shuddering while panic clawed my ribs. I'd faced him down once before but didn't have the gumption to do it again. I told myself to calm down—he was most certainly dead. Had to be.

Jay asked, "How do you know it's his?"

Chet told him, "He zoomed past us once while me and Roger was dragging home firewood and practically freezing to death. He'd only been out of prison a short time. Tootled his goddamn horn and waved."

"Fellas, maybe this solves the mystery of where his bootlegging money went: he got paroled and bought the car to celebrate. That was a few years ago; could be Miss Peterson forgot he owned it, or he sold it before they met."

"Unless Papa's not dead," Chet said. "Maybe somebody else got his face blown off in Papa's office and everybody guessed it was him, but he's still keeping time with Mama. And now we're gonna have to deal with the sonofabitch all over again."

Though he'd voiced my own worst fear, I elbowed him and tried to sound nonchalant. "You've been watching too many scary movies on base. If Rienzi was here, she'd follow inductive and deductive reasoning." They stared at me, and I shrugged. "You remember how she talks. Half the time, I can't figure what she's going on about."

Chet pointed at the car that was as dark as my port-wine birthmark. "Okay, what does her conductive reasoning tell you?"

"Somebody who knew Papa bought his car and is visiting Mama."

"*Visiting*—that's one word for it."

Checking the rearview mirror, as if there'd be any other traffic on that lonesome road, Jay asked, "Should we wait here or barge in on them?"

The question brought forth an incident I'd tried to forget, when I had stumbled upon a view of Mama with the husband of Mrs. Gladney. "M-m-maybe we should leave them be," I said, ashamed of the quaver in my voice. "We can come back later."

"Then whatchu wanna do now?" Jay asked. "We've lost too much daylight to dig for treasure at the old home place."

"I'm hungry again," Chet said. "I vote for Trudy's—I mean Dora's."

Our oldest brother grinned. "All that flirting in town got to you too, huh? Roger told me about you and that colored girl—seeing a little of the world's made you broad-minded."

"Stuff it."

"Hey, I don't hold it against you; Roger's got hisself a half-Japanese honey. I only know white girls, so I was thinking about dropping in on the Turners and see if Geneva would sit up with me awhile. Maybe I can invent a way to mend her broken heart, or at least distract her from her woes."

Not a minute before, we'd all been looking down on Mama for her apparent tryst even as we were conjuring fantasies of our own. Whenever I judged someone, life made me out to be a hypocrite.

"While y'all look for love," I said, "I'll check on Darlene and give her our gifts." I opened the truck door and retrieved the .38 Special and box of bullets, which I tucked into my baggy pockets. "Happy hunting, you Don Juans."

The straightest route to our sister's place was to pass Mama's home, cut through the fields we used to sharecrop, and follow a goat trail to Darlene's doorstep. I heard Jay turn the truck around and drive back toward the highway while I followed the lane until it ended at the ramshackle house of my youth.

I'd spent most of my seventeen years walking that route in bare feet, wearing a threadbare work shirt and hand-me-down overalls. Each week, the clothes had needed to last until Monday—washday in the country—when I'd put on an identical outfit for the next seven days. Those had been the only duds I'd owned.

Now I wore not only shoes but socks and boxers too, and I'd gotten used to indoor bathrooms, a daily shower and shave, brushing my teeth, and putting on a clean uniform every morning. I didn't need to get a whiff of my armpits to know I was overdue for a scrub.

It amazed me how quickly I'd adjusted to a new way of living. If circumstances forced me back here, I wondered how long it would take before I returned to bare feet and a meager bath each Sunday. How long before the life I now lived seemed like the daydream of the hayseed I used to be as I rested for a spell in someone's barn loft?

I made a wide curve around Mama's house, braced for raunchy laughter echoing from inside. Or worse sounds. But only a crow's caw broke the silence.

The bullet hole Papa had made years before in the bedroom wall was still there. Looking through it at Mama with Mrs. Gladney's husband had driven me to quit the school where he was the principal, go to work and live in the sawmill, take on Papa, and trick the military into accepting me early. All because I'd been curious about what another boy was peering at through the wood siding.

As I started across the neglected barn lot and garden that comprised the back yard, a man said, "Hey."

I nearly jumped out of my skin. On reflex, I lifted my fists like a boxer.

The stranger stood on the back porch wearing a sky-blue checkered suit with a dark tie and matching pocket square. A gray fedora shaded his eyes as he took a final puff from a cigarette. He ground it out against the sole of his two-tone shoe and pocketed the butt. "I don't think we've ever met," he said, his speech marking him as a townie, maybe from as far north as Atlanta.

Reminding myself I was no longer a boy but an airman in the US Army, I unclenched my hands, squared my shoulders, and said, "I'm Roger MacLeod. This is the house I grew up in."

"Yes, I know all about you." He walked to the edge of the porch and leaned on the top rail, which gave me a good look at his tanned, handsome face. His eyes matched the blue of his suit. "I'd seen you often enough through binoculars when you were younger—both you and your brothers—riding with your father on his monthly whiskey runs. Mance always brought one of you kids to the Ashers' still in Florida to make sure we wouldn't shoot at his truck. The clever SOB used you boys like shields." He gave me a movie-star smile. "I'm Ed Bascom."

His name clicked. I remembered rude comments I'd overheard Papa make over the years. "The revenuer?"

He laughed. "My official title is agent with the US Department of the Treasury."

"And you're here on official business, seeing if my mother is selling illegal liquor?"

"No, this is a social call. Your mama and I go way back, thanks to me tracking your father. May he rest in peace."

"Eddie," Mama said, walking onto the porch while she bobby-pinned her hair, "who are you—oh, hey, Bud." She'd put on the store-bought emerald dress with the umpteen white buttons Darlene had worn earlier. "Mr. Bascom invited me to supper."

"In Papa's old Chrysler."

"He's got a good memory," Bascom said to my mother. "Takes after you." Turning back to me, he said, "Your father sold me the car after he went into the lumber business. That was his way of saying it was nothing personal, me dogging your old man and him giving me the slip all those years."

Mama told me, "You'll have to fend for yourself. There's some biscuits in the pie safe and a little buttermilk left and, thanks to Eddie, souse and ham and all is keeping in the smokehouse."

"I'm going over to Darlene's first to see how she's faring. You remember your injured daughter and how poorly she felt this morning?"

"I recollect her perfectly well, and don't you take that tone with me. You ain't so growed-up that I couldn't give you a walloping." She shook her head at Bascom. "You hear how ungrateful he is? They're all like that, even after I slaved away for them all those years."

He smiled down at me. "Go easy on her, okay? She's got a lot on her plate. Get yourself something good to eat in town." He took a silver dollar from his pocket and flipped it toward me.

I let it fall at my feet in a puff of dust. The money would've constituted a fortune when I was younger—and could again if my nightmares came to pass and I had to return here for whatever reason. As I set off for the fields without another word to either of them, I wondered whether I'd look back on this show of defiance and kick myself.

The sun set, and the air turned a little cooler but far from winter-cold. I rolled down my sleeves and buttoned the cuffs as I strode through the countryside, navigating with ease in the near dark, pleased I hadn't become so accustomed to electricity on the airbase that I was helpless in the gloaming. Walking across the fallow, sunbaked fields felt like stepping on pie crust as an inch or two of sandy loam crumbled and compacted beneath me with each footfall.

One thing country life had over living in town was that the night sky offered up a show. The Milky Way, dozens of constellations, the bright half-moon—what Rienzi would've called waxing gibbous—along with a sprinkling of planets and the zip of shooting stars were all there for me to take in as I ambled along.

After a half-hour of listening to my shoes trample earth, dry grass, and weeds, and smelling wood smoke and cooking on the breeze, I saw a few dim lights from Darlene's house. A ragtop prewar Plymouth was parked near the front porch: Wyatt Weaver had come home from guard duty. Unless Darlene was following in Mama's footsteps and had a different man there. She was on husband number five already, so it was possible that I'd hiked from one love nest to another.

Still, I needed to make sure she was on the mend. I stepped onto the front porch and knocked.

A few seconds went by, and a man snapped, "Well? You gonna get the goddamned door, or do I have to do everything around here myself?"

The door opened at last, and Darlene's battered face peered out. In the porch light, her bruises and split lips looked even worse than this morning, but I knew firsthand this was a stage in the healing process. Her good eye widened, and the undamaged side of her mouth turned upward. "Bud, you're here for supper." She pitched her voice louder than she needed to.

"I just wanted to check on you. Don't put yourself out on my account."

"How often do I get to entertain my baby brother?" She turned, still shouting with genuine-sounding cheer, "We've got company, Wyatt. Come meet Bud."

From the kitchen at the end of the hall, a bottle tipped over, rolled off the table, and shattered on the plank floor. "Goddammit," Wyatt grumbled.

"I should go," I said. The revolver and bullets felt heavy in my pockets.

"No, really." She clutched my arm, her grip desperate. "Please stay."

CHAPTER 9

DARLENE LED ME INTO THE FRONT ROOM. A STAINED APRON covered her dull, faded housedress, putting me in mind of how I found Mama the day before.

I removed the .38 Special and box of bullets from my pockets and handed them over. "We got to thinking you might need some protection." I listened to her husband muttering in the kitchen. "In case Harvey and Rutha come back, I mean."

"That was sweet." She bussed my cheek and set the items on a nearby shelf.

I followed her down the swept hall and into the kitchen, where pork chops sizzled in a skillet on the stove. A naked lightbulb dangled overhead, like at Mama's, but the rafters weren't home to dozens of spiders. Even in her condition, my sister had tidied up the place. She'd told Jay, Chet, and me that her husband liked everything "just so."

At the table were three mismatched chairs and a stool. Wyatt Weaver, a small, pudgy corporal in a wrinkled Army uniform, slouched at the head of the table, one arm thrown over the ladderback of his chair. In his other hand, he clutched a brown bottle of beer.

Several empties stood near his elbow, their caps near his dusty boots. An arc of drizzled liquid curved across the tabletop to the edge. Below, shards of brown glass lay scattered on the otherwise-clean wood floor; darkened pine boards marked ground zero. The room smelled like stale beer and frying pork.

"Your timing's perfect," Darlene said. "I can't eat 'cause of my mouth, so you can have my portion." She retrieved a whisk broom and dustpan from the corner. I made a move to help her, but she shook her head and said, "Wyatt, this is Bud. Remember me telling you about him?"

"Please call me Roger," I said, putting out my hand. "Good to meet you."

He saluted with the bottle and kicked a chair toward me. I took that as an invitation to sit. Though I wanted to be anywhere but around a drunk, I sat.

Darlene stooped nearby, expression tight with pain, and swept up the glass.

Wyatt said, "She told me all y'all's in the service too. Where you stationed?"

"Lackland, in San Antonio."

"Army Air Forces. A flyboy." He shook his head. "Looking down on us from your goddamn tin can in the sky while we do the hard work of keeping this country safe."

I pointed at my birthmark. "They won't let me fly—pilots aren't allowed to have distinguishing marks. Instead they're teaching me procurement." I rolled my eyes, trying to show disdain for the job to placate him. "You're the real soldier; I'm just playing at it."

He sat straighter, his arm nudging the two empties closer to the table edge. "Poor baby. You come home to cry about it to your mama? That's what this one does all the time." He pointed the neck of his bottle at Darlene, who dumped the brown shards into a garbage pail. "I always know where I can find her. Instead of doing chores, she's boohooing at Reva's place. Good-for-nothing. That's what she is." He drained the remainder of his drink.

Darlene gathered four more bottles from a small icebox and plunked them in front of him as neatly as a bowling alley pinsetter.

She snatched the two near his arm and the bottle from his hand. The effort made her wince, elbows bending inward toward her battered ribs.

My barrack-mates called empty beer bottles "dead soldiers." I hoped it wouldn't take too many more drinks before Wyatt was dead to the world. As my blood rose, crimson blurred the edges of my vision. I caught myself grinding my teeth in anger.

The way he treated Darlene made me wonder if she'd invented the visit from Harvey and Rutha. I asked him, "What did you think when you found her like this?"

"First I thought she had a guy on the side that done it. Then she tells me about your daddy's people." He scowled at me. "Not sure I believe her—I liked your daddy just fine. Sold high-quality shine to my old man."

Regretting my visit more and more, I called to Darlene, who was forking porkchops onto two plates. "Can I help with anything?"

Wyatt placed the lip of a fresh bottle against the table edge and slapped down, knocking off the cap, which joined the others beside his boots, along with splinters of wood. "Why you wanna do women's work?" He guzzled more beer and snorted. "Always knew you airmen was sissies."

My sister glopped mashed potatoes from one pot onto the plates and added English peas from another before setting the meal before us with rust-spotted flatware.

"Get him a beer," Wyatt ordered.

From my Lackland experiences, I knew if I told him I didn't drink, the sissy comments would intensify. "I don't want to put a dent in your supply. Sweet tea's fine. Or well water."

"Beer," he insisted. Rather than take from his three reserves, Darlene delivered another from the icebox.

I left the cap on and rotated my plate so the vegetables were closest to her. "Can't you have them at least? They won't need much chewing."

"I'll eat after y'all finish." She added with a slight smile, "Remember how we had to wait for second-table at the old home place on Sundays? And it always took forever for the grown-ups to finish their dinner. Reckon I'm used to it."

Head down, sawing into his pork chop, Wyatt seemed to be ignoring us. Grateful for the reprieve, I said, "Second-table—you still feel like a kid? I haven't felt that way in a long time."

"Maybe just a longing for it." She cut her eyes at her fifth husband. "I had to grow up pretty fast, just like you boys."

I wished I knew somebody who would be kind to her, but the only good men I could name were too young for her or too old or in San Antonio. Maybe I could take her with me and help her find a better life out west. "Hey," I said, "you ever consider—"

Wyatt slapped down his fork. "Goddammit, can't a man eat in peace? It's as noisy as the chow hall in here." He took another swig, eyeing me. When he spoke again, he slurred his words even more. "I heard you MacLeod boys think you're tough. Your daddy was, no doubt about it, and maybe Chet can look after hisself. But you and Jay? Sissies, that's what I say." He jabbed my shoulder with his free hand. "Chet's not here to fight your fights. Hunh?"

Retreating to the stove, Darlene said, "Nobody wants to fight you, Wyatt. Bud's our guest. Mind your manners, now."

"Don't you tell me what to do, good-for-nothing." He jabbed me again. "Right, flyboy? Nobody can tell a man what to do in his own house. A real man anyways."

The scene reminded me so much of our childhood I wanted to scream. Darlene should've known better than to talk back, but she was playing Mama's role as she'd seen it countless times.

In one respect, this was still better than suppertime when we were young—back then, there was no hoping to outlast Papa. As a kid I had to take whatever punishment he dished out. But I didn't have to put up with bullies anymore.

A memory flashed: Chet beating Hugh Bradley to a pulp with brutal efficiency. My hands balled into fists, and a deeper red colored my vision. Stirring things up instead of calming them down seemed to be what all the MacLeods did. Even though I was a bastard, maybe I wasn't really any different from them.

Fighting for self-control, I forced myself to ignore Wyatt and cast my gaze around the kitchen. On the wall near the back door was the old single-shot rifle missing from Mama's house. She'd probably given it to Darlene and her husband as a wedding present.

"C'mon," he said, giving my arm another poke. "You're letting your food get cold anyhow. Let's have it out while your worthless sister reheats it."

"Don't you talk about her that way," I said, the chill in my voice sounding more like Chet than me.

"She's my wife. I can do whatever I want. Not that she makes me wanna do very much." He looked her over, sneering.

I stood. "Stop it. Last warning."

He finished his beer and slammed the bottle down. "Thought I was getting a real hot-to-trot gal—what everybody says your mama's still like—but she just lays there, flat as a board and dry as a bone, with her eyes squinched shut."

Darlene gasped. She put her hands over her face and began to sob.

"Get up," I told him. My heartbeat hammered in my ears. The crimson haze now tinted everything I saw, a world bathed in blood.

"That's what did it, hunh? Baby brother taking up for big sister. Or was it bringing your mama into the mix? You a mama's boy still pining for her tit?"

I grabbed my full beer bottle and clubbed the top of his head, expecting the glass to break like in the Western picture shows. Instead it stayed intact and rocked him back.

He looked dazed. I hoped the blow and all the alcohol he'd consumed would send him to sleep, but he blinked and then pushed to his feet, standing a few inches taller than me. "That the best you got?" He raised his fists. "C'mon, fight like a man."

Growing up, I'd been in countless brawls with Chet and lost them all. The bout I'd won against Hugh's youngest brother, Buck, was more from luck than skill.

But I didn't want to outbox Wyatt Weaver. Literally seeing red, I wanted to destroy him.

As he edged toward me, leading with his left hand, I scurried around the other side of the table, angling toward the back door.

One thing I just discovered that I had in common with Chet was his killer instinct.

I snatched the rifle from the wall and cocked it. Aiming at Wyatt's chest, I pulled the trigger.

CHAPTER 10

THE HAMMER FELL ON A SPENT ROUND. ITS SURPRISING CLICK sounded loud, despite Darlene's crying. I couldn't recall another time when the rifle wasn't ready to fire.

Other options sprang to mind. Darlene had left the revolver and bullets in the front room. It would have only taken me a few seconds to retrieve them. Even closer was the large, rusty carving knife lying on the counter. Or the rifle butt could've served as a club.

Wyatt looked as if I'd slapped him awake from a dream. "What the hell are you doing? I wasn't trying to kill you, just trade a few punches. What kind of lunatic fixes to shoot a man in his own home?"

He was right. I'd lost my mind.

My disappointment turned to horror at what I had almost done.

The red haze lifted. I began to shiver. In my hands, the rifle felt as heavy as a canon. I dropped it and bolted through the back door.

Down the steps and across their field, I fled like I was the one in the iron rifle sights. I didn't get far before pitching forward as if shot. On hands and knees, I puked.

The night air made my clammy skin even colder. I heaved until my stomach knotted and my throat burned. A stream of tears drizzled into the stinking mess; the thirsty ground seemed to be pulling them from my eyes.

Bye-bye, baby. Papa's words from years ago just before he'd tried to shoot Mama in the face at the Cottontail Café. Before I'd saved her but also ruined everything for me and my brothers. Before I'd learned so much about my family and my place in it.

Back then, though, I never would've believed this newly revealed truth about myself: I was indeed Papa's son in all but blood, as capable of murderous violence as he'd been. Strange that it had only surfaced now, when I was defending my sister's honor, instead of all those times when I could've been protecting my own.

I kneeled with my butt on my heels, shaking. For an insane moment, I contemplated going back inside the house to find a coat. A fit of mad laughter juddered through me, followed by more weeping.

Another voice in my mind, this one Jay's from earlier: *Every day I wake up telling myself not to be like the people I came from but the person I wanna be*.

Thinking about how disappointed in me he would be made the tears fall even faster.

Footsteps in the tall grass ended my crying jag. This was it. No doubt Wyatt had loaded the rifle and come out to do to me what I'd tried to do to him—just as Mama had ultimately done to Papa after his failed attempt to murder her. The cycle seemed fitting and proper. It granted me a strange sense of peace.

Still on my knees, I bowed my head and waited for the bullet. My soul would go to Hell, I supposed. Papa wouldn't be surprised to see me arrive. No doubt he would be there with Uncle Stan, the two of them probably shackled together in misery for all eternity. Maybe the demons would task them with teaching me to swim again, but this time, instead of Foster's Drain or Fan's Wash Hole, it would be in the Lake of Fire.

"Bud?" Darlene said.

I turned as she came closer, and I staggered to my feet. I saw in the moonlight that her face was as wet with tears as my own. "Sorry for all that," I said, sniffling and wiping my cheeks. "Reckon you won't have me over anymore."

She stared into my eyes. "Were you really trying to kill him?"

"For a second, anyway. Why wasn't the rifle loaded with a fresh round?"

"Lazy me and lucky him. I got to thinking after y'all brought me home how I need to take up for myself if Harvey and Rutha come back, so I tried practicing." She pointed behind her. "Put one of Wyatt's empties on a fencepost yonder and took a shot. The rifle's jerking or whatever it's called—"

"Recoil."

"Yeah, that. Danged thing hurt my shoulder and ribs so bad I didn't try a second time. Just put it up and went back to housekeeping. I'll try tomorrow with the little gun you done brought."

"You saved his life—probably mine too. Even if Sheriff Reeder would've let me off because we're kin, the Army might've gone after me for murdering a fellow soldier."

"But why'd you wanna kill him?"

My face flushed. "'Cause of what he was saying about you."

"I hear that and worse whenever he's home."

"So why haven't you shot him yet?"

She shook her head. "Bless your heart, baby brother, that's no way to go through life—killing everybody you get crosswise with. He ain't nearly as bad as my earlier husbands. Least he don't raise a hand to me."

"But you deserve so much better. Rienzi and I never talk ugly to each other."

"Beggars can't be choosers." She glanced toward the house. "I better go in. He's surely done eating by now."

"You mean after nearly getting killed, he went back to his supper?"

She shrugged. "He was starting in on your portion when I came out. With another beer or two in him, he'll fall into bed and sleep till noon."

"I wish I could save you from him."

"I'm the oldest, remember? I oughta be looking after you."

"Everything's catawampus in this family. Why should that be any different?" Mindful that I smelled like vomit, I gave her a quick peck on her salty, unbruised cheek. "I'll stop by again when he returns to base."

"He'll be home a few days. It's why I done laid in so much beer."

"You take care."

"Speak for yourself. You've changed. And it ain't for the better."

CHAPTER 11

I SHUFFLED BACK TOWARD MAMA'S. FROM THE HEIGHT OF THE moon, I knew not much time had passed, so the house was probably deserted.

If Jay had found Geneva Turner at home, he would've turned on the charm and talked her parents into letting him sit up with her on their porch—and invent a fix for her broken heart. If he struck out there, most likely he would've driven to Colquitt or Bainbridge to flirt some more with the town girls.

Assuming Chet's nerve didn't fail him and his money didn't run out, he would keep ordering and eating at Dora's until closing time. Maybe he would even muster the courage to trade a word or two with Trudy. And Mama for sure wouldn't be home yet from her date with Ed Bascom, the revenue agent. Figuring she'd returned to her old habit of seduction in exchange for sustenance, though, I needed to steer clear of the house until well after midnight.

I veered toward the woods. During warm nights in years past, I would've joined Nat Blanchard for some fishing with cane poles on Spring Creek or talk with him and his wife Leona in their cozy little home, but both were now lost to me forever. "Rest in peace," I murmured. I only hoped the person I wanted to see would still be there.

Walking through the forest, my shoes sounded much noisier against the deadfall than my bare feet had done when I was a kid. I navigated by moonlight just like in my youth and found some of the old trails I used to follow.

Wanda Washburn wasn't traveling the paths as I was, with the heart-pine torch she called her flambeau lighting the way. Instead, tracking the sweet scent of burning wood, I finally found her where I should've started my search: at her small cottage, deep in the woods.

She sat with her back to me near a low campfire in the clearing that comprised her front yard. Notched posts on either side of the rock-ringed firepit supported a horizontal bar from which hung dented buckets and pails of varying sizes. Their scorched metal undersides glowed orange.

The colored woman stood, as tall and straight-backed as ever, wearing a man's shirt and overalls. She stirred something in one container, sniffed the contents, tapped it into the bucket, and set her spoon on a rock at her feet. "Mr. Roger," she called, still not facing me. "Robert Bryson said he gave you a lift home when you was hitching on Wednesday."

"Yes, Miz Washburn," I said and walked toward her. "May I join you?"

"An ole woman's always glad for company." She made room for me on the log. I sat beside her, and she said, "Your daddy's killing brung you back?"

"Yes, ma'am. Jay and Chet, too, but only until Sunday." She didn't reply, and a torrent of words spilled from me to fill the silence. "I can't believe how much has gone on since I enlisted, with Nat and Leona passing and their son and his family going up North. Mama shooting Papa and taking up with his old enemy, that revenuer Bascom. Papa's brother and sister threatening Mama and whupping Darlene over some rumor of money. We weren't here but a few hours when Chet drove a man to kill himself, and tonight I nearly—" I clacked my teeth together before completing the confession.

She stirred whatever boiled in another pail. Steam from pungent herbs tickled my nose. "There's been a lot of commotion, that's for sure," she said.

Thinking she didn't have anything more to say about it, I cast about for another subject. "Anybody see the Woman lately?"

"Not that I heard. I'm starting to wonder if folks can't see haints no more."

"Well, it's my fault nobody's seeing the Dutchman. I mean, your mama's spirit light." I stared at my hands in the fire glow. "After she...passed through me or whatever happened, I thought I'd always feel special, but I've gone right back to being me."

She patted my knee. "That's enough, sonny. Can't 'spect to go through life a-sparkling. It'd be a burden, sure enough, being so different from everybody else."

I glanced around at the home she'd made for herself in the back of beyond. Lovingly tended gardens bordered the cottage. From the porch rafters, bunches of roots, wilted leaves, and dried flowers hung upside down like bats. At least this little piece of my childhood hadn't changed. Still, it finally occurred to me how far she'd chosen to live from all others, coloreds and whites alike.

"Miz Washburn, you've done a lot for me over the years, but can I ask you for one more thing?"

"This have to do with what happened tonight?"

I began to correct her, the words "almost happened" ready to spring from my mouth, but I realized she was right—something *had* happened. It was just my good fortune that it'd been an attempted killing instead of cold-blooded murder. I gulped down that response and instead replied, "Yes, ma'am. I tried to shoot Darlene's husband."

"You don't need anything from me to fix that."

"But I wanted so badly to do it. I need something to take away the hate in my heart. To wipe out that violence I never knew was inside me. What if I see red again, and this time the gun's loaded?"

"Say I gave you a potion you believed bone-deep would cure you. Then you return to Texas and get your heart broken, an ache so bad you can't breathe—"

Despite the fire, a fit of shaking seized me. "You mean Rienzi's fixing to break up with me?"

"I ain't saying that, but what if she did? You gonna hitch your way back over here and ask for a dose of my medicine to fix your heartache? Later on, you'll get knocked on your fanny by another bolt from the blue—wouldn't you come a-knocking again? Soon enough, you'd be on my doorstep day and night, asking me to mend every little thing that ails you."

"But you have powers. Way back when, you cursed Robert Bryson, and then he couldn't swallow until you lifted the spell."

"That's 'cause he believed I could do. He took his power and gave it to me without ever once thinking he had any control. No reason why you should go and do the same."

She placed her palm over my heart. Her hand felt as hot as the pails over the fire must've been, making me flinch. "Roger, don't you never ever give nobody control over how you feel or what you do. You can't change other folks, but you can always choose how you act. Don't want to be like your papa, all full of rage and violence and such? Decide not to. Nobody makes you do a thing."

"But—"

"Go on now." She shooed me off the log. "I gotta mix up a poultice for a child that is really and truly ailing. You think on what I said and see if it don't make sense by the time the rooster's crowing up the sun."

Feeling off-kilter as I tried to get out of her way, I staggered to the edge of the firelight and considered her advice. "Um, goodbye, in case I can't get back here before I need to leave for Texas."

"Don't you fret about that none. We'll see each other again—in this world or the next. And what a grand time we'll have then."

I left her as she carefully ladled contents from three pails into a fourth, creating a plume of yellow smoke. My return through the woods seemed to go much faster—a good thing, because my head buzzed with Wanda's words and my lingering horror at what I'd nearly done, and I wanted to lie down somewhere.

As I neared Mama's home in the moonlight, I reckoned I would make a pallet out of any moldering hay still in the barn loft and spend the rest of the night there. I headed that way but stopped when I noticed the back door of the house open. Bracing for cries of passion, I heard a pained groan instead, the sound of an injured man.

I crept up the porch stairs and looked into the dark kitchen. A memory came to me from when I was a barefooted child: Nat's huge, warm hand holding mine as he guided me and murmured reassurances to overcome my fear of the dark. Now I was comfortable at night, sometimes even preferring it, but I still shuddered as I considered who I might find. Maybe Papa's ghost had attacked Ed Bascom for romancing Mama. Maybe Bascom had shot another of her lovers. Maybe Harvey and Rutha had ambushed someone else.

I took a few steps inside and angled left toward where the kitchen table and benches would be. It took me a few tries blindly grasping overhead to find the length of twine, but I finally yanked down on it and the light bulb flashed to life. I blinked at the sudden brightness and the scene before me.

The toes of my shoes were less than an inch from a gaping hole in the floor. Boards had been stacked neatly on the long bench seat, which, like the table, had been shoved aside. Instead of just revealing the crawlspace under the house, there also was an empty enclosure the size of a suitcase.

I had spent most of my life eating just above that secret spot.

Another groan tore my attention away from that mystery. Behind me, propped against the stove, Chet sprawled. Dried blood caked his nose and mouth.

CHAPTER 12

I HURRIED TO THE ICE CHEST ON THE BACK PORCH AND, repeating my actions of the day before, chipped off a hunk for Chet. I wrapped it in a rag and handed him the cold bundle, which he placed against his swollen jaw.

"Was it Rutha?" I asked.

Even in his battered state, he looked like he wanted to knock me into next Tuesday, so I added in a rush, "Harvey, I meant."

"No." Grunting, he sat up. "It was Sheriff Reeder's deputy: Brooks."

The thought of the lanky guy in the too-big uniform beating Chet made me laugh.

He glared at me. "I ain't feeling so poorly that I can't take your head off."

"Sorry. It's just...how'd it happen? Did he ambush you?"

"No, I did that to him." Chet peered at the ice pack, now stained red with his blood, and reapplied it to his face. "Hitched back from Colquitt, saw a beam of light sweeping around inside the house. I snuck in here and got the jump on him. But he slipped my punch like your Rienzi can do, and he hit me harder than anybody's ever socked me." He worked his jaw in a slow circle, wincing all the while but forcing himself to complete the circuit. "It wasn't a fair fight, though. He used his big, metal flashlight. Felt worse than Papa's baseball bat."

I pointed at the suitcase-sized hidey-hole. "Did you see what he took?"

"Brooks was empty-handed—except for that flashlight." He looked past me. "Think that was down there the whole time we was growing up?"

"I reckon. It looks as old as the wood around it. Whatever Papa kept in there could be what his brother and sister are after." I shook my head. "Maybe we lived above a fortune for years. Remember that time I spilled well water on the kitchen table, and it leaked through and soaked Papa's pants?"

"Yeah, he backhanded you twice. So hard the second time, I thought your head would fall off."

"Maybe that water drained down into the hiding place and soaked the money hidden there. Could be he removed the money that night and spent it on himself and his other families."

"But it's like what Mama said. If Papa had money, why'd we live like this?" He waved his free hand at our meager surroundings.

It would've killed him to know he'd pantomimed Mama's gesture exactly, so I didn't point it out. Instead I sat beside him, propped against the stove with my legs straight out. I couldn't help but notice that his legs were longer by a good three inches. Even with everything I'd been through, I wondered if I'd always feel like a kid beside him. I sighed and said, "Maybe it was his rainy-day money, and what with prison and then taking up with the sawmill widow, he forgot about it."

"Doesn't seem like he ever forgot a red cent."

"Well then, what's your theory?"

He scowled. "That's another of your Rienzi words. I don't theorify, I conjecturate."

"Okay, and...?"

"And I think it was empty all along. Papa probably got the big head when he struck his bootlegging deal with the Ashers—figured so much money'd be rolling in, he'd have to hide a bunch of it from Mama so she wouldn't spend it all on herself. If we tear up the boards in the other rooms, I'll bet we find more secret places, likewise empty. Because he never did make much as the middleman."

"What's that mean?"

"You know, the guy in between the Ashers cooking up the moonshine and the men pouring the liquor from the five-gallon barrels Papa delivered into those Mason jars they sold to customers." Chet swiveled his jaw experimentally again with less wincing before he returned the ice pack to his face. "He probably couldn't charge too much, or he'd have to answer to both sides—the Ashers would raise sand with him if he made their shine too expensive, and the retailers would find a cheaper source."

"How do you know so much about this?"

"Remember how I hoboed before enlisting? One of the jobs I took was with a guy in Kentucky who did the same thing as Papa, but with bourbon instead of white liquor. Priced hisself out of business and got his dumb ass shot to pieces the very same day."

"Speaking of getting shot full of holes, how was your date with Trudy?"

"It wasn't a date. I was hungry, is all."

"Get your fill?"

He growled in reply. I rested my head against the iron stove behind us, saying, "Funny how Brooks knew about the hidey-hole but we didn't. Was he in uniform?"

"Yep. Maybe doing the High Sheriff's bidding."

"How did Sheriff Reeder find out about it? And why would he care?"

"Hell if I know." Another glare at me. He bobbed the rag-wrapped ice chunk in his hand as if weighing a potential weapon. "I think I liked you better when you stuttered. It kept you from asking so many damn questions."

"I can't help it." Snatching the bloody ice pack from him, I placed it against the top of my scalp where a headache had commenced to throb. "When Jay came up with his plan for us reuniting, I thought we'd just loaf around and have some fun. Now everybody's getting beat up, and there are people dying and almost dying, and—"

"Wait. Who almost died? I only walloped Hugh Bradley."

I took a breath, let it out slowly, and told him about my attempted murder of Wyatt Weaver.

Chet took it all in without interrupting. Then he frowned and asked, "When shooting Wyatt didn't work, why didn't you club him to death with the rifle stock? That's what I woulda done."

"But Darlene was right—I overreacted. What he did wasn't a killing offense."

"What he said about her offends me right enough to kill him. Let's go finish the sonofabitch." He jumped to his feet. His eyelids fluttered, and he swayed and had to brace himself against the stovetop. "In the morning," he murmured, eyes closed, chin down. "We'll kill him proper then."

Footsteps thumped across the back porch, and Jay entered the kitchen, puffing away on a Lucky Strike. Cherry-red lipstick streaked his mouth, cheeks, and neck. "Hey, fellas. Who're we killing?"

SITTING CROSS-LEGGED ON THE KITCHEN floor, we were still making plans about what to do with Wyatt and Brooks when Mama finally got home. We fell silent as Papa's Chrysler raced up the sandy driveway. No doubt Mama and Bascom could see the light seeping through the closed shutters.

Not that having her sons home put the kibosh on her romantic plans. After a lengthy interval—during which Jay and I stared at our shoes, and Chet gnawed what remained of the ice chunk—her high heels finally clip-clopped onto the front porch and into the house. Bascom's footsteps didn't accompany hers. He drove away much slower than when he'd arrived, like a man savoring his success.

Mama walked down the hall and peered into the kitchen. Her lipstick, a darker red than Jay's new girlfriend's, had smeared beyond the border of her mouth, and her emerald dress was wrinkled and misbuttoned from neckline to navel. She nodded at Jay. "Well, at least one of you is making the most of your leave. Chet, you in another fight, or did a girl get rough with you?"

Chet pointed at the hiding place Brooks had revealed under the floor. "Sheriff Reeder's deputy ransacked this here kitchen and then clubbed me. You know about that secret spot?"

"Oh my stars." She hurried over to the hole. "Was that here all this time? What'd Brooks take out of it?"

"We think it was empty. But he knew about it somehow, when none of us did."

Jay said, "Maybe it was part of the house when it was built. Mama, is the landlord still the same guy that's always owned this place?"

"No, it's mine now, free and clear."

My brothers and I traded a look. I asked, "How'd you manage to buy it? We got divvied up among your sisters years ago because you couldn't even afford the rent. Remember? You gave me away to my real father and crazy Aunt Arzula and nearly got me killed."

"I recall perfectly well. And you'll mind your tone if you wanna keep sleeping under my roof."

Jay flipped his spent butt into the sink. "Can you at least tell us how you came by the money?"

She lifted her chin and peered down her nose at us. "It was a gift. Eddie Bascom bought it and signed the deed over to me. No strings attached."

I eyed her mussed face and misbuttoned dress but kept my mouth shut.

CHAPTER 13

MAMA COULDN'T—OR WOULDN'T—SHED ANY LIGHT ON THE hidden spot under the kitchen table, so my brothers and I quit our interrogation and turned in. We slept on the floor of the front room again atop pallets of old quilts. The discomfort and my brothers' snores reminded me of the barracks at Lackland.

On Friday morning, we replaced the floorboards Brooks had pulled up and moved the kitchen table and benches back into place. Mama served a breakfast of eggs, sausages, and biscuits and ate at the counter, what Lonnie used to call the cook's table. She stayed as silent as we did.

Though my brothers and I all needed a bath and a shave, we'd donned yesterday's clothes on the off chance things went catawampus with Darlene's husband. No point in blooding fresh duds. But wearing the same outfit again and reeking as I did reminded me once more of the life I'd escaped and my deepening fear of fate forcing me to return to it.

Chet's wounds had begun to scab over, and dark bruises replaced the swelling around his mouth and nose. Traces of Geneva's lipstick remained on Jay's face and neck despite him rubbing a wet rag over his skin. The only signs I carried of our most recent adventures were on the inside: opposing feelings warred within me about what I'd almost done to Wyatt and what we now planned for him.

We bolted our food, Jay thanked Mama on our behalf, and we piled into her pickup for the short drive to Darlene's. With the windows down due to another warm morning, Jay managed to get through two cigarettes before we arrived. Our first task was to remove our sister from the house and potential harm. We found her on the front porch, trying to sweep away the ever-present sand and grit.

Her face looked a little less gruesome, and she moved with more ease than the day before. After we clambered from the truck and congregated on the steps below her, she glanced toward the closed front door and whispered, "I'm fine. No need to waste your leave checking on me."

Chet said, "We came for Wyatt."

She looked at me instead of him. "What did you tell them about last night?"

I said, "Everything."

Still keeping her voice low, she replied, "Then they know nothing really happened except you went out of your head for a spell."

"Darlene," Jay said, sounding sterner than usual, "Wyatt's the one who's lost his mind, messing with the MacLeods." He stepped onto the porch. "This won't take but a minute."

She blocked the doorway, holding her broom at port arms.

We had anticipated her likely interference and switched to Plan B. Chet said, "C'mon, Roger, we'll do this the hard way." He and I darted toward the rear of the house. I heard Darlene's shoes rattle the stairs as she hobbled down in pursuit of us, leaving the front door undefended.

Chet and I dashed onto the back porch while our sister hissed curses at us and tried to catch up. By the time we entered the kitchen, Jay had retrieved the revolver from the shelf where I'd told him he would find it. He gave me a nod and disappeared inside the bedroom.

I heard a soft click. He'd thumbed the hammer of the .38 Special.

Darlene shouted, "Wyatt, watch out." She pushed past us and hurried to the bedroom doorway, with Chet and me now following her.

Perched on the edge of the mattress, Jay had forced Wyatt into a sitting position against the headboard, with the barrel of the gun under the man's plump chin. Our brother-in-law looked with wide eyes from Jay to the three of us clustered in the entrance. Sweat had begun to darken his strap undershirt. The air reeked of the beer that had oozed out of his pores overnight.

Darlene screamed, "Don't!"

"I won't," Jay said, voice deadly calm, "if ole Wyatt here clears out of this house and your life and never looks back." He pushed the muzzle harder into the soft roll of skin, which tilted Wyatt's head. "Hmm? What do you say, Wyatt? We'll let you live if you do that right now, and you never, ever talk to our sister again, write her, or even look her way. You'll move to the base barracks and put in for the first spot that opens up outside of Georgia, even if it means going to the other end of the world."

Chet stepped into the room and pointed his finger like a second gun. "Don't think that us returning to our duty stations makes a lick of difference. We're putting the word out to all our friends around these parts. If you come back here, you'll be dead before the sun even moves a jot in the sky. Got it?"

"You've all gone crazy," Darlene shrieked. She grabbed my arm. "Bud, this is your fault."

I shook her off. "No, it's Mama's for not teaching you better about men. We're saving you from yourself."

Wyatt rasped, "If you shoot me, you boys will hang for sure."

I said, "You forget—the High Sheriff's our cousin. He always looks after family."

"Okay," Wyatt sputtered, "okay, you win. She don't mean nothing to me no how."

Crying, Darlene staggered down the hall and into the kitchen. I knew she'd thank us one day. We still had to make sure Harvey and Rutha stayed away, but at least Husband Number Five wouldn't plague her anymore.

"First step, get your clothes," Jay said, keeping the revolver in place. "We'll drop you off at the base."

"But my car..."

Chet said, "It's Darlene's now. You're lucky we're not kicking you out in your skivvies."

While they watched him pack two battered suitcases, I took the key to his Plymouth from the nightstand and entered the kitchen. Darlene slumped at the table, where overlapping rings from Wyatt's countless beer bottles marred the wood surface. She cried into her cupped hands.

"Here," I said. I placed the key beside her elbow.

"You ruined everything," she bawled.

"We made everything better. We're giving you back your freedom."

After another minute of weeping, she wiped her reddened face and scowled at me through puffy eyes. "Freedom to starve. Freedom to freeze to death come a cold snap."

"What do you mean?"

"Wyatt's the breadwinner. I don't have any money for food or rent."

"You have his car. Drive to Albany or Macon or up to Atlanta again and get a job. Sell it if you have to and start building your nest egg."

"And die alone? You three would like that, wouldn't you? For me to never marry again, live out my days as a spinster—all the while thanking y'all for my *freedom*."

I retreated a step. "We just want you to be happy. For you to find someone who'll treat you like you deserve."

"But what about what I want? You ever think of that?"

I dropped my gaze, unable to meet her fierce stare. "So, um, what do you want?"

In the hallway, Jay said, "Move it." He shoved Wyatt ahead of him, the revolver aimed at our brother-in-law's head as they marched toward the front room. Suitcases held together with straps swung from Wyatt's hands.

Chet took point, walking ahead so the man wouldn't be tempted to bolt.

Darlene swiped at fresh tears as she watched them leave. "I wanna be taken care of. Have somebody I can count on. Wyatt did that, but now you're running him off."

"But the way he treats you, talks about you—"

"I told you last night, it's a damn sight better than getting beat like a rug. Who gave y'all the right to play God and decide what's best for me?"

"We're your brothers. We're supposed to look out for you."

She indicated her bruised face and missing teeth. "You didn't save me from Harvey and Rutha—the real problem."

I tried my last gambit. "Rienzi says it's better to rely on yourself, not to depend on anybody else."

"Sounds like you rely on her plenty. Careful you don't scare her off too."

CHAPTER 14

CHET RODE IN THE PICKUP BED WITH WYATT TO MAKE SURE he didn't jump out during our drive to the Army base. In the truck cab, I finally had elbow room, and the day was warming nicely, but I huddled against the passenger door, chilled by Darlene's words.

Jay pulled onto the highway. Between puffs of his cigarette, he said, "Mission accomplished. We got Wyatt so scared, he didn't realize I put the gun on the shelf on our way out the door."

"Here's hoping Darlene won't use it on us next time we check on her."

He glanced over. "What do you mean?"

"You didn't hear her caterwauling?"

"Yeah, but—"

"Those were angry tears. She's fit to be tied."

"Once it sinks in that ole Wyatt won't be talking ugly to her again or running her down to anybody else, she'll dance a jig."

"She said she can't afford to buy food or pay the rent."

He tapped the wheel for a moment. "Well, she can stay with Mama until she gets herself sorted out again. With that revenuer paying Mama's bills, Darlene can live high on the hog."

"She did say she wants to be taken care of," I allowed. "But I think she had a man in mind to do that."

"A man will be doing that—Ed Bascom. And even better, she won't have to spread her legs for him."

The way Mama does, he didn't have to add. It bothered me that we really hadn't made the situation any better for her or Darlene.

Somehow, I thought we MacLeod boys would size up the situation and fix everything well before our leave ended. But if I considered how we'd handled things in the past, I was forced to admit that nothing had ever gotten fixed. All three of us had merely saved our own hides instead, escaping into the military rather than solving the problems at home.

True, we were just kids then—and some might've said all three of us still were—but I'd always thought of us as battlers, able to handle whatever life dished out and then counterpunching like hell. In reality, though, we were survivors, rats able to scurry to safety from a sinking ship but never giving a thought about plugging the leak.

After I voiced this to Jay, he shrugged and flicked the remnant of his smoke out the window. "I was worried about Mama until we found out Bascom was seeing to her. Harvey and Rutha won't wanna mess with a federal lawman. He solves all our problems."

"But what if he's just one more problem *we* have to solve?"

"How do you mean?"

I folded my arms. "I don't trust him."

"That's 'cause he's poking our mother. But she's always done things this way, even when she was with Papa. If we're rats fleeing a capsizing ship, then she's the unsinkable Reva MacLeod, doing whatever she has to, even when that meant giving us away. She'll go from one fella to another for the rest of her life and do just fine."

"But she doesn't look fine, even with Papa's sworn enemy paying the bills."

"Give it time. Could be that Bascom is her knight in shining armor."

"I think he's a good-time Charlie in a shiny suit."

Jay laughed as he made the turn toward the German POW camp where Wyatt was stationed and my friends and I used to trade homemade biscuits with the prisoners for cans of evaporated milk and other Red Cross rations they received. The paved road dead-ended at a gatehouse with a uniformed MP posted out front. Jay braked to a halt twenty yards away.

From the truck bed, Chet growled, "Remember what I said." He tossed the suitcases into the dirt on the shoulder of the road.

Wyatt jumped over the side—maybe a display of bravado to show us who the real man was—but he landed badly and yelped as he turned an ankle. Chet hopped down with ease.

I slid over so he could join us in the cab. For once, I sat between him and Jay. We were out of birth order. It felt wrong, like it was bad luck.

Jay wheeled the truck around, and my last view of Wyatt Weaver was of him limping toward the gatehouse, swaying side to side with the weight of his bags. I asked Chet, "What did you tell him to remember?"

"A few months back, I talked to a guy who'd fought in the South Pacific. He told me all these vicious things the Japs did to anybody they captured. Apologies to Rienzi, but they were evil bastards. I told Wyatt those stories, warning him that he'd get even worse if he disobeyed our orders. He actually peed his pants. Reckon the MP will have a good laugh at his expense."

I said, "At least we didn't have to spill any blood. What's next, digging for gold?"

Chet touched the bruises on his mouth. "No, we gotta pay a visit to Sheriff Reeder's deputy."

The High Sheriff had an office in the Miller County courthouse, where Chet had beaten Hugh Bradley to a pulp. Lawyers in suits and felt hats and secretaries in dresses and high heels strolled up and down the exterior marble steps. The old shame from my school days of being a rube among townies turned me into a fidgeting, self-conscious mess. Even if I'd been in my Class A uniform, I would've felt underdressed.

Inside, the footsteps on polished floors and the chatter of those with business in the courthouse echoed around us, creating a clamor that made my head throb. Jay snagged a passing policeman and asked for directions to Reeder's office.

We took a flight of stairs to the second floor. Past the courtroom and down one hall, we spotted "Miller County Sheriff's Office" stenciled in black on a pebbled-glass door. Behind it came the rapid clack of typewriter keys, putting me in mind of the Army Air Forces procurement office I worked in at Lackland.

I asked my brothers, "Do we knock?"

Chet barged in.

A pretty secretary looked up from her desk. Pale fingers with blood-red nails were poised over her machine. The smart little hat that perched on her head bore an olive feather in the band, which matched the color of her jacket. She asked, "Can I help you, young man?" Looking past him, she added, "Um, young men."

Chet said, "We're here for Brooks. Where's he at?"

"The *deputy* is yonder at the county jail." She peered at the wounds on his nose and mouth. "I'm supposing you're familiar with the place, bless your heart."

Jay put his long arm around Chet's shoulders and turned him toward the exit. "Thank you kindly, ma'am. We'll be on our way."

As soon as they were back in the hall, I closed the door and followed them.

Chet shook off Jay. "I swear to God, we're wasting all our time chasing people this way and that and coming up empty, like they're haints." He raised a fist and appeared to look for something to punch, but everything nearby—except us—was made of stone, wood, or glass. With a growl, he dropped his hand.

Jay took the lead down the staircase. "What I need to invent is some way to track everybody so we can find them easy. Maybe—"

"Dammit, Jay," Chet bellowed. "I'm sick of your invention talk. Just shut up a minute."

I'd never heard Chet raise his voice to Jay, let alone cuss him. I wouldn't have dreamed of doing it.

Instead of getting his back up, though, Jay gave Chet a smile. "Steady, big man. We'll find him and fix this. We'll fix everything, sure enough."

Chet grunted in reply. The cords in his neck stayed rigid. "You're a lot more confident than me."

"I've got faith is all. Roger, you with me?"

"Always." I looked from one brother to the other. "Us against the world, right?"

"Maybe so," Chet said. He dodged around a pair of men in suits and fedoras and slipped outside.

Jay and I took our time catching up to give him a chance to cool off.

We reached Chet a block away on the sidewalk. He stood stock still, facing Mama's truck. Leaning against it, dressed in overalls and woolen shirts, were my old nemesis Buck Bradley, his older brother Mike, and their dad. All three held hunting rifles.

CHAPTER 15

Too bad Jay hadn't invented a way to make us invisible.

He jabbed his thumb toward the courthouse. "Lotta lawmen and judges thataway. Be a quick trip to the gallows if you shoot us in cold blood."

The Bradley boys' father, Leo, pressed his rump against the grille of Mama's truck, as if bracing himself. He raised his rifle. "Y'all gotta answer for Hugh."

"We didn't kill him," Chet said. He stepped forward, which caused Buck and Mike to lift their rifles too. "He did that to hisself."

"After you and your freakshow brother there went and jumped him."

The night before, I'd tried to shoot a man. Now three men were about to shoot us. *Live by the gun, die by the gun* and other useless warnings clouded my thoughts. My insides felt like they had melted and were draining into the hollow, rigid trunks of my legs.

I glanced behind me, hoping somebody was coming to our rescue, but no one headed toward us, and those walking up and down the stone courthouse steps were probably too far away to understand any screams for help. None of the cars going by even slowed down. Maybe the drivers thought we were just some country bumpkins having a rowdy family reunion.

How bad would the rifle bullets hurt before they ended me? Would they feel like fire or ice? I wanted to hold Rienzi one more time and tell her how sorry I was that I wouldn't be with her forever the way I'd promised.

Leo said, "Y'all are coming with us." He gestured with his rifle at a battered, rusty, brown Nash 600 nearby that looked like it had tumbled down a hill.

Chet said, "What if we don't?"

"Then we shoot you dead right now and take our chances with the goddamned law."

Out in the street behind the Bradleys, car horns began to honk. A truck had paused, blocking the westbound lane—a Sunbeam bread truck. Jerry was at the wheel, peaked cap pushed up on his head. He seemed to be studying us.

Thinking he needed a sign and wanting to distract our would-be killers from the commotion Jerry was creating, I raised my hands in surrender and told my brothers, "We better do what he says."

Chet started to turn on me but then looked past the Bradleys at the traffic jam with Jerry at its front. "I reckon so." He raised his arms high overhead.

Jay followed our lead. "We can't all fit in that jalopy of yours," he said. "How about I ride with you and Mike, and Buck here drives our Mama's truck with Chet and Roger beside him?"

"Quit your stalling," Leo said. "I'll cram the freak in the trunk if I gotta."

Buck said, "Yeah, I'll break Bud's arms and legs to make sure he fits good." He grinned at me and stroked the rifle butt.

More car horns joined the chorus. Mike Bradley shifted like he wanted to check the ruckus behind them, so I took two steps toward our firing squad to hold his attention. My brothers did the same, which made the Bradleys aim at us.

With no oncoming traffic blocking him, Jerry revved his engine and tore in our direction. Hoping to protect my brothers from gunfire, I pretended to stumble, dropping my hands to the pavement to catch myself. All three rifle barrels tracked me.

Jerry rammed the rear of Mama's truck, shoving the front tires over the low curb and pitching all three Bradleys onto their faces. Leo and Mike dropped their hunting rifles as they sprawled on the concrete. Buck managed to hold onto his. Jay and Chet scooped up the two loose guns.

Buck pushed to his knees. Blood ran from gouges in his nose and forehead and most of his knuckles. "Freak," he yelled at me and raised his firearm.

I sidestepped, grabbed the barrel, and yanked the weapon from his wounded hands. Fury over what he and his family had almost done consumed me. The red haze once again blurred my vision. Unlike at Darlene's, this gun was no doubt loaded.

My old enemy got his feet under him, looming over me even more than he had when we were children. Jay and Chet covered the other two and shouted for them to stay down.

Jerry jumped from his truck in his deliveryman uniform. His peaked cap tumbled off as he ran toward us and hollered my name.

I remembered facing Buck on the schoolyard, boxing gloves covering our fists, kids encircling us and screaming for Buck to destroy me. New voices clamored in my head now, ordering me what to do to *him*. It was time to kill or be killed.

One voice cut through the hubbub, though: Wanda Washburn's, telling me not to give my power to anyone. If I murdered an unarmed man, I might never get that power back.

The red haze dissipated, and my mind cleared, allowing me to remember what had ended our boxing match years before. Instead of turning the rifle around and shooting Buck, I looped it low and swung upward, catching him under the chin with the walnut stock. My massive uppercut laid him out, just like on the playground. His head thudded on the truck hood before he tumbled to the pavement, senseless.

Exhaustion flooded through me. The rifle went from being a club to a cane as I leaned on it for support.

"Hunh," Jerry said, surveying the three prone Bradleys. "Guess you boys didn't need much help after all."

Jay told him, "You helped plenty. Thank you." He rushed through an explanation for why Leo and his sons were holding guns on us.

"I'm glad my route took me in this direction, but yer mama ain't gonna appreciate that big dent I put in her truck bumper." He patted my shoulder and headed off some men in suits who hurried over now that the hubbub had ended.

"She won't even notice," Chet growled. "Too busy getting her own bumper rammed. But I reckon these three ain't damaged enough yet." He aimed his confiscated rifle at Leo's head.

"No killing," Jay said.

"They were gonna do it to us." He and Jay stared at each other for a moment. Then he snarled, "Fine." Taking a page from me, he swung the rifle like an ax, chopping the butt down on the back of one of Leo's knees and then one of Mike's. Both men howled in pain.

Chet looked at Jay, grinning. "I better do the other ones."

"That's probably enough as is." He put Leo's gun in Mama's truck and then considered the dirty whitewalls on the Nash. "Course, kneecapping their car might not be a bad idea." He withdrew a knife from his pocket and flattened the two closest tires.

More horns honked, this time from the eastbound lane, where Jerry's vehicle was jutting into the traffic. He turned from the growing crowd and asked, "Want me to get a cop?"

"We're heading that way anyhow," Chet called. On the way to the truck, he stepped on Mike's neck, grinding his heel and making the man yelp. He tossed the rifle onto the seat.

I leaned into my old friend. "Thanks for everything, Jerry, including the arsenal."

He looked over his shoulder at me. "Lemme shake loose of this mob so I can get my truck outta yer way."

"You got us started over the curb—we can just hop it. Meet us for dinner at Dora's around noon. We're buying."

I checked on Buck to make sure he was still breathing, while my brothers rolled Mike and Leo out of the way. The two bloodied men cursed us as they held their injured knees.

Leo spat, "We ain't done with you sonsabitches."

Chet snatched the remaining rifle from me, spun it end over end as smoothly as a drill-team captain, and slammed the butt down between Leo's legs. The man squealed and writhed as he covered his privates. Chet said, "Only we can talk about our mama that way, even if it *is* the God's honest truth." He jabbed Leo's unprotected stomach. "Got it?"

Jay climbed into the truck, fired up the engine, and beeped the horn. "Come on," he said. "Enough fun and games."

Chet joined us in the truck. I sat in the middle. Once again, we were out of order.

Jay stomped the accelerator, jumping the back wheels over the curb. He steered past the three Bradleys before dropping from the sidewalk onto the street again. Given the bumps I felt under the tires and the cries that followed, it's possible we ran over someone's hand or foot. Maybe both.

Chapter 16

We rolled through Colquitt in silence, the Bradleys' three rifles lying across our laps. I didn't know about my brothers, but I was too caught up with imagining how close we'd come to getting murdered to want to chitchat.

Finally Chet said, "I shoulda shot them all when I had the chance."

Jay shook his head as he took a deep drag on a cigarette, his cheeks deflating. "Then the Colquitt police would be hauling you down to the calaboose in handcuffs. Instead you're riding in style to the county jail with us." He sat taller behind the wheel, as if driving a new Cadillac rather than Mama's beat-up truck.

"And armed to the teeth instead of defenseless," I said, inspecting the single-shot weapons. Despite being well used, they'd been maintained much better than Leo Bradley's Nash. "These will come in handy if they make another run at us."

Chet jabbed me with a sharp elbow to the ribs. "I thought you was all ajangle yesterday over almost shooting Wyatt. Now you're fixing to go to war?"

"It's not murder if somebody's trying to get you first. Then it's just protecting yourself. I'd fight a thousand Bradleys to get back to Rienzi." Before they could question my loyalty, I added in a rush, "And to protect our family, of course. Us against the world, right? I love y'all."

"Aww," Jay said. "He loves us. I love you, too, fellas." He turned the truck toward the Miller County jail. After a pause, he said, "Chet? Hey, buddy, you wanna add your two cents about brotherly love?"

Chet peered at the walnut rifle butt I'd used to uppercut Buck. Some of my old rival's blood had dripped on it. He murmured, "What woulda happened to us if Jerry hadn't come along?"

"We'd have figured something out," Jay said and parked across the street from the Miller County jailhouse. Sheriff Reeder didn't merely keep prisoners inside those brick walls. He conducted public hangings out back. What was more, he and his family lived there. We were about to invade his home, where he regularly executed folks. Now that we were here, being his cousin didn't feel like it offered any sort of protection.

I asked Jay, "What if we didn't escape? Would we be dead now?"

"Naw, something woulda broke our way. We survived Papa—that makes us invincible."

I nodded toward the jail. "Are we going to be dead soon enough anyway?"

"Surprise is on our side." He scooped up the three barrels and nodded for Chet to lift the three stocks. "Still, better to set these on the floorboard than walk in with them—no point pushing our luck."

Three rifles underfoot made it hard for me to exit the truck. I ended up having to scooch across the seat like a little kid.

Drawing on the dusty side of the pickup, Jay finalized a Plan A and a Plan B and gave each of us a role to play. Before we could lose our nerve—or at least before I could lose mine—we crossed the street and walked inside the building.

Brooks sat at a desk near the front door in his oversized clothes doing paperwork with a pencil. The pink tip of his tongue poked from the corner of his mouth. Nobody else was around, so we went with Plan B, stopping shoulder to shoulder across from him.

The deputy glanced up at us, and from the way his head jerked and eyes watered, he must've bitten his tongue. He dropped his hand to his holster. "Ain't a good idea squaring off with a lawman."

His voice sounded high-pitched and shaky, like a boy caught stealing. "Gallows are out back if my bullets don't finish you first."

I was getting sick of people threatening to kill me. Before anger could settle in, though, I recalled Reeder saying that Brooks could shoot the eye out of a crow at fifty paces. He might've looked awkward, but he was also lethal, and he had gotten the best of Chet in a fight. Good to bear that in mind.

Jay swung his arm in front of Chet to hold him in place. Grinning, he said, "No call for threats, deputy. We just came in to report a crime."

Brooks studied us. "Whereabouts was this crime?"

I played my part, saying, "Over to the courthouse. Mr. Bradley and two of his sons drew down on us."

His shoulders relaxed, but he kept a hand on his gun. "Oh, that there's a town police matter. Best to take it up with them." He glanced down at his paperwork. My favorite teacher, Mrs. Gladney, would've been mortified by his handwriting. "I gotta get back to this."

Chet pushed Jay's arm away, which wasn't part of either plan. He raised one leg and kicked the desk against Brooks, pinning his gun hand under the table. Chet launched himself across the blotter. He seized the deputy's shoulders and toppled his chair backward. Our middle brother ended up sitting on Brooks's narrow chest, legs trapping the deputy's arms and fist drawn back. He roared, "I gotta county crime to report."

Faced with a new Plan C, Jay and I rushed around either side of the desk. Jay grabbed Chet's raised arm.

Brooks winced, "Ow, you bounced my head off the floor."

"Kinda like you bounced your flashlight off my face? After robbing our house?"

"Hey, buddy," Jay said in a soothing voice, "the sheriff could walk in any second now."

"We're kin—he wouldn't do anything to us."

I crouched to put my face near Chet's. "Brooks is Reeder's grandson, remember? That makes him our cousin too. Would you really beat up one of your own?"

Chet glared at me. "It never stopped me from clobbering you, way back when."

I swiveled my head to look at Brooks, hoping to give him a chance to apologize. "Isn't there something you can say to keep him from doing to you what he did to Hugh Bradley?"

Brooks squeaked, "How bad did he clobber you?"

The question made me frown. "No lasting damage. Why?"

"'Cause we're more than cousins." He stared past me, focusing on Chet. "We got the same daddy."

CHAPTER 17

WITH HIS FREE HAND, CHET BUNCHED A FISTFUL OF THE deputy's uniform shirt. "That's a lie. You'll say anything to keep me from whupping you."

Speaking fast, Brooks cried, "It's how I knew where to look in your house. Years ago, he told me about it."

Chet rocked back, his grip slackening. Instead of resisting Jay, he now seemed to be held up by our oldest brother, who, like me, was still gawping at Brooks's news. We all peered down at him, and Chet muttered, "You got his eyes and nose and hair, same as Jay. Same as me."

Same as Tommy Rush, I thought, picturing Papa's other bastard son, who I'd met—and punched—years ago. I realized there could've been a hundred people running around South Georgia with Papa's features, given all the tomcatting he'd done.

That hadn't been his worst sin, of course. The times Papa beat and humiliated my brothers and me—and shot Mama—all flashed through my mind. I asked Brooks, "Was he good to you?"

"Yeah, he treated me fine, but I never saw him much." Pinned, he used his chin to point up at Chet. "If you're not going to hit me, can I at least get off the floor?"

Jay yanked Chet to his feet, freeing Brooks, who crab-walked back a few paces. Our half-brother lurched upright. He tucked in his shirt and rubbed the back of his head. "You know, I wouldn't have shot you."

Chet touched the wounds on his mouth and nose. "That's too bad. I'd have punched you for sure and would still be punching you if these two hadn't stopped me."

Before my brother could go to war again, I said, "Brooks, does your daddy—well, the man who thought he was your daddy—did he know that our papa and your mama, um, got together?"

"I don't think so, but Sheriff Reeder did. My mama's his daughter. I got my suspicions that he introduced Mance MacLeod to your mother to lure him away from the family."

Jay lit up a Lucky Strike and ground out the spent match underfoot. "Then something like a year later, they got hitched, and here came Darlene, me, and Chet. And Roger showed up too."

Brooks glanced at me, frowning. I shrugged. "I'm a bastard like you. Mama cheated with one of her brothers-in-law."

Chet said, "Kinda makes your head spin, trying to keep track of all the bed-hopping."

"Fellas, it's making my head spin not being the oldest brother anymore," Jay said. "Brooks, what were you expecting to find in that hidey-hole anyway?"

"A long time ago, our daddy told me he'd stashed some money there."

"How much?" I asked.

"He didn't say." Brooks rubbed his face, mirroring what Chet had done earlier. "Sorry for walloping you…brother of mine. You came in swinging, and I just reacted."

Chet folded his arms. "We ain't done yet. I'm biding my time is all. Did you at least get what you came for last night?"

"No, there wasn't anything in there. He lied to me."

"Or he took it out a while ago," Jay said. "Unless somebody else found it first."

"The High Sheriff's here," I said, looking out the front window as Reeder's car stopped in front of the building. "What I can't figure, Brooks, is why you picked last night to look for it, when you thought it was there since we were all kids."

Brooks squirmed but finally replied, "I'd forgotten about it until I was leaning against the cruiser, listening to your mama tell about the problem with those two, Harvey and Rutha. I wanted to be the hero by coming up with the money that'd solve everything. Prove myself to my grandpa and make y'all proud of me, so you'd welcome me into your family—" the front door opened, and Reeder stepped inside as Brooks finished with "—when I told everybody the truth."

"The truth about what?" the sheriff asked, tipping back his campaign hat as he studied the scene with the desk askew and chair tipped over.

"About Mance MacLeod, sir."

"Goddamn that sonofabitch. He was nothing but trouble. I shoulda shot him dead back when he started sniffing around your mama. It woulda saved Reva the trouble."

I glanced at my brothers and new half-brother. They all looked like they wanted to point out that they wouldn't exist if Reeder had killed Papa back then. What made me feel even worse was that maybe I still would've been born if Mama had stayed true to form. I couldn't imagine living in a world without my brothers.

Chet asked Brooks, "Why not tell us yesterday morning about the money you thought was there, when y'all stopped by to gig me and Roger about Hugh Bradley?"

"'Cause of your mama. She probably doesn't know about me. It seemed pretty hateful to tell her she wasn't our daddy's first choice."

"As if your mama was," Chet grumbled.

Brooks put his hands on his hips. "Now look here—"

"Fellas," Jay said, "that's getting us nowhere fast. Sheriff Reeder, we're grateful you turned Papa loose on Mama—I'm kinda partial to being in the world—and Brooks, we're mighty proud to welcome you into the fold. But this has turned into another snipe hunt, so we gotta get going."

Brooks put his hand out. "I like having some brothers finally. I grew up with six sisters."

Jay shook it. "We'll come by and say hey before we head back to our bases on Sunday."

Brooks offered Chet a handshake next, but he simply nodded and marched outside.

To save our new kin further embarrassment, I stepped in, saying as I clasped his palm, "Welcome to the family—such as it is." I let go and asked, "Did Papa tell you about any other places where he hid some money?"

"Sorry, no. I wish I had some way to help y'all."

"If we think of something, we'll let you know."

The sheriff hitched his thumbs in his gun belt. "As long as it's legal."

"Yes, sir," Jay said. "Or we'll keep it outside your county." He ushered me out the door.

We found Chet across the street staring at the rear of the orange truck. "Jerry really did do a number on this," he said. "I ain't sure the tailgate can drop down." He tried to rattle it, but it was frozen in place.

"We've got bigger problems than that," I said. "Reeder and Brooks won't do anything about the Bradleys unless they try something outside the town limits. Darlene's going to lose her home 'cause we scared off Wyatt, and Harvey and Rutha are still gunning for Mama."

"On the bright side," Jay said, mashing his spent Lucky Strike with the toe of his shoe, "we got us three rifles and a new half-brother."

"Who doesn't fight fair," Chet replied, touching scabs on his mouth again. "Y'all notice just now how Reeder didn't bat an eye when we was talking to Brooks about the hidey-hole and other places Papa coulda hid money?"

"Yeah," I said, "that's why I asked about any other secret spots. The sheriff didn't even look curious."

Jay glanced back at the jailhouse. "So either Brooks told him about coming up empty, or he somehow knew that was a dead end already—which would mean he's a lot more involved in this than we thought."

Remembering the shovels in the truck bed, I said, "Maybe we can still dig for gold and silver at the old home place?"

"We could do that from now 'til Sunday and not find anything," Jay said. He looked at the sun. "It's almost noon. With only a day and a half before we need to catch our buses, we gotta focus on sure things."

"Dinner at Dora's is a sure thing," Chet replied.

I sidled out of punching range. "Is that your stomach or tallywhacker talking?"

"You promised Jerry we'd buy him dinner there, so this is on you."

I checked my pocket money. If we ate the rest of our meals at Mama's, I'd have just enough to get an RC Cola sometime during the long bus ride to San Antonio.

Though I wanted to stay no matter how long it took to get things sorted out, no way could I risk going AWOL. The military police would have no problem catching me, and I would've undone everything I'd fought so hard for. Jay said we needed to focus on certainties. The one sure thing was that we only had thirty-six hours to fix all our family's problems.

CHAPTER 18

I COULD TELL DORA'S DINER WAS HOPPING EVEN BEFORE WE stepped inside. When I opened the door, the noise that crashed over me from the clamor of at least twenty conversations and the jukebox blasting "Hey! Ba-Ba-Re-Bop" was so overwhelming, I barely noticed the aromas of frying food and cigarette smoke.

Colored tradesmen and women occupied every table. Two waitresses hurried between them, a pot of coffee in one hand and a sweet tea pitcher in the other. Trudy grabbed orders from her mother and another cook, scooted to the cash register to ring up customers, and handled refills at the counter. Jerry sat there in his Sunbeam uniform with an open stool on either side of him—his peaked cap and clipboard reserving them—but all the other seats were taken.

I cupped my hand and hollered at my brothers, "Y'all sit. I'll say hey to Jerry and eat standing up in the corner."

"No, you sit," Chet said. He grinned so wide, it threatened to reopen his split lip. The sight was as rare as a hen's teeth and just as spooky. "I'm gonna help out."

Before we could reply, he weaved among the customers and hustled behind the counter in time to save a plate of burgers that was teetering on Trudy's overloaded tray.

Her expression went from shock to relief to gratitude. Like Brooks, she used her chin to indicate direction. Chet delivered the order to a man in dungarees who looked just as startled as she had. While Chet's back was turned, Trudy's expression softened further. She was clearly smitten.

Jay said in my ear, "Either he'll get hisself and Trudy lynched, or they're gonna change the world."

"Chet could take on the whole Klan and win, so my money's on the second thing."

"No, your money's buying lunch. Now pick: cap or clipboard?"

I took the stool on Jerry's left, setting his peaked cap beside him. We helloed each other and shook hands. I leaned in so he could hear me. "Thanks again for saving us."

"Yer welcome. Couldn't have my favorite servicemen KIA'd in their own town."

Jay placed the clipboard by Jerry's right elbow. "What happened after we got gone?"

"The local cops showed up. Buck was still out cold, Mike was babying the foot you ran over, and Leo kept switching from cradling his broken hand to cupping his balls to rubbing his knee. Made it look like a game." He pantomimed it for us. "Y'all got blamed for everything, of course, but there were enough folks about to persuade the coppers otherwise. Seeing as how nobody got shot, and Leo and his boys were already put through the wringer, they got off with a warning."

I said, "Weren't the Bradleys hacked off at you too?"

"No, they only got y'all in their sights, so watch yer backs. When I left them, they'd slapped Buck awake and were dealing with them flat tires."

Chet topped off the tradesman's coffee on my left and asked us, "Whaddya have?"

"Cheeseburgers, fries, and RCs all around?" I raised my eyebrows to Jerry and Jay, and they nodded. I sat up straighter and proclaimed, "If you're quick about it, sonny, there might be a tip in it for you."

"No tip, and you'll have more than that forehead scab to pick at." He threw a hook so fast I felt the breeze pass by my nose before I realized what he'd done. "Order up," he called to Dora. "Three fries, one cheeseburger, two SOS's."

Dora turned and stared at him. "The only shit I serve in my place is the lip I'm fixing to give you. And you don't wanna know where I'm gonna stick those shingles." Shaking her head, she slapped three more patties on the cook table.

Chet slunk off to spell Trudy at the cash register, where a line had formed.

Jay lit another cigarette and tapped Jerry's arm. "The Bradleys are the least of our worries. We still can't find Harvey and Rutha to set things straight, and now Darlene's gonna lose her house." He and I took turns telling him about my run-in with Wyatt and our solution to his contrariness.

"Let me get this straight," he said. "You only got a day and a half to fix yer family's problems, but you keep making things worse instead?"

I hung my head. "Yeah, that's about the size of it. I reckon everybody'd be better off if we hadn't come home."

"Don't know about that, but it sounds like you need a better plan than the thrashing around y'all been doing. You're like a trio of drunks trying to catch a dollar bill in a windstorm."

Jay's eyes widened. "Hey, I know how we can make some quick money to pay off Papa's people and maybe have some left over to set Darlene up. We'll get whiskey from the Ashers and sell it."

Looking past Jerry, I replied, "We'd need money to buy it from them."

"How much you reckon?"

Jerry blocked our eye contact and said to Jay, "Yer solution to all this bad stuff happening is to go into bootlegging, which could get you killed or jailed?"

"Well, instead we could rob a bank," he replied. "We could take Mama's truck up to Albany or even Columbus, where the banks are bigger and nobody knows us. With the Bradleys' rifles, we'd look like—"

"You'd look like a bunch of kids, but that wouldn't stop a security guard from plugging you. No, boys, if that's the best plan you got, I'll get Sheriff Reeder to lock you up until yer leave's over, for yer own good."

Chet delivered three plates of cheeseburgers and thick-cut fries with RC Colas. "I heard that last bit. Did y'all tell Jerry we now got a lawman for a brother?"

Jerry looked from Jay to me, frowning.

"A half-brother," I explained. "Here's what happened."

Between bites of hot and greasy deliciousness, Jay and I described our encounter with Brooks.

"So," Jerry said, polishing off the last of his fries, "another plan that didn't work out how you meant it to, but at least you didn't scare off your new relation like you did with Wyatt."

"See?" Jay replied. "We're on a roll."

"Rolling off a cliff, sounds like."

Chet and Trudy took plates of food from her mother. They stepped into each other's path and then both sidled right and then left, as if dancing. After a moment of mutual glowering, they broke into laughter. I hadn't heard Chet laugh in many years.

He let her go by. As she passed him, the fingers of her free hand grazed his. The contact was fleeting and made to appear accidental, but Chet jerked like she'd goosed him. He practically floated to the waitress waiting to receive the order. That woman seemed none too pleased by their shenanigans.

I was happy for him and Trudy, but seeing their flirting and maybe the promise of something deeper gave me a sharp pang of longing for Rienzi. If she'd been sitting beside me just now, witnessing what could've been two people falling in love, I imagined she would have put her arm around my shoulders and hugged me close.

Instead I was sitting between a whippet-thin colored laborer, who looked a mite uncomfortable eating next to a white boy, and Jerry. My old friend wiped his mouth with a paper napkin and said, "Better hope they keep that in here. Even so, any number of these folks won't care for it neither."

Jay stubbed out his Lucky Strike in a tin ashtray. "Guess we got enough problems without starting a race war too. Talk about spelling disaster."

The question he'd asked earlier about how much we'd need in order to buy moonshine from the Ashers lined up in my brain with "spelling," and I knew I had to try something. I owed Mrs. Gladney a visit anyway.

CHAPTER 19

MY FORMER TEACHER AND FIRST CRUSH GREW UP IN WHAT had been the largest house in town and now lived in an even bigger one—a wedding present from her father, who owned the general store and much else of value in Colquitt. A fence of wrought iron surrounded the three-story stone building, which boasted turrets and parapets and other medieval architecture that would've looked more suitable in an Errol Flynn movie. The only things missing were a drawbridge and a moat.

I closed the gate behind me and took my time walking to the front door so I could brush off my day-old clothes. There was nothing I could do about my odor; it had been a long time since I'd had a shower. I stared up at the huge, metal-banded front door and wondered whether I should've looked for the servants' entrance or not come here at all.

Before I could talk myself out of this latest poorly considered adventure, I used the iron door knocker to rap on the oak a few times. While I waited, I turned so I could admire the manicured yard, pruned shrubbery, and flowerbeds sporting pansies and mums.

The door opened, and a colored maid named Lucy, who wore a gray uniform that matched the shade of her hair, asked, "May I—" She stopped speaking when she caught sight of my birthmark. "Oh, Mr. Roger, hello."

"Hello, Miz Lucy. Is Mrs. Gladney home?"

"She's visiting over to her folks' place with her daughters, but they'll be back directly. Would you like to wait for her in the study?"

"Yes, please." I wish I owned a watch, having promised Jay I'd only be away for thirty minutes, which included a ten-minute walk here and another ten back to Dora's.

She beckoned me and led the way through an impossibly high-ceilinged parlor of stone that echoed the feudal theme of the exterior and smelled like wet cement. The second-story balcony looming over us would've been perfect for pouring boiling oil on any intruders.

I wondered how Valerie Gladney saw the place where she lived. Maybe she looked up there and recalled a scene from *Romeo and Juliet*. Or perhaps she fantasized about pushing her awful husband, Walton, over that railing.

Hopefully my former principal and sworn enemy was anywhere but at home. For the first time ever, I would've even been glad if he were with Mama at that moment.

I followed Lucy down a long hall with closed doors on either side. The age of chivalry theme didn't extend to this part of the house: instead of flaming torches inserted into iron wall sconces, small decorative lamps atop narrow tables lit the corridor at regular intervals. I thought of Mama's single bare bulb in her kitchen and decided she would love to move in. Having demonstrated her marksmanship on Papa, she could earn her keep by standing guard in a turret, maybe armed with a crossbow. And, of course, that would mean Mrs. Gladney wouldn't have to share a bed with Walton anymore, the thought of which pleased me to no end.

At last we arrived at a carpeted room lined with overflowing bookcases and outfitted with numerous flowered couches and armchairs and more tables and lamps. Due to the spring-like weather, the fireplace wasn't lit, but a huge glass chandelier provided plenty of warm light. Glossy magazines fanned across some of the tabletops; fresh-cut flowers in crystal vases graced others and added a sweet scent to the air.

She said, "This is the missus' most favorite room."

I could see why: a lifetime of books to read and not a single thing from a Prince Valiant comic strip. "It's beautiful," I said. "Does she spend her days in here when she's not teaching or playing with her girls?"

"Mm-hmm. Nights, too. Lots of times even sleeps on that longest sofa." She shook her head. "I'll come in many a morning to find her counting sheep with her finger between the pages of one book or another. Please sit wherever you'd like. Do you care for sweet tea or lemonade or a Co-Cola?"

"I'm fine, thanks. Please don't go to any trouble on my account."

"It's no trouble. You was always her favorite, so it's the least I can do."

"Oh." I blushed as she beamed at me. "Um, a Co-Cola, then, please."

"Coming right up."

I studied my options for sitting. If I'd still been a kid in love with her, I would've made a beeline for the sofa with an afghan draped across the back and plenty of pillows and imagined I could watch over her and keep her safe while she dreamed. Now, though, choosing a spot where any female other than Rienzi slept felt wrong, so I picked an upholstered chair that faced the hall. Before trying it out, I dusted off the back of my trousers again. I should've asked Lucy for a towel to sit on.

She returned bearing a tray with a capped, frosty Coca-Cola, a bottle opener, a cut-glass tumbler that put every jelly jar I'd ever drank from to shame, and an ice bucket with bird-footed tongs. I thanked her, and she left again. Even though I'd just had an RC Cola at lunch, I wanted the Coke because it was more expensive and came in a smaller bottle: a taste of luxury. A fella could get used to this life. I wondered if instead of asking Mrs. Gladney for money, I should beg her to adopt me and Rienzi, and *we* could be the ones standing guard with crossbows.

Footsteps thudded down the hall, much too heavy to be Lucy's or another woman's. Walton Gladney appeared in the doorway, filling the large space. He was even rounder than when I'd seen him in Mama's bedroom. The buttons of his white dress shirt strained to contain him, and the legs of his dark dress slacks bulged like sausage casings. Most of his hair had beat a hasty retreat from the top of his head.

Without thinking, I lapsed into the role of the dutiful student and got to my feet.

"You," he said. "I thought you'd run away to the service."

"I did, sir, but my father died, so I'm back until Sunday."

"Did your misbegotten brothers return too? Are we never to be rid of the MacLeod boys for good?"

My temples started to throb. "I'll be out of your, um, hair soon enough. Sir."

"I want you out of my *house*."

"Yes, sir. Once I talk to Mrs. Gladney."

"She doesn't want to see you." He strode toward me, reaching out with a meaty hand.

I snatched the Coke bottle and shook it until foam built up inside. As he came closer, I set the bottle opener against the cap and pointed the primed cola-sprayer at him.

He halted. "That will go flat in just a few minutes."

"Maybe so, but I reckon it'll still slosh out at a good rate. Be a shame to mess up your snappy outfit."

Eyeing me, he took a step back. "What do you want with Valerie?"

"To say hello while I'm in town."

"I'll give her your regards. Now, scram."

I went with the weapon I should've used to begin with. "Are you still having relations with my mother?"

"No, I got all she had to give and moved on to something better." He smiled and hitched up his belt.

Now I wish I'd grabbed the fireplace poker instead of the Coke. "I'll never understand why Valerie married you."

"And I'll never understand why you were her favorite, you smug little bastard."

Two girls, age five and three, squealed and giggled as they scampered past the doorway, heading deeper into the house. Mrs. Gladney entered the room. She wore a long-sleeved blouse in navy blue and a matching pleated skirt with a white belt and white gloves. Her low-heeled shoes hadn't made a sound outside, probably because she weighed so little now. Since I'd seen her almost a year ago, she must've lost at least thirty pounds, making her look even more unhealthy than Mama, despite her coiffed blonde hair and careful makeup.

"Language, dear. Little pitchers have big ears," she said, her voice sounding reedier than before. "Do like them and run along."

CHAPTER 20

MR. GLADNEY FACED HER. "UM, ALL THAT STUFF YOU MIGHT'VE heard...I was just teasing him."

"We'll talk about it later." Her flat tone reminded me of when she'd get onto a misbehaving student.

"Lucy will need to summon a fumigator after Bud's gone. He probably has head lice or worse."

"Go, Walton. I want to talk with him."

He lumbered from the room, and she closed the door behind him. Turning, she said, "Sorry I wasn't here when you arrived, Roger. You would've been spared that ugliness."

As if I were back in the classroom, I stood straighter and used my best English. "It's not your fault, ma'am. How much of our conversation did you hear?"

"Enough to know the leopard likes to brag about never changing his spots." She crossed the room faster than I thought someone who looked so sickly could move. I managed to set the Coke bottle and opener on the tray before she hugged me. I felt the bones in her chest and arms but also a fierce strength in her embrace. "It's so good to see you," she murmured, stepping back. Then a disapproving scowl darkened her expression. "You smell like cigarette smoke."

Relieved the Lucky Strikes masked my body odor, I said, "It's from my brother, Jay. He picked up the habit in the Army."

"I hope you don't. It doesn't matter what the commercials say—I think they're unhealthy."

"I'm saving my money for a more expensive vice anyway. Someday I'll need to figure out what that is, so I can partake."

She gave me a fleeting smile. "Lucy said your father's passing brought you home."

"Yes, ma'am."

"I know what kind of father he was to you, so it feels strange to offer you condolences, but it's also rude not to do so. What should I say?"

"What you just said is fine, thank you."

"Where are my manners? Please sit and stay a while." She chose an upholstered chair near mine.

I waited until she settled before I did the same, proud of my manners but unable to stop myself from following this up with a rude question. "If you don't mind me asking, ma'am, have you come down with something?"

She touched her styled hair. "I know I must look a fright. It's been weeks since I've gone to the beauty parlor."

"Your hair's as pretty as ever. It's that you look so, well, skinny."

"Oh." She removed her gloves, placed them on a side table, and peered at her pale left hand. The gleaming wedding ring spun with ease on her finger as she played with it. "I just haven't felt like eating much in a long time. It doesn't offer pleasure anymore. Nothing seems to, except for my girls and teaching."

Having been half-starved for most of my childhood, I thought someone living with so much plenty but choosing not to eat must've been touched in the head, but my old teacher didn't seem crazy. It was a reminder of how impossible it was to imagine—let alone understand—someone else's life and choices. Maybe that's why I enjoyed reading so much: it was the closest I ever got to comprehending another person.

I said, "If you still want me to teach in the classroom beside yours someday, ma'am, that won't happen if you waste away to nothing."

She smiled, clearly indulging me. "All right then, I promise to remember that at mealtimes. What else can I do for you?"

Mindful that I was already overdue back at the diner, I summarized the traumas of the past few days, skipping over the part when I'd tried to kill Darlene's husband. "All in all," I said, "my family's in a terrible fix unless we can get enough money to make Harvey and Rutha go away and still leave something leftover to set up Mama and Darlene in better circumstances."

"So, you came here to ask me for a loan?"

"Yes, ma'am." I stared at my dirty fingernails. "One that my brothers and I can't pay off anytime soon."

"Roger, look at me." She stared at me for a moment. "You can imagine what I think of your mother."

I nodded, forcing myself to meet her gaze. "Because of her and your husband?"

"In part. There's something even worse, though. You weren't any poorer than many students at school, and some were even worse off than you. But you had a more tragic childhood than all my other pupils did. That wasn't due to awful luck—it was awful parenting."

"Yes, ma'am. Papa was a monster."

"He was," she said, her expression softening in a way I remembered from back in my schoolhouse days: the combination of a smile and frown and wet eyes, a look of pity I'd grown used to. "But I don't think you've ever known a mother's love either."

My own eyes teared up, and I had to breathe deeply to keep from crying outright. "I reckon not, but I still want to help her."

"That's what makes you such a fine son. And that's why it's even harder to say no."

"If you're worried about not getting paid back—"

"I don't give a fig about that. The problem is, I don't have the money to give you."

"But..." I gestured at the chandelier and massive room full of furniture and books.

She shook her head. "Everything is in Walton's name. I even need him to accompany me to the bank if I want to withdraw any money. The husband controls everything."

I balled my hands into fists. "That ain't—isn't—right. Didn't your father have this house built for you as a wedding present?"

"It was part of my dowery, a payment to Walton for taking me off my father's hands."

"Is that why Mr. Gladney does whatever he feels like?"

She blinked at me and took a moment to compose herself. "You've certainly become more outspoken, Roger. Did the military give you that confidence?"

"Maybe so, ma'am. That and trying to keep up with a much smarter girlfriend."

Looking relieved by the turn of our conversation, she said, "I'm so glad you're still with Rienzi. Is she waiting for you in San Antonio?"

"No, ma'am. She isn't the type who sits around waiting for anything or anybody. She's studying and doing science and trying to take in everything the world has to offer. I'll be lucky if she even notices I've been gone."

"You still have a lot to learn about girls. I'll bet she misses you as much as you miss her. I'm going to miss you too." She stood and held her arms open to me.

I gave her a goodbye hug. After we separated, I said, "I'm glad we had the chance to catch up."

"Sorry I can't help you. I'd ask my father, but he's up in Atlanta somewhere, on the start of a business trip. And, of course, my mother is in the same situation I'm in." She paused and then snapped her fingers. "Wait. If she knows what hotel he's staying at, we could call long distance and leave a message about wiring some money. Or we could send a telegram."

"Thank you, ma'am, but no. My brothers and I couldn't impose on a stranger. Even if we did, though, the banks will close shortly, and there's no Western Union nearby. We need cash, and we need it now."

"What are you going to do?"

I thought back to Jay's suggestions at Dora's. "I reckon we're going on our own business trip."

CHAPTER 21

PARKED BEYOND THE GATE IN FRONT OF MRS. GLADNEY'S home, Jay and Chet sat in the truck with the windows rolled down. Smoke curled upward from a Lucky Strike between Jay's fingers. On the street below his car door lay a half-dozen spent cigarettes but only one match: he was chain-smoking.

They'd wrapped the Bradleys' rifles in a mildew-spotted blanket they'd found somewhere and put the bundle in the bed with the shovels. Both of them scowled in my direction as I walked around to the passenger door. I was used to that from Chet but never from Jay.

Chet glared at me through the open window and refused to move. He said, "You got any notion of how long you kept us waiting? I coulda been helping Trudy the whole time."

"Sorry, I went as fast as—"

"Daylight's wasting," Jay snapped, sounding gruffer than I'd ever heard. "Your old teacher come through for us?"

"Can I get in, please?"

"Chet," Jay said, as if commanding a dog.

After Chet scooted over for me, I climbed in and shut the door. "Sorry, I struck out again. Mr. Gladney controls her money, and you know how he's always had it in for us."

"Dammit." Jay pounded the steering wheel. "I really thought she'd loan us whatever we needed. Now what do we do?"

It scared me that my brother with the head full of inventions and plans had come up empty. His unexpected anger and the worsening predicament we were in made me stammer, "I-I-I think we should go with the plan you came up with at Dora's."

"What? You really want to rob some banks?"

"The other one. With the Ashers down in Florida."

Once I explained it to Chet, regaining confidence as I did so, he said, "But we need money to buy their whiskey before we can sell it for a profit."

"What if we stole some?" I asked. "They can't exactly run to the police or some fed like Bascom."

Jay said, "Don't you remember how many armed men always hung around their house? They'd kill us for sure." He elbowed Chet. "Thanks to this one here, we almost got shot once today. I ain't fixing to invite some Florida cracker to finish the job."

Chet jabbed him back. "Hey, what's eating you? I've never seen you so ornery."

Jay flicked the remainder of the cigarette into the street. He raked his fingers through his dark hair, where sweat made the individual strands standout like they were pomaded. "Fellas, we're running out of time. We've been driving all over hell and gone and coming up empty everywhere we turn." He peered at the sun, which glowed behind thin clouds. "This time Sunday, we're all gonna be on separate buses heading back to our duty stations with everyone worse off for our coming here."

"I don't guess the brass would give us a leave extension," I said, "until we've put all those problems to bed?"

Chet snorted. "No chance. And if we go AWOL, the MPs will show up, club us over the head, and haul our sorry asses off to the stockade." He touched the back of his scalp.

"You went AWOL before?" I asked.

"No, I got locked up for fighting. They also fined me and busted me back to private."

"Aha, so that's why we're the same rank." I tried to sound playful to lighten the tension, but I felt him bristle beside me.

He stared straight ahead. "Jay, can you just drive? Anywhere. If we're on the move, maybe something will happen, or we'll think of a fix. Sitting here just makes me want to start punching everybody."

"Yeah, okay." Jay fired up the engine. "Roger, Jerry refused to let you buy his lunch, so we used your money for gas." He checked the mirrors and stomped the accelerator, making the truck lurch forward.

"Not the reunion I had in mind," I said. "Sorry again."

"It's not *your* fault," Jay said.

"Meaning what?" Chet shot back.

"Meaning we almost got murdered by a problem you started. If you hadn't humiliated Hugh, he wouldn't have killed himself, and we wouldn't have the entire Bradley clan gunning for us. You do the same thing in the Army, beat another soldier half to death?"

"Not quite half."

"Why?" I asked, bracing for a body blow.

Chet merely glanced at me. "He was making fun of one of the mess hall janitors, this colored guy with a fearsome scar on his face, somebody just trying to do his job."

Jay turned us toward US Highway 27. His voice softened a bit. "Did he see action in the war?"

"Dunno, we ain't never said two words to each other. But something about the way he carried hisself reminded me of Lonnie." He smiled, looking wistful. "Remember that loose-limbed swagger of his, like being on the bottom rung of the world didn't bother him one bit?"

I said, "So, when that other soldier started poking fun…"

"Yeah, it was like he was gigging Lonnie. I lost my mind."

"How long were you behind bars?"

"A week. They woulda held me a lot longer, but the one I flattened was a known screwup, and everyone agreed he had it coming. Plus, a captain who heard about the fight wanted somebody with what he called a 'killer instinct' for his boxing team, so he pulled some strings."

Jay grunted. "Okay, so you got us driving on 27. Where to?"

"How about home?" I asked. "See if Mama got another visit from Harvey and Rutha?"

Chet grumbled, "And what if Bascom is visiting her?"

"I'm not looking through anymore peepholes, I'll tell you that." I leaned my face into the whipping air. "You smell that smoke? It's too warm to use a fireplace. Maybe somebody's burning trash?"

Jay pointed to the column of gray on the horizon. "Pretty big trash fire."

Chet said, "And pretty close to home. Maybe Mama set that Chrysler ablaze, the one Papa sold the revenuer."

I began to get a bad feeling that only worsened when we started down Hardscrabble Road. Way too much smoke for anything but a housefire. Images of my Uncle Stan and Aunt Arzula dead in bed as flames consumed the room around them tormented me.

"Damn," Jay muttered. He tried to go faster on the dirt road, but the washboard surface made our teeth rattle and threatened to shake the truck apart, so we approached the conflagration with our dread far outpacing our speed.

"As much as I get crosswise with Mama," Chet said, "I sure hope she wasn't in there. I know she'll get the same in hell, but it's too soon."

We turned onto the lane leading to our childhood home. Through our open windows came the crackle of flames devouring wood.

An inferno engulfed our low-slung, ramshackle house. The floor had begun to collapse into the breezeway. Orange sparks swirled around the stacked-stone pillars like cavorting demons.

I was so busy worrying about Mama, wondering where she would stay now—assuming she was alive—and fearing that our uniforms and civvies had burned up along with her things that it took me a moment to notice a car parked a safe distance from the disaster. Though I recognized the black Hudson Super Six with its humped hood, chrome highlights, and Texas plate, it was so out of place, I chalked it up to a heat mirage.

Then the driver's door swung open, and Rienzi Shepherd stepped out.

CHAPTER 22

BEFORE JAY COULD FINISH BRAKING, I SHOVED OPEN THE passenger door and jumped. I stumbled but managed to stay upright, passing the truck at a dead run as it squealed to a halt. Even as far away from the house as we were, I had to push through the odor of charred wood.

Rienzi looked exactly as she did when I'd seen her the previous weekend, but my surprise made everything about her seem more beautiful. Her black hair was in a pageboy style that swooped in to touch her delicate face, perfectly framing it. Dark eyes, pale skin, slender figure—the blend of Asian and European traits made her prettier than if she'd only possessed one or the other.

The shock of watching my childhood home burn competed in my mind and gut with the astonishment of seeing her again much sooner than I could've hoped for. Tragedy and ecstasy. Depthless sadness and ethereal joy. The two shouldn't have been able to exist in the same moment, but here they were, pulling me apart like taffy.

As I drew nearer, I noticed the dark smudges on her shirtwaist, a favorite of mine with blue and white stripes. The hem of her calf-length skirt was dirty too—no, burned. Ash dusted her low-heeled shoes.

She lifted her arms and caught me in an embrace. Always in balance, she absorbed the collision, seeming to flow while she turned my momentum into a gentle spin. I held her so tightly, I felt her chest rise and fall with each rapid breath. She seemed to be as excited as I was.

The panorama over her shoulder shifted as we twirled, showing me Mama's house in flames, the sandy front yard that hadn't been weeded or raked in a year, Jay and Chet standing outside the truck, spindly pines and leafless oaks, and then her father's Hudson. The fire was behind her again as we slowed.

Even this far away, the noise of destruction forced me to raise my voice instead of talking to her gently, the way I wanted to. "How..." I began. "What happened?"

"Always with your imprecise questions." She put her cool hands on my cheeks and kissed me hard. It wasn't the passionate smooch she'd given me at the bus station in San Antonio. Instead it felt fierce, almost angry, with teeth just behind those soft lips. She eased her head back but kept her hands on my face. This close, I saw the crimson rimming her eyes. "You scared me," she gasped, throat raw as if from crying. "At first, I thought you might've burned alive."

"Is anybody in there?"

"Not that I could see."

Excitement and relief turned to upset as I realized the risk she'd taken in coming here. I said, "You shouldn't have driven all that way alone. It was too dangerous."

She dropped her hands to my shoulders. "I had my boy disguise on until after the last time I stopped for fuel: overalls, hat, the works."

"But what are you doing here anyway?" I realized how that sounded, and added, "Um, not that I mind, since it all worked out okay."

"Winter break from UT was boring. I'd already read everything in the local library, Dad was deep into writing another paper, and I was lonely." She gave my arms a squeeze. "I missed you so much."

Mrs. Gladney was right—I still had a lot to learn about girls. "I missed you, too, but did you really have to steal your father's car?"

"Borrowed it. He'll understand. Buses couldn't get me here fast enough."

I remembered one of our conversations from years ago, when she told me she memorized bus schedules for fun. Finally calming down, I took a breath and asked, "When did you get here anyway?"

"Not soon enough. The fire had already spread everywhere."

Jay and Chet walked up. Rienzi took a step back, breaking contact with me. My formerly oldest brother said, "Sorry to interrupt y'all's reunion, but did you see if Mama or anybody else is in there?"

"Yeah," Chet said, "and what started it anyway?"

"I opened the shutters and looked through all the windows, but I didn't see anyone. The fire was in every room, so I couldn't get far inside. I think somebody set it—I smelled gasoline."

The house rumbled as a wall fell in along with part of the roof, sending up a fireball and a burst of smoke and sparks. I said, "Did you see who?"

"No, but a car not too different from my dad's nearly ran me off the road as it was heading toward the highway."

"Fleeing the scene of the crime," Chet muttered. "Was it a Nash 600?"

"I don't know car models."

"Well, I'll be dogged. I thought you knew everything."

She folded her arms. "Not yet. Describe the Nash 600, please."

"Brown with a big ole hump of a hood and lotsa chrome, but beat-up and rusty."

"That's an accurate description of the one that almost hit me. Do you know whose it is?"

Jay growled, "We do." He stared daggers at Chet. "Leo and his sons fixed their tire problem and came here. Now our mother not only has two maniacs threatening her, but she also has no house, no duds—nothing. Plus we lost our uniforms and civvies."

Rienzi said, "I managed to rescue Roger's knapsack and your two duffels and put them in the car." She opened the trunk with a key. In addition to our carryalls, she had also grabbed the greatcoat I'd used as a blanket the night before.

I thanked her with a kiss on the cheek, lugged my brothers' gear out of the trunk, and set the oblong bags at their feet. The olive drab exteriors were sooty but intact.

"Well, that changes everything," Chet snapped. "I hope the Army sends you a medal."

"Hey," I said, getting between them, "you better stop talking to her that way."

She stepped around me. "Roger, you don't need to fight my battles."

Jay yelled, "Everybody just shut up a minute. We got bigger fish to fry. Like who started all this." He glowered at Chet again.

"I didn't make them do that." Chet gestured at our home. "Just like I didn't make them come after us or make Hugh kill hisself."

"But you set it all in motion because you always take things too far."

"No, I'm too restrained." He turned his pointing finger at me. "If anything, it's his fault. He stopped me from killing Hugh. If I'd a done that, nobody woulda known about the fight. Or I coulda shot Leo and his boys when they were laid out on the ground, but *you* stopped me then. Either way, the Bradleys wouldn't be after us, and our house would still be standing."

Before I could protest, Jay shouted, "Why don't you kill every living soul so nobody can do anything to you ever again? Including us—so nobody can blame you."

Chet balled his fists and sneered as he appeared to quiver with rage. Instead of punching Jay, though, he snatched up his duffel and stomped back to the truck. Once behind the wheel, he made a sharp turn that threw sand and dust every which way and drove back toward US 27.

I told Jay, "He'll come to his senses and be back soon enough. Unless he decides to hunt down Leo and his boys using their own guns."

"I hope he stays gone awhile, whatever he's up to—I'll need all that time and more to forgive him."

I took a step back. "Uh, w-w-what happened to us against the w-w-world?"

"Open your eyes, Roger. As soon as we got back together, everything went to hell. We've been at each other's throats all day. Maybe there ain't no *us* no more. Maybe there never was."

As I tried to stammer a reply, he slammed his cigarette pack against his open palm, nearly ejecting one into the dirt, and broke two paper matches before getting the third to light. He took a deep drag that made the tip flare like the conflagration behind us. Through a haze of smoke, he said, "Look, I'm sorry. It's just that things only got better for you, me, and Chet once we left here and went our separate ways. You got your future right here with Rienzi. Go back to Texas. Get on with your life. And forget about this place."

I was having none of that. "With luck, Harvey and Rutha will think Mama's tapped out now and leave her alone, and the Bradleys will call it even."

"Sure, Roger. We've been all manner of lucky lately." He shouldered his bag and plodded past the Hudson, heading toward the side yard.

"Where are you going?" I called.

Jay paused and looked back at us. "To Darlene's. Maybe Mama's visiting with her."

Rienzi asked, "Can we drive you there?"

"No, I need to walk. Alone." He trudged away, head down and puffing on his cigarette, staying far from the house as it continued to burn.

Waves of heat made him ripple and warp until I couldn't recognize him anymore.

CHAPTER 23

Lightheaded and nauseated, I swayed as my eyes burned. I wanted to blame it on the smoke from the inferno, but I knew better. "I can't believe what just happened. It feels like I lost two brothers in two minutes."

Rienzi said, "You look scared."

"That's 'cause I am."

"Come here." She hugged me hard and then clasped my hands in hers. "It'll be okay once everybody calms down."

"I don't know. It's more serious than that. Chet's never been riled at Jay before, and I've never seen Jay so low."

"It sounds like everything goes back to the Bradleys and whoever Harvey and Rutha are. Can you tell me about them?"

"Long story." As I'd done for Mrs. Gladney, I summarized what had happened since my arrival on New Year's Day. Because I was talking to Rienzi, though, I included my attempted murder of Darlene's husband. She deserved to know everything about me. Maybe she'd decide I wasn't suitable boyfriend material, but it wouldn't have been fair to hold back on her. Besides, I felt so blue, a perverse part of me wanted to see if things could get any worse.

As always, she took in everything I told her like a scientist studying data—no judgment in her expression, just curiosity. Her only interruptions were requests for clarification. As ever, precision was her watchword. By the time I finished, we were both leaning against the dusty, bulbous fender of the Hudson, which was so wide we could've sat on it like a bench.

She said, "You and Chet have a problem with anger. While I'm glad you went from failing to shoot Wyatt to choosing not to shoot Buck, you did still hit him so hard with the rifle butt that you knocked him out."

As I began to defend my actions, she patted her cool fingers against my mouth and continued, "Remember when we first met? I asked about your port-wine birthmark, and you tried to punch me. You also told me about hitting your other half-brother, Tommy Rush, outside the diner. Violence never solves anything, but it seems to be the choice you make when you're mad. Do you think you're that way because of how your father beat you?"

I shrugged. "Mrs. Gladney told me I've never known a mother's love either."

"That makes two of us, but at least yours is still alive. I have a loving father, though, so maybe it's not a fair comparison." She sighed. "If we're going to have a future together, I can't be afraid of you or your predisposition when you become upset."

"I'd never lay a hand on you."

One corner of her mouth tilted up. "Not in anger maybe, but you can be very handsy when we make out."

I played along, liking the change in subject. "You are, too, but you're usually twisting my wrist or pinning me or flipping me across the room. Isn't that resorting to violence?"

"Only when you go too far." She leaned in and kissed me tenderly. "I'm still not ready to do everything you are. When you show respect, though, we always have a very nice time." One more kiss, even more sensuous. "That was the kind of reunion I thought about while driving here."

"Instead, some loony firebugs nearly ran you over, you risked your life saving our gear, and you witnessed my family falling apart along with our mama's house."

"I think it was just a falling out with your family instead of a falling apart. It's fixable."

"Promise?"

"I do."

Hoping it wasn't the last time I ever heard her say that, I tried a little humor to further lighten the mood: "Can my violent predisposition be fixed?"

"If you put your mind to it instead of your fists."

We jumped when the rest of the roof gave way with a tremendous clatter, snapping the single electrical cable that had been connected to it. Still fixed to the top of a nearby pole, the wire whipped around as if it were alive and thrashed on the ground Jay had crossed minutes before, spitting sparks.

Other than some upright framing beams that flared like torches, most of the house had collapsed. The foundation pillars looked like stubby tombstones in a fiery graveyard.

It was a good thing Mama wasn't around. Losing all her clothes and gifts from various lovers would've sent her into the blaze to try to salvage something. Where would she live now? And where would we stay until Sunday? I reminded myself the only "we" now consisted of Rienzi and me. What Chet and Jay would do before hitching rides back to the Colquitt bus depot was anybody's guess.

I said, "I'd offer you a cool, shady spot to rest after your long drive, but the place I had in mind just caved in. Reckon we could use the barn, find a stump in the woods...or climb into your backseat."

She looked me over. "You're not mad at me for pointing out a shortcoming?"

"No, I reckon I've got plenty more of them. I want to be worthy of you, so I'll do whatever it takes to make you proud of me."

"I love you," she said.

"God knows why." I hugged her to me. "I love you too. Sorry I stink."

"I can't smell anything but woodsmoke." She gave me a squeeze and returned to leaning against the fender. "Should we drive somewhere and figure out what to do next?"

"We could try my sister's to see if Mama's there. Even if she isn't, we can break the news about the house. If Jay hasn't beaten us to the punch, we can warn Darlene about why he's going to be so put out when he arrives."

"Okay, I'll pilot, and you navigate. That word comes from Latin: *navis* means ship."

"You're still reading about ancient mariners and such?"

She nodded. "You thought it was dangerous for me to drive from Texas on my own? Well, try conning a boat across the ocean with only the stars to guide you. At least I had a Rand McNally *Road Atlas*."

"Getting lost isn't what bothered me about you driving all this way. The issue is what passes for pirates in these here waters."

"That's why I also borrowed Dad's revolver."

"Criminy, not another gun." I nudged her with my elbow. "I thought violence wasn't the answer."

"It's not when you're lashing out in anger." She nudged me back. "But when you're in mortal peril or seeking justice, the appropriate amount of violence, judiciously applied, can be a righteous act."

Broadening my accent, I replied, "I only got about half of that, little lady, but I reckon what you mean to say is that if some feller's shooting at me, I oughta shoot back."

"Albeit judiciously."

Frowning, I said, "That there's Greek to me too."

"More like Middle English and Latin."

Imagining a dunce cap on my head, I slunk around the front of the Hudson and got in the passenger seat, glad now that my brothers weren't here so they couldn't see me being outwitted and then driven around by a girl. On the other hand, there was no other girl I wanted to be with.

She made my head hurt and heart burst at the same time.

CHAPTER 24

COMPARED WITH EVERY VEHICLE I'D EVER RIDDEN IN—from Papa's Model B Ford truck to Robert Bryson's Pierce-Arrow straight-eight to Army jeeps—riding in the Hudson was like sitting in an upholstered chair after you'd spent your whole life with your backside on the floor.

Though cut off now from the housefire, I still smelled the woodsmoke on our clothes. At least it masked my BO even more than Jay's Lucky Strikes had, though I worried all those odors would soak into the cloth seat. "To get to Darlene's," I said as we approached the highway along Hardscrabble Road, "turn right."

"*Starboard*, you mean, sailor."

"I'm in the Army Air Forces, not the Navy."

"Well, I think of my dad's car as a ship. Left is *port*. The hood is *fore*, and the backseat and trunk are *aft*."

"Okay, I'll give it a try. I reckon I've heard Popeye talk that way at the picture shows."

She made her voice gravelly, saying, "Well, blow me down."

From spouting Latin to quoting cartoon characters. I couldn't help but laugh.

After a truck rumbled past, she turned to follow it, smoothly shifting gears. Rienzi drove the same way she did everything: in the most efficient, expert manner possible, with no wasted motions. Her hands stayed at ten and two on the steering wheel, grip confident but not too firm. She kept a light touch on what Robert Bryson had called the "foot feed" so she could maintain the same safe distance behind the truck, decelerating as needed without having to stomp the brake pedal and clutch. Watching her, it struck me that I could be living in one of the science fiction tales I used to read, where the hero fell in love with a beautiful, fascinating girl who turned out to be a robot.

"Up ahead," I said, "we'll pass a house with a goat out front. Just afterward, make a right...I mean a star-bored."

"If the goat has wandered out back, how will I know it's the correct house?"

"If that goat's moved an inch, it'll mean Judgment Day has come and all our problems are solved."

She glanced over with a frown, the first time she'd looked away from the road, and I explained, "It's made out of rusty coffee cans. The lady living there is touched in the head."

"Maybe she's an artist who's chosen to sculpt with those because there's no marble around here. Lots of people who're called crazy are simply different and more creative than the rest of us."

"So, uh...am I different?"

"Yes, that's why I love you. Plus, you're crazy." She giggled and made the turn past Old Lady Fitzsimons's place. The goat statue, rusty brown and leaning to one side, wore a jaunty bonnet on its head. Railroad spikes jutted through the brim like horns.

She kept our speed low on the dirt road. I guided her through three more turns at increasingly obscure landmarks: a tumbledown barn with a tree growing through the roof, the ever-expanding trash heap where I'd found the moldering Bible I made use of to scam my way into the Army Air Forces, and a busted wagon where a generation of teenagers had carved their names and documented their loves and hates before someone had set fire to it.

When we finally arrived at Darlene's, my sister was sweeping the porch, moving with more ease as her injuries continued to heal. She set aside the broom and watched the Hudson come closer. Out in the country, it was rare to see an unfamiliar automobile drive up. Even shading her eyes from the sun, she probably couldn't make out Rienzi and me behind the windshield. From the grim set of her mouth, I wondered if she thought her husband had stolen a car and come for her.

Rienzi parked behind Wyatt's ragtop Plymouth and shut off the engine. We pushed our doors wide and climbed out. Seeing us made Darlene look even more sour.

The front door opened. Jay stepped onto the porch and lifted his hand in greeting. A cigarette burned there, clamped between two fingers. He didn't look happy to see us either, but then again, he hadn't looked happy all day.

As relieved as I was that he'd beaten us there to deliver the bad news, I couldn't relax. My brother and sister's matching moods underlined how serious our troubles were.

Without a word, Darlene went back to sweeping. She dug in harder with the bristles, as if punishing the sandy dirt that had dared to blow onto her porch.

"Hey," I called, but she didn't reply. To Jay, I asked, "Is Mama inside?"

"Nope, but the good news is that she's with Bascom. According to Darlene, they stopped here this morning before heading up to Columbus for the day."

I indicated our sister. "She knows about Mama's home, right?"

"Yep. Ain't said boo to me since I told her. Instead she's been beating her house into submission."

She whirled on him and pointed the broom as if she'd affixed a bayonet to the handle. "Don't y'all talk about me like I'm not here, and don't talk about *my* house. It ain't mine—nothing is."

Our sister's comment reminded me of Mrs. Gladney's lesson about her situation and made me realize Rienzi was in the same position. I swore that when we got married, things would be different for her.

Darlene swung her broom handle in my direction. "I thought at least I could move back in with Mama, but y'all took that away from me too. Now where am I gonna go when the rent's due?" A fit of sobbing overtook her. She screeched, "I wish you'd never come home."

Rienzi gave me a prodding look from the other side of the car. I held up my hands and told her, "I keep trying to do something. It's all I've been doing since I got here, but everything keeps going catawampus."

Rienzi shook her head and marched toward the porch. "Darlene, I realize we don't really know each other, but if you want to come live with me and my father in San Antonio until you get back on your feet, you're welcome to join us when we drive back on Sunday."

Jay nodded his approval, but I hated this option. Having Darlene under the Shepherds' roof was liable to drive them around the bend. And my sister skulking around their household would definitely put a crimp in any romancing I might try when I was off duty and her father was away from home.

Darlene said, "I'd miss my friends too much."

Rienzi asked, "Can one of them let you stay in their home?"

"No, they're all working on families of their own. We never see each other anymore—we only write."

Instead of pointing out the flaw in not wanting to miss seeing friends Darlene never saw anyway, Rienzi replied in a gentle voice, "A letter from San Antonio will still reach them; it just takes a little longer. You'll like it there. It'll be a return to city life, like you had in Atlanta."

"I dunno about living with a bunch of Orientals."

Rienzi sighed. "My dad's white, and I'm half-white. That's three-quarters of us you'll be able to tolerate. Versus nothing tolerable about your present situation."

"But what about the car?" My sister jabbed the broom toward Wyatt's Plymouth.

"You could follow us in that if you'd like."

"I'm broke. What will I do for gas money and lodging along the way?"

"I can pay for those things." From the confident way Rienzi said it, I guessed she'd mooched from her father's wallet too. He was very patient and understanding, but I wondered whether her extensive "borrowing" and then showing up with a quarrelsome stranger to live under his roof would finally push him past his limit.

"But I get lonesome real quick, and it's a long drive, and the radio's busted. Who am I gonna talk to?"

Rienzi's shoulders rose and fell as if she were taking a deep, calming breath. I bet she was regretting her offer. "You can talk to yourself. I often do it. Sometimes it's the only intelligent conversation I have all day."

Even if that dig was directed at me, I had to stifle a laugh. I said to my sister, "We could drive your car to Colquitt or Bainbridge on Saturday and find someone who'll buy it. That way, you can ride with us and have a nest egg you can start building on."

"What if everybody around these parts is too poor to buy it?"

"Then we'll take it up to Albany or even Columbus."

"I dunno, that seems awful far. I don't like being in a car that long."

Unable to contain my growing frustration, I shouted, "If that's too far, how long do you think the drive to Texas is?"

"Don't you yell at me. You're the one who made this mess to begin with."

"No, Harvey and Rutha did that when they beat you as a warning to Mama."

"Harvey didn't lay a hand on me. It was all Rutha."

"What the hell difference does that make?"

Rienzi caught my eye and patted her hand in the air, as if tamping down something.

I offered to Darlene, "Look, I'm sorry for hollering. We're trying to fix your problems, but you keep punching holes in our ideas."

"Maybe you need better ideas." She resumed sweeping, flinging the dust off the porch in our direction.

Jay said to her, "Some time ago, when Mama gave us boys away, y'all ended up staying at the old home place. Could you and her do that again?"

"No. Aunt Lizzie caught Mama and Uncle Roscoe canoodling instead of helping her go through Grandma's things. Grandma left Lizzie and Roscoe that house, so Mama's banned from there."

Like Uncle Stan had been, after I came along and Grandma put two and two together. Someone had finally punished Mama directly for her sins—and at the worst possible time.

I said, "How about staying with Aunt Maxine and Uncle Jake? They're real nice."

"They moved to a farm outside of Valdosta last year. That's so far away, I might as well be in Texas."

Instead of going down that rabbit hole again, I asked about whether Mama's other two sisters could take them in.

"They're both dealing with lots of sickness at home. I can't remember which, but one of our cousins came down with TB and another's got the plurzy."

"Pleurisy?" Rienzi asked.

Darlene shrugged. "Never heard of that. All I know is it's plurzy or dropsy or some such. Anyhow, they got their hands full."

I admitted defeat. "Okay, I reckon we'll sell Wyatt's car somewhere for you tomorrow, and you can ride with us to San Antonio on Sunday. Better pack your bags."

She set her broom against a porch rail. "That won't take but a minute. I ain't got outfits galore like Mama."

Tempers had settled, so it didn't seem like a good time to remind her that Mama only had the clothes on her back now—thanks to our war with the Bradleys.

CHAPTER 25

DARLENE FINALLY INVITED US INSIDE TO SIT, SO WE GATHERED around her kitchen table on the three mismatched chairs and a stool. She set a Mason jar of well water before each of us except Jay, who accepted one of Wyatt's leftover bottles of cold beer. The sunshine through the open windows was enough that we didn't need to turn on the naked bulb dangling overhead. In the cone of light, dust motes zigzagged in the same chaotic motion that summed up my actions so far that week.

I said to Jay, "Mama's not coming with us to Texas, so we still need to get her situation sorted out."

"Bascom will take care of her." He stared at me from across the table. "Why do I gotta keep telling you that?"

"But he could be gone in a blink, just like all the others."

"Don't you talk about Mama like she's some kinda strumpet," Darlene said. "She just gets lonely, is all. We have that in common. If she'd took Papa back, none of this would be happening."

I turned on her. "You mean, after he did time for trying to kill her?"

"Don't you know it's Christian to forgive and forget, little brother?"

"It's stupid is what it is. He would've made sure he succeeded the next time he took a notion to murder her."

"Never. He just lost his head that one time."

Jay rapped on the table, getting our attention. "No. That weren't the only time he was fixing to put one of us in an early grave. Some years beforehand, he tried to shoot me dead."

"What?" I said. "When was that?"

He lit a fresh cigarette. "The winter I was eight. Chet was six, and you were five."

"I was ten then," Darlene said. "Why didn't I ever hear about it?"

"Mama swore me to secrecy. Said what happened was a coincidence, but it would still scare y'all so much you wouldn't be able to stand to be around him."

"I already couldn't," I said. "What's the difference?"

"You used to idolize him," he replied. "He'd pick you for a run to the Ashers or to go on some errand with him, and you were walking on air—you've forgotten about that, is all. Like I sort of forgot about what really went on until Darlene said what she just did about him only losing his head the one time."

Darlene said, "You gonna finally get around to telling us what happened?"

"Papa took me hunting deep in the woods with a very narrow path between the trees. He told me to follow behind him, and we walked like that for a while, single file. I noticed his rifle tipping back more and more on his shoulder until the barrel was aimed right at me. Instead of gripping the stock, he'd looped his finger inside the trigger guard and held the butt steady with his other hand."

"Sounds like a dangerous thing to do," Rienzi said.

"That's what I thought. So I stepped to the right where the trees didn't hem us in as much. No sooner had I'd done that then he squeezed the trigger." He rubbed the stubble on his chin. "I saw some action in the war, but I was never as close to enemy fire as that day. Papa spun around and had this expectant look on his face that turned to startlement. And then it became something else when his eyes met mine. Maybe he had a feeling akin to shame—I ain't sure, because it's the only time I saw him with that expression."

I asked, "Did he try again?"

"No, he blinked hard, like he hoped he'd see something different when he opened his eyes again. Then he said hunting accidents happen all the time, but we got lucky and that I should keep my mouth shut about it. *No point in worrying everybody over nothing*. Then he told me his stomach was bothering him and led me back home.

"Later, I was looking for something to write on to practice my times tables, and I found a bunch of new-looking papers in that ratty desk in the front room. They had my name on 'em, along with Chet's and yours—" he looked at Darlene "—and yours, Roger. I took them to Mama because I couldn't read most of the words. She said it was life insurance Papa must've taken out on us, and she explained how it worked."

My head was spinning from his story. With all the times Papa had acted like he wanted to kill me, maybe the only reason he didn't was because he hadn't kept up on the insurance premiums, so he couldn't cash in. Steeling myself, I asked, "Was Mama a part of it?"

"I don't think so. She acted surprised and peeved, like he'd bought the policies without mentioning anything to her. That's when I relayed the story of what happened in the woods. She gawped at me but then shrugged it off as a coincidence. Just like Papa, she told me not to tell anybody so as not to spook y'all."

Rienzi murmured, "Sometimes correlation does imply causation." When I tilted my head at her, she elaborated for my benefit: "*Coincidence*, my foot."

Darlene wrapped her arms around herself. "You reckon he thought about killing me?"

Jay replied, "He mighta had designs on us all. Anyways, I told you about that to say it was a good thing Mama didn't try to take him back—and it's equally good she ended up getting revenge for us."

Darlene shook her head. "She never told me she shot him."

Our brother said, "It's not something you brag about. Even with your cousin as the High Sheriff."

I fingered the chewed-up edge of the table where Wyatt had knocked off his beer bottlecaps. "God knows I've got more than a few bones to pick with Mama, but we owe her all the same. I say we go to the Ashers today and get some whiskey she can sell to make enough to pay off Harvey and Rutha and leave some to get her back on her feet."

Rienzi said, "Isn't selling untaxed liquor illegal?"

"Yes, but so are assault and threats of harm and everything else Papa's brother and sister are doing. And so is stealing your father's car and gun and money."

"I told you I just borrowed all that."

Jay shook his head. "I'm sorry I ever suggested going down to Florida. Those Ashers are scary people. Even Chet's afraid of them."

Rienzi looked at me. "How much does it cost to buy some whiskey from the Ashers?"

"Probably more than you *borrowed* from your dad. They aren't gonna give it to us on credit, so we'll have to steal it. But that's the nice thing about swiping something that's illegal—it's not like they can go to the law about it."

"That sounds exciting," Darlene said. "I always envied you boys setting off on a big adventure to see the bootleggers every month while I had to stay home. If y'all are heading to Florida, then I'm going with you."

CHAPTER 26

DARLENE SAT IN THE BACKSEAT OF THE HUDSON, AND I RODE shotgun beside Rienzi and gave her turning directions. Technically, I was riding *rifle*, because we'd brought along the weapon I'd tried to use to kill Darlene's husband. That felt like ages ago.

Jay had shown no interest in reacquainting himself with the Ashers, which was smart but also a shame because he was a far better shot than I was. He'd confessed to feeling bad about his parting with Chet and wanted to bury the hatchet before they needed to catch separate buses on Sunday. We dropped him in Colquitt at Dora's. The pickup Chet took wasn't parked there, but hopefully Jay could get a lead on his whereabouts.

I tried to convince Darlene to go with Jay, but she refused to budge. After we left our brother at the diner, she peppered me with questions about the bootleggers. The thought of my sister nattering all the way to Texas and then burrowing into Rienzi's home like a tick made me feel resentful and angry enough already, but here she was, also denying me what little time alone I could've had with Rienzi. Even if that time was spent going to Florida and stealing illegal whiskey from a passel of gun-toting maniacs. And possibly dying in the process.

Darlene leaned forward and folded her arms on the top of our seat, as close to inserting herself between me and Rienzi as possible. "I thought y'all only visited the Ashers at night."

"That was when Papa had business with them—buying their liquor, not snatching it."

Rienzi's fingers fidgeted on the steering wheel, something she only did when agitated. I figured Darlene was annoying her as much as she was aggravating me, but then Rienzi said, "Explain it again: why isn't there an alternative to breaking the law so your mother can get on her feet?"

"She's got nothing now and no prospects. A man like Bascom will demand who-knows-what from her, now that she's over a barrel. The only thing she has left is her pride, and he'll take that away from her lickety-split."

"I like Agent Bascom," Darlene said. "You ain't spent any time with him. If'n you did, you'd know he has feelings for Mama."

"No doubt. I'm sorry to say I've seen firsthand the *feelings* men like Bascom show her."

"You got a dirty mind. He's always been a perfect gentleman when he brings her by."

My mind flashed to Mama's misbuttoned dress, but before I could respond, Rienzi said, "Roger does have a dirty mind, but it's understandable. He probably developed certain ideas growing up around barnyard animals."

Darlene snorted in my ear. "Farm boys are like that for sure. I married enough of them to know. You wouldn't believe some of the things they done tried. While I was sleeping this one time—"

"Please hush," I said as my face heated up. "Y'all are making me feel guilty, and I haven't even done anything."

"But he tried to, right, Rienzi? And he ain't even proposed to you yet, let alone married you, but he'll take whatever he can get. That's boys in a nutshell."

Rienzi patted my knee. "I love him all the same. But none of this gets at my question."

"We're forced to do something crooked because everything legal takes too long to pay off. Turn right up there, just past that rusted-out Model T in the ditch." After she made the turn, I continued, "If Mama got a job in town on Monday, she wouldn't collect her wages until week's end. What's she gonna eat until then? Where's she gonna live?"

Darlene offered, "Since I'm going to Texas with y'all, she could live in the house me and Wyatt are renting—at least until the rent's due. And she could eat whatever's left in our fridge and her smokehouse, unless that burned down too. Also, I got a bank of sweet potatoes and collards in my winter garden she can harvest."

Rienzi glanced over at me. "Well?"

"And what if it takes her more than a week or two to find work—or even more likely, what if her boss fires her on day one for smarting off and word gets around so nobody else will hire her? The food on hand will soon be gone, and the landlord will kick her out. Then she'll be at the mercy of Bascom or whatever new guy has taken a fancy to her."

"That's logical. I can see your mother having difficulty holding down a regular job. But I still don't like the idea of two wrongs making a right."

"Growing up with Mama and Papa, it was nothing but wrongs, but we turned out all right."

Darlene slapped my shoulder. "*Nothing but wrongs*? I can't figure what you mean—Papa never laid a hand on me, let alone tried to shoot me like he did Jay, and Mama always treated me fine."

And maybe not coincidentally, she was the only one of us four who didn't learn any survival skills. As much as I ached to get into another fight with her—let off a little steam and give voice to my ever-growing resentment—there was no point in launching into one.

I choked down my anger and turned my attention back to Rienzi. "Anyway, it's hard to take the moral high ground when you're barely treading water."

She hummed in reply, which I'd learned was her way of conceding a point temporarily but leaving the door open for future argument.

I continued to direct her down a series of paved and dirt roads in Seminole County, where Papa had grown up and raised Harvey and Rutha following their mother's violent death. A drunken brawl between their father and uncle had ended with them wrestling over a shotgun and accidentally blowing her in two. Neither man had drawn a sober breath after that. When each one had passed on and Papa burned their bodies, he told me, they had so much liquor in them that the flames were blue.

Maybe Harvey and Rutha were back in their old stomping grounds. If they suddenly appeared like a couple of haints, though, I'd have no idea who they were—but surely Darlene would let out a yelp. The thought of them somehow ambushing us as we jounced along piled on another layer of tension I didn't need.

At last we crossed the Florida border, but I couldn't relax because soon we'd be entering the county where the Ashers made their whiskey.

I pointed to the sandy shoulder of the road up ahead. "Pull over yonder. Please and thank you."

"Why there?"

"It's even rougher backroads from here, and I need to remember the way. It all looks different in the daytime; plus, I haven't made this trip in a long time."

After a couple wrong turns, lots of backtracking, and the increasing feeling I would never find the right route—or even figure out how to get us back home—I recognized the live oaks at a crossroads. Papa had stopped there one time to introduce me to Sheriff Roger Timberlake, the man Papa had named me after as one of his many bribes. I remembered the fat lawman scaring the bejesus out of poor Lonnie and Papa frightening me half to death with his threats if I embarrassed him in front of the sheriff.

"Okay," I announced, "I got my bearings. It should be easy from here."

I was wrong, of course, but after one more false start, my memories grew clearer and my directions became more accurate. Graded dirt roads turned into wagon trails and then cow paths. Tall grass scraped beneath the car as a swamp closed around us. We still had a good hour of daylight, but the thick stand of tall pines created a dusky gloom.

Finally we arrived at the tunnel of trees and undergrowth that marked the entrance to the Asher lair.

CHAPTER 27

RIENZI POINTED DOWN THE TUNNEL MADE UP OF GREEN AND brown growth. "So, do we just drive in there, snatch the nearest container, and make our escape?"

"Let's grab two," Darlene said, "and we'll all be rich."

I shook my head. "Selling their whiskey won't make us rich. It'll be enough to make some bank and give Mama a decent start, is all."

"But the more we steal, the decent-er that start will be."

"You gotta understand that they put their liquor in five-gallon wood barrels. That's about fifty pounds each. Yeah, we gotta get more than one, but we're gonna run out of space in here right quick. We can't get greedy."

"We'll steal judiciously," Rienzi said. "Is this the only way in or out?"

"I got no idea." Staring at the thick growth on either side of the path, I said, "I recall the Ashers had this boy Chet's age named Seth who would hide in the trees along the path. He'd yowl like a jungle cat and drop onto Papa's truck holding a sawed-off shotgun and wearing this ring of raccoon tails around his waist. Not a stitch of clothes on him, and he cussed like a grown man. He's frozen in my mind that way; it's strange to think of him as eighteen now. I wonder if he escaped into the military like us."

Darlene shifted behind me. "He sounds…interesting. I wonder if he still runs around naked."

I was about to make a joke about her already planning on husband number six, but Rienzi said, "We could literally swamp my dad's car looking for another path, so I guess we'll have to take our chances. What's on the other side of this passageway?"

"A clearing. Assuming everything's the same as before, there'll be a rotting house and an old barn, which is where they keep the whiskey."

I traced on the palm of Rienzi's hand with my forefinger so she would know what was to the right, left, and dead ahead when we came through the tunnel. Plus, it might've been my last chance to touch her before we got a nasty surprise. "We always came on a moonless night to make it harder for revenuers like Bascom to get a bead on us during the drive. There'd be a campfire in the middle of the clearing with a bunch of Asher men sitting around it in chairs. I guess they were kinfolk; they all were big guys with bushy beards." I clasped her hand, hoping my plan wasn't a huge mistake that would get her hurt or worse. "Of course, that was on the one night each month when they expected Papa to show up with money and leave with whiskey. Maybe nobody will be around during the day. And with a nearly full moon tonight, they won't be expecting a whiskey runner anytime soon."

Rienzi asked, "Were the women outside too?"

"I never saw any, just this girl named Nadine who was my age." Sitting beside the love of my life but recalling someone I'd thought a lot about as a kid—always fantasizing about rescuing her from this place and being rewarded with a kiss—made me feel unworthy.

As if reading my mind, she cocked her head at me. "Was she pretty?"

"Kind of plain. And she smelled like woodsmoke."

"I smell that way now. Do I remind you of her?"

"No, you're completely different."

"How often did you see her?"

"Just a few times. Why are you baiting me?"

"From what you told me about the girls you knew—Cecilia and others—you developed feelings for them easily."

Darlene whacked my shoulder again. "Oh, he fell in love at least once a week. My friends would come over to spend the night, and he'd moon over every one of them."

"And here we are, about to visit the home of another girl you used to know. Maybe you're hoping to see Nadine again."

"No, I'm hoping to steal her daddy's liquor and not catch a bullet in the back for my troubles. I don't give a fig about her."

"Okay, just checking."

She eased one foot from the clutch and the other onto the accelerator, and the car started into the tunnel. Twisted branches scraped both fenders and raked the glass and roof with crooked fingers.

Darlene said, "I'm getting a spooky feeling. Maybe me and Rienzi should stay here, and you should go up the path and bring back the barrels."

"That's a long way to lug almost fifty pounds—and I'd have to do it quite a few times."

"You're not as strong as Jay or Chet, but you could manage it. Don't you want to keep your sister and girlfriend safe?"

"With the trees and undergrowth so close, I don't think I could open my door if I wanted to."

The canopy shut out any remaining daylight and magnified the rattle of the Hudson engine as we rolled closer to the clearing. Ahead, I made out the firepit, where there was no hint of smoke or embers, and the steps leading up to the Ashers' porch. All seemed quiet and still.

Rienzi said, "We're not exactly stealthy. Maybe I should back out of here before it's too late."

Something rapped hard against the trunk of the Hudson. Then twice more.

Rienzi stopped the car, and we all turned in our seats. Through the narrow back window, a broad-shouldered man was illuminated in the red brake lights. He raised a club.

No—it was a sawed-off shotgun.

CHAPTER 28

Good God Almighty, another gun was being pointed at me. There was no way I could maneuver the rifle inside the car. Rienzi caught me looking at her purse, which contained the pistol she borrowed from her father, and shook her head. She was right of course—a blast from the shotgun might kill us all before she could even take aim.

Darlene ducked beneath the level of the window. I expected her to start crying and praying, but she only seemed to be holding her breath.

"Keep going," the man ordered, shouting so we could hear him. "Stop in the front yard."

Voice quavering, I murmured, "I'm so sorry I got y'all into this."

Rienzi lifted her foot from the brake and kept the car rolling forward just fast enough that it wouldn't stall. She didn't reply.

"Don't you wanna tell me this was a terrible idea?"

"No," she said, keeping her voice low, "I don't want my possibly final words to sound resentful. Wait, that sounded resentful. What I meant to say is *I love you.*"

Her words gave me strength. "I love you too. Which is why this was a terrible idea."

"He doesn't know our intentions or even who we are. All he can surmise is that we're from Texas because of the license plate. We could say we're old friends hoping to visit Nadine."

"I got nothing better, so let's go with that."

The Hudson entered the clearing, a huge sandy area that used to be dotted with clumps of stiff weeds, like hairs sprouting from a patchwork of moles. Now, though, the sand was clean and raked in a pattern of concentric circles centered around the firepit. To the crows flying over us, it must've resembled ripples emanating from a stone dropped into a pond.

Rienzi said, "It seems a shame to mess up the design with our tires." She stopped the car before we reached the outermost ring and switched off the engine.

Darlene sat up and reported, "He's still behind us with his shotgun. Goodness, he's a big feller. Really much of a man."

He strode up on Rienzi's side and peered in through the driver's window, weapon at the ready. As Darlene had said, the fellow was tall and sturdy. He'd torn the sleeves from a pale, crewneck work shirt and wore it open, like a makeshift vest, revealing a thick-muscled torso and arms browned by the Florida sun. His legs were encased in denim pants he'd sheared off at the knees. He stood too close for me to tell whether he wore shoes, but he didn't seem the type.

His tanned face showed only light stubble. I realized he was younger than I'd thought.

He squinted past Rienzi and said, "Hey, you're Mance MacLeod's son."

So much for our Texas alias. The birthmark on my face always told on me.

Though the glass distorted his voice a bit, something in it sounded familiar. Always ten steps ahead, Rienzi cranked down the window so I could talk without shouting. "Seth?"

Darlene piped up. "The naked boy?" She leaned on our seat again, as if to get a better look.

He lowered his weapon a few inches and said, "It's Bud, right?"

"Roger." As with Jay and Chet, Seth had matured into a man while I somehow remained kid-like, stuck in time.

Seth grinned, revealing grayish teeth. "I liked playing cat and mouse with your daddy's pickup. Things wasn't never the same after he got sent to the big house. Lotsa guys took over his route—fought over it more like—but nobody's lasted."

"Yeah, if nothing else, Papa was reliable." Reliably brutal, selfish, and evil. He'd been all manner of consistent.

"Yeah, that's the word for it." He mouthed *reliable* a few times, as if memorizing it. Then he said, "The latest one got hisself nabbed by the revenuers, from what we hear. So I reckon some other chucklehead will give it a go before long. Wait." He peered at me harder, as if putting his whole face into it. "You ain't that chucklehead, is you?"

"No, I'm just riding with my girlfriend here and my sister. We came to pay a call on Nadine. Is she still around?"

Instead of relaxing, he raised the shotgun again. "She ain't gonna wanna see you, after what you done."

Darlene slapped my shoulder. "What'd you do to poor Nadine?"

I raised my hands so quickly, I stubbed my fingers on the metal-backed ceiling liner. "Nothing. I never said two words to her." Trickles of sweat dampened my armpits.

He growled, "She was sweet on you. Told our ma you'd come for her someday. You even went and kissed her."

Rienzi looked at me. "Do tell."

"Not by choice." Each heartbeat throbbed in my overheating face. "Seth, you were in on it, remember? You and Angus forced our faces together and made me kiss her."

"That ain't her recollecting. You wasn't *reliable*, 'cause you broke her heart." He thumbed back the hammer. "The ladies can stay in this here car, but you get out."

"Okay, j-j-just don't hurt them. If Nadine w-wants to have it out with me, fine. I'll refresh her memory about what really went on."

After I climbed out, he directed me with the barrel toward the front porch. I took a few steps in that direction, and he shouted, "No, dummy, go around the circle. We like it neat."

Their mother must've taken more interest lately in the appearance of the Asher homestead. Now that I was in the open and making a wide loop around the firepit, I could see fresh planks here and there on the barn. The lichen had been scrubbed away. And the porch had been rebuilt from yellow pine that could've come straight from the Ramsey sawmill.

I had never met Mrs. Asher but counted on her being more reasonable than her son—and daughter. It flabbergasted me that Nadine had entertained the same rescue fantasies about me as I had replayed over and over while I did chores and fished and daydreamed in one barn loft or another all those years ago. From her tearful reaction back then, I'd figured she hated the very sight of me. Strange to think that she'd only grown to hate me later for not following through on a promise I'd never made and over feelings we'd never shared.

From the other side of the circle, Seth kept pace and maintained his aim. Eyeing the thick woods that surrounded the clearing like a stockade, I knew it would've been impossible to escape. And anyway, I couldn't abandon Rienzi and Darlene. As in my dealings with Papa, I just had to take my licks and hope I didn't get killed.

CHAPTER 29

SETH MOTIONED ME ONTO THE PORCH, WHICH SOMEONE lacking carpentry skills had rebuilt. The wood joints were sloppy, and whoever hammered the boards together bent quite a few nails. There wasn't a screw in sight, so the whole thing would probably collapse in a few years. Maybe Ray and his kin had done the work while nursing hangovers after one of their whiskey benders. Despite all this, the new porch looked better than the sagging mess on which Seth and his older brother Angus had forced me to kiss Nadine so many years ago.

I listened for the sound of male voices beyond the closed door and shuttered windows but couldn't hear anyone. "Where's your daddy and brother and all?"

"Open the door."

I did as ordered and stepped inside. Seth prodded me forward with the barrel. Because it had been sawed short, that meant he was right behind me. Rienzi probably could've done one of her fancy moves to disarm him, but I hadn't learned those tricks. Whenever she'd showed them off to me, it was because I'd gotten too fresh, and she was flinging me across the floor or making sure I couldn't move.

We were in a long, narrow space that seemed to be a combination living room and storage shed. Chairs with busted-out cane bottoms and scarred tables with lit kerosene lamps kept company with saws, rakes, and all manner of other tools. Weapons galore, but nothing worth risking my life to grab. "Where to?" I asked.

"Hallway on the right."

As we walked that way, single file, he called over my head, "Hey, you'll never guess who come by."

From the hall, I smelled crappies frying, but I was too tense to salivate. Up ahead was a dimly lit kitchen and the sound of a whisk rattling inside a tin bowl. I asked, "Is your mama used to you bringing guests to supper at gunpoint?"

"You ain't a supper guest, and Mama's dead and gone."

We entered the kitchen, where a few kerosene lamps hung overhead from nails bent into hooks. The fire in the woodburning stove made the room stifling.

A suntanned young woman about my age set her bowl on a weathered wood countertop, a long braid of hair swinging behind her. She wore an apron over a faded housedress that had been made for a shorter, plumper person. The hem ended just below her knees, revealing browned, bony legs and sandaled feet, and the sleeves rode up in her armpits. Folds of daisy-print cotton bagged on either side of her waist over the drawstrings of the graying apron. Despite the ill-fitting clothes, she carried herself regally, with a straight back and lifted chin. She seemed to look down her nose at me, the way I imagined Cleopatra might've done when viewing a barge slave.

"Bud MacLeod," she said, her voice high but somehow stern. After a moment, she frowned. "Ain't you recognized me yet?"

"Are you Nadine? Sorry, I never heard your voice before."

"You got some nerve coming back here after all these years. I'd have Seth shoot you where you're standing, but I just scrubbed the kitchen."

"Um, are you s-s-sore because your family ganged up on us when we were kissed—I mean *kids*? All that teasing wasn't my fault any more than it was yours."

"I could tell you was nice. The onliest nice boy I ever knowed. But you wasn't nice enough to come for me."

Seth emphasized her comment by prodding my spine with the shotgun barrel, making me jump.

"We were little. What could I have done?"

She forked over the breaded fish in the skillet, which bubbled with lard. "Not forget about me when you got older."

"I was too busy trying to survive to worry about anybody else."

Now, I realized, I was worried about everybody else but doing a terrible job at surviving myself, let alone helping them out. Maybe I would've been better off just minding my own business.

Seth said, "He got him a girlfriend now. She's looks kinda funny, but he's sweet on her for sure. Brought his sister along for the ride. At least one of them's from Texas, judging by the license plate."

"I'm in the Army Air Forces there, and that's where Rienzi lives."

Nadine said, "She's your girl?"

"I like to think so."

"So I'd say you're surviving pretty good—got you that Army job and a sweetheart. Who coulda been me, if you gave a good goddamn."

I didn't know what to say. If I told her I used to think about her all the time, I'd look like a louse for forgetting about her. But if I told her so much had happened to me since my last trip here that I never thought about her again, she'd think I was a heel. Both were true, marking me as a louse and a heel. But as sorry as I felt for her, would I have given up one second of my life with Rienzi to be with Nadine? Not a chance.

I said in a rush, "Look, I did give a damn, but I couldn't do anything to help you. If you want to raise sand with me about that, then so be it, but I'm not going to apologize for not doing something I never could've pulled off anyway."

Seth asked, "Want me to take him out back and shoot him where we buried the others?"

I heard him take a step away from me, probably to avoid blood splatter. Before Nadine could answer, I made a beeline for her. If he pulled the trigger, she'd probably die too.

She darted to her left, but I snatched her around the waist and put her between me and Seth, using a favorite hold of Rienzi's to pin her. I guess I'd learned one of those fancy moves after all.

As a kid, she'd been weak and scrawny, but now I felt the tight bundles of muscles that came from scraping out a living in a swamp. Her long braid was trapped between us, locking her head in place. I placed my face beside hers and smelled the woodsmoke scent I'd always associated with her, along with sweat and cooking grease.

"Everybody just calm down," I said, my heart pounding. "There won't be any killing. I don't want to hurt Nadine, but I'm not fixing to get hurt either."

Seth asked her, "What do I do?"

She squirmed in vain. "Put the gun down."

He guided the hammer forward and set the weapon at his feet. "What else?"

I said, "Better take that skillet off the fire and put the fish on a plate. They smell like they're done."

With a nod of permission from his younger sister, he wrapped a rag around the cast iron handle and followed my instructions. Eyeing me, he seemed to consider using the pan of bubbling lard as a weapon, so I turned Nadine to keep her between us. He went back to the entryway, within easy reach of the shotgun.

"See?" I said in her ear. "I give so much of a damn that I kept your supper from getting ruined."

"Why are you here anyway? Is your daddy wanting to go back in business with us?"

"No, he's dead. Killed by my mama in December."

"How'd she do it?"

"With his old revolver, all six shots."

"I done the same."

"You killed your father?"

She stiffened in my arms, and Seth looked as if he wanted to snatch up the gun and fire away. "Never," she said.

The heat of the kitchen and the danger I was in made my pores open wide. I blinked sweat out of my eyes as it trickled down my face. "What then?"

"Daddy got cut real bad on a piece of metal last year, fiddling with the still. The infection took hold and killed him. A little later, some kinda fever carried Mama away."

"So who'd you shoot?"

"Angus had went south by then, but some family stayed behind. Uncle Mitch tried to force hisself on me, so I grabbed the gun off his belt."

Seth said, "Yeah, I heard the shooting and come a-running. Uncle Tyler was gawping at what was left of his brother and fixing to draw his own gun, so I blasted him. Everybody else skedaddled after that, and we never seen them again."

"Then you're not making whiskey anymore?" The thought of all this being for nothing crashed down on my shoulders. My hold on Nadine loosened. She struggled to break free, but I managed to pin her again.

"Oh yeah, we are," she declared. "We ain't as good as Daddy and them, but we make do, and we got us some help now: a runaway Seth found in the swamp."

"I'm glad to hear that, because we need as many barrels as we can cart away."

Seth said, "Dammit to hell, you put us through all this, and you just wanna buy some shine?"

"That's the thing—we don't have the money, so we aim to, um, take it on credit. We'll pay you back as soon as we can."

Nadine hissed, "You got some gall, breaking my heart and now coming down here to steal our liquor."

A clatter sounded beyond the back door, like overlapping footsteps mounting a porch. I glanced behind me, confirming a solid wall was there, and dragged Nadine backward until we were safely tucked in the corner.

"Open the door," a female voice outside said. She sounded like another teenager. "Then hands back on your head—while you still have one."

In marched Darlene with fingers laced atop her crown, elbows pointing outward, followed by Rienzi doing the same. Bringing up the rear was a towheaded girl of maybe eighteen in ratty overalls and a dirty work shirt. She pointed a revolver at Rienzi's back.

CHAPTER 30

EVEN WORSE THAN THE THOUGHT OF DYING MYSELF WAS getting Rienzi and Darlene murdered. I would've broken down and begged for their lives except I had to keep ahold of Nadine.

Seth asked, "Whatchu got there, Brindle?" He hefted his shotgun and smirked at me.

"Caught these two snooping around the still." She saw us in the corner, my arms clenched around Nadine. "What's going on in here?"

Rienzi gave me a hard look. I didn't know if that was for getting us into this mess to begin with, embracing a girl I used to have a crush on, or resorting to taking a hostage to stay alive. If we survived, I knew I would learn the answer.

Once again, I expected Darlene to be a nervous wreck, but she had frozen statue-like, eyes fixed on some distant point, so inert that she almost vanished when I didn't focus on her. I realized she'd learned survival skills after all—no doubt at the hands of husbands who'd beaten and humiliated her.

Nadine said, "Brindle, if Bud here don't let me go on the count of three, shoot that one near you first—she don't look like his kin, so it's gotta be the girlfriend. If that don't seem to bother him none, shoot his sister next."

I released my grip on her before she could start counting.

Rather than dash away, she turned and slapped me hard across the face. "Now I see how you really are, I knowed I wasted my life dreaming on you."

Rubbing the hot patch she'd left on my cheek, I said, "If it makes a difference, I didn't mean you any harm. I was just trying to keep from getting killed."

Nadine stepped out of Seth's line of fire. He said, "What's to keep us from shooting all y'all now?"

I shrugged. "Mercy?" He laughed, but I persisted. "We haven't really done anything. If you let us go, we promise to never come back."

"Haven't done anything?" Nadine spat. "You broke my heart twicet now."

I indicated Rienzi and Darlene. "But they're innocent."

Brindle poked Rienzi in the spine with the gun muzzle, making her—and me—flinch. "No, they're whatchu-call-em…witnessers."

Rienzi addressed Nadine. "If you kill us, you'll never learn how to make whiskey faster and better. After only a cursory glance, I spotted at least six ways you can improve your fermentation and distillation processes. I bet I can find another twelve if I take my time."

"What are you going on about?"

"Chemistry, thermal and fluid dynamics, and proper ingredient storage, to name a few."

"In simple English," I coached. "Pretend you're talking to me."

"If I show you how to make tastier whiskey and fill more barrels faster, will you promise to let us go?"

Seth asked, "How do we know you ain't fooling just to save your skins?"

"Because I won't only tell you. I'll show you by making the improvements, and you'll start seeing the results before we leave."

Nadine looked at her brother. "The still ain't producing like it did in Daddy's day, so we really ain't got nothing to lose. If she's funning, we'll kill them all."

"About that." Rienzi swept Brindle's legs while snatching the girl's revolver. She aimed at Seth before he could react. With her free hand, she withdrew the gun from the purse on her shoulder and tossed it to me so I could cover Nadine. "My ideas flow more freely when people aren't pointing these things at me."

Darlene marched over to Seth and relieved him of his shotgun, giving him a lingering once-over. Rienzi, meanwhile, helped a stunned Brindle to her feet. I think I loved her more in that moment than ever before: she not only turned the tables but also acted generous in victory. She was forever teaching me how to be a better person.

"Okay," she announced, "let's bring that still of yours into the twentieth century."

Chapter 31

After inventorying the materials the Ashers had on hand, Rienzi led us out back to a clearing near a free-flowing creek where they had placed their distilling operation. She put everybody to work except Darlene, who stood over us with Seth's weapon like a gun bull surveying a chain gang.

Though Rienzi and I kept our sidearms at hand, Nadine and the others seemed to forget their previous threats after a while. They threw themselves into remaking their still: everything from the way they built a fire in the stone furnace below the large copper pot to the best means of storing the bulk cornmeal, malt, and yeast to keep water and critters out.

Rienzi limited her vocabulary to make herself understood and described various types of more efficient stills they might construct in the future if they could come by the resources. I wasn't sure whether she was dreaming up newfangled contraptions on the fly, as Jay did, or taking chemistry experiments she'd read about and applying them to this backwoods laboratory.

The well-built fire Brindle had learned to create brought welcome light and heat now that the sun had set. I dusted off my hands and stretched my back, feeling the pistol in the right side of my waistband press against my shirt. Without thinking, I'd put it in the same spot Papa had kept his Colt. And now here I was, helping the next generation of his former business partner's family improve their product. All because he'd picked me on occasion to be a human shield during his bootlegging runs to thwart his sworn enemy—who was now bedding Mama.

I finally understood irony.

Rienzi had taught the Ashers and Brindle to continuously stir the mash as alcoholic steam rose and collected in the copper cap arm, which carried the vapor down to a large crate known as the worm box. The spiraled copper pipe inside, which everybody called the worm, was now properly submerged. Cold creek water flowing over it forced the steam to condense back into liquid alcohol. A newly fashioned spout at the base of the worm fed the drizzle of whiskey through a cheesecloth filter—replacing the nasty burlap sack they had been using—and into one of the five-gallon wood barrels I remembered so well from my childhood.

Seth dipped a gourd ladle under the spout and collected about a tablespoon of clear liquid before he sampled the batch. He smacked his lips. "I'll be damned. It goes down smoother than what Daddy cooked up in the old days."

Darlene pointed his shotgun at him. "Then you don't mind us trading it for our lives?"

He dropped the ladle and held up his hands. "No, ma'am. Seems like a right fair deal."

"I don't agree," she said. "We're also gonna take as many barrels of whatever liquor you got on hand as we can fit in our car, and—" she gave him a wink "—y'all got yourself a new partner for the South Georgia run. But don't you be calling me no chucklehead."

"What?" I asked. "You're fixing to taking over Papa's old route?"

"Why not? I've always been a night owl, and the revenuers ain't likely to shoot at a woman driver any more than they'd open up on some man with a young'un. From the bank we make on this haul, I'm fixing to trade in Wyatt's car for a truck with a working radio."

"Now remember, we've gone through all this so Mama can buy off Harvey and Rutha and have enough left over to get back on her feet."

"There'll be plenty to go around, little brother. Don't you worry none."

But worrying was all I'd been doing—when I wasn't mucking things up.

Seth sniffed the discarded burlap sack and licked the wet spot where an earlier batch of shine had trickled through. "Whaddya think, sis?"

Nadine looked at the night sky, where a nearly full moon had just topped the tree line. "We got more than two weeks before it'll be full dark again, so there's lots of time to resupply." She nodded at Rienzi's improved still, where Brindle continued to stir the mash. "'Specially with this making faster than before."

She turned to me. "One thing, though. I never wanna see you again."

"Fair enough. I wasn't wild about our reunion either."

A hurt look passed across her face, and then she put her back to me. "Brindle, keep stirring. Me and Seth will help them load up, and then I'll spell you so y'all can eat. I woulda fixed some cornbread, but I got interrupted."

"Fried fish is good on its own," Brindle said. "Hey, Rienzi?"

"Yes?"

"Sorry for poking you with that gun. You taught me a bunch and probably saved my bacon."

Rienzi slipped Brindle's revolver alongside their tools in a wood box the size of a footlocker. "What do you mean?"

"I reckon they was fixing to bury me with their uncles if I didn't do whiskey-making any better."

"It's science, mostly. When I get home, I can mail a textbook to you."

"The mail rider don't come here." Brindle gazed at the bubbling mash. "And I can't read no how."

"Well, you're a quick study and learning the best way possible: by doing. If you ever want to work on your reading, you'll pick it up in no time."

The girl smiled and switched hands on the paddle.

Seth said, "Y'all park near the barn doors, and we'll load as much as she'll take."

It turned out that too many barrels in the trunk pressed the wheel wells against the top of the tires. Rienzi figured out that distributing the weight within the full interior, including the front seat, enabled us to carry an extra two hundred pounds of whiskey.

Seth and I put the final barrels on the back seat beside Darlene, and Nadine slammed the suicide door. My sister called through the open window, "I'll be back for more during the new moon."

"This time with money," Nadine warned.

Seth lifted the sawed-off shotgun Darlene had propped against the barn siding. "I'll be watching for you from the trees."

She smiled at him, looking pretty despite the purplish-green bruises on her jaw. "You ever been married?"

"No, you?"

"Lots of times. Fixing to get divorced again. You got something going with Brindle?"

"No, she don't cotton to fellers."

"Then me and her ain't a bit alike. See you soon."

Rienzi started the Hudson and put it in gear.

I told Nadine, "Play it straight with my sister, okay? She's had a hard life too."

"Long as she's straight with me. It'll be funny doing business with another gal."

"There's a lady in our county who runs a sawmill. Maybe times are changing."

"Don't hold your breath." She glanced at the sandy soil between us and then back up at me. "I'm sorry for putting y'all through the wringer. Rienzi set us up good. And you and me...we ain't exactly enemies now."

I touched my cheek, which was still puffy where she'd walloped it. "But we're not really friends either."

"Yeah, just maybe-coulda-been-somethings."

"Maybe. Well..."

I pivoted toward the car, but she tugged on my sleeve, stopping me. "There's something I always wanted to ask. All them years ago, they made you kiss my cheek, but not the other way around. Why's that?"

"Could be they knew you were braver than me, so they thought it was funnier to make me do it."

"You think I'm brave?"

"Making illegal liquor in the back of beyond and selling it to desperate men two and three times your age? You betcha."

"But not brave enough to kiss you goodbye in front of your clever girlfriend."

"That's good, because I plan to marry her, and also 'cause I want to make it home in one piece."

She put out her hand, and I shook it. "Have a good life, Bud."

I didn't bother to correct her. "Take care of yourself. You deserve a happy ending."

For the first time ever, I saw Nadine smile.

The interior of the Hudson smelled of high-proof alcohol and old wood. Once I settled into the front seat and propped my elbow on one of the two barrels between us, Rienzi said, "That was a very formal parting."

"I'll take it after having guns pointed at me all day—all week, it seems like."

"Back to Darlene's home?"

"No, folks buy this stuff at night, and Darlene needs to learn how to sell it. We'll try as many people on Papa's list as I can remember. Our last stop will be the first person I probably should've seen when I came home. Y'all ever had your fortunes told?"

CHAPTER 32

ONCE WE'D GOTTEN BACK ON A DIRT TRACK WIDE ENOUGH that it could reasonably be called a road, I said to Rienzi, "Thanks for saving our hides back there. If I'd gone on my own, I'd probably be some alligator's supper by now."

"Hasty decisions can kill."

I caught the edge in her voice. "That look you gave me in their kitchen could've killed. Are you still peeved because I had to hold Nadine so close?"

Enough moonlight came through the windows that I could see her disappointment. "No, that wasn't it at all. I was upset—and still am—because you risked your life to save someone who didn't ask for your help and doesn't want it. I admire you for trying to be everybody's hero, but you can't make decisions for your mother or for Darlene or me or anybody else. It's foolish of you and unfair to us."

"Yeah," Darlene said from the backseat. "You decided what was best for me and got Jay and Chet to go along."

I replied, "You're setting up to fill Papa's shoes, and you've even sunk a hook into Seth—would you really take Wyatt back if you could?"

She slapped my shoulder yet again. "Don't pretend everything's okay now thanks to you. If you had your way, all this shine would be for Mama's benefit, and I'd have no house and no nothing else but a car I ain't got the money to put gas in. And I got two eyes in my head—I can see that you don't care for me going with y'all to Texas. So I'm making do. It ain't giving me a silk purse from a sow's ear, but it's my decision—mine."

"Sorry I'm ruining everybody's lives by caring too much."

Rienzi patted my arm atop the barrel. "Now don't get pouty. Think of it this way: What if I decide that you'd be happier as a civilian, so I somehow make sure you're drummed out of the military? Would that be fair to you, even if I'm right?"

"Of course not, but does that mean I can't help anyone who's in trouble?"

"No, but they have to want and need your assistance."

I bounced my fist on my knee. "It's so blasted hard to stand by while people make bad choices. Especially when I can get them to do something better for themselves." Replaying those words in my head, the magnitude of my arrogance became clear to me. I groaned, "Good God Almighty," and knuckled my eyes, feeling like I was waking from a bad dream. "I reckon I owe everybody an apology."

"Accepted," Rienzi said and turned north to take us closer to Georgia. It was a good thing she remembered the route to the Ashers and could mentally reverse directions; I was so caught up in my thoughts I forgot to pay attention.

Darlene said, "So, you done living our lives for us?"

"I won't interfere anymore, promise. And I'm glad you're going to do something you look forward to." I nudged Rienzi and asked, "Can I still give advice?"

"Yes, but ask permission first."

"Darlene, can I advise you about selling whiskey to the men we're going to see on our rounds? I remember how Papa handled those things, and they can be a squirrely bunch."

"Please do. I ain't got the faintest notion how to go about it."

I relaxed against the seat, feeling the yoke of being responsible for everybody else's lives lift from my neck and shoulders.

"Feel better?" Rienzi asked.

"Yeah. How about you?"

"No."

"What is it?"

"I hit you with that retort about how hasty decisions can kill, but I keep thinking about my own spontaneity, driving all the way from Texas just so I could see you a few days early. It might've killed me if something had gone wrong. Instead, it saved your life. Does that mean everything—prosperity, tragedy, *everything*—depends on dumb luck?"

"Maybe so. That's why I wanna see the fortuneteller."

WE WOUND A SERPENTINE PATH through the counties of southwest Georgia, startling some folks awake when I rapped on their door and being met by more than one gun barrel. Despite the week I was having, I still couldn't get used to that reception. Yet, once the men answering our knock heard us out, nearly every one of them ran a hand over their mouths, as if they each had a powerful thirst that hadn't been quenched in some time, and they had customers in the same fix. These were retail bootleggers, the ones who earned extra money selling small quantities to the public in the backrooms of stores, behind government buildings, and door to door.

Times were still tough, and many couldn't pay for a whole barrel, so we poured whiskey into however many Mason jars they could afford for us to fill. This was something Papa never stooped to do in his day. But it allowed Darlene to ingratiate herself and learn to negotiate, and it started the process of getting them comfortable conducting business with their former supplier's daughter. One of them even gave us the leftovers of his fried chicken supper when he heard our bellies growl.

By midnight, Rienzi and I were competing to see who could yawn the biggest and loudest, while Darlene acted as if she had enough vim to carry her until dawn. We still had three barrels, one on the front seat and two beside my sister. A box we'd scrounged during one of our stops held a jumble of crumpled and folded dollar bills and a pirate's chest worth of assorted coins. Darlene kept it on her lap and had taken to running her fingers through the loose change like she was playing a tune. She'd definitely made bank on what we'd managed to sell.

I said, "Last stop for now. We'll sell the rest tomorrow—wait, it's now Saturday. We'll sell the rest tonight. Take a left past that pine so tall it blots out the stars."

Rienzi negotiated the turn from dirt road to cart path. She asked, "Is this your mystical teller of fortunes?"

"Don't poke fun. Posey's the real thing—has the second sight and all."

"Yeah," Darlene said, "I heard me some stories."

"But it's not possible to see beyond the present. Maybe she can predict things with some accuracy because she plays the odds."

"Firstly, Posey is a man, and secondly, you shouldn't say things aren't so just because your science books can't explain them. One time, these two couples graduating high school asked Posey to tell their futures. Only three of them got answers—Posey told one of the girls she had no future. On the ride home, they wrecked their car, and she was killed."

"Was he right about the other three's futures?"

"Letter perfect. But that's not all he can do. Uncle Jake went to him once because he couldn't find his revolver. It'd been his father's in the Spanish-American War, one of the few valuables our uncle owned. He'd looked everywhere for it but came up empty. He drove down here and opened his door, but before he could even set foot on the ground, Posey hollered from the porch that the gun was under the front seat. Sure enough, that's where our uncle found it."

Darlene said, "I heard from Mama that Uncle Jake asked Posey the best time for them to move to that farm near Valdosta. He hardly did anything without Posey's say-so."

"See?" Rienzi said. "That's the thing. People give up their free will and hand over their life savings to some charlatan who knows a few tricks."

"You sound plenty sure of yourself," I said, "but I remember you shimmying up a tree so you could escape a spirit light no scientist can account for."

"Fair point. Here's the real problem, though: if Posey can see the future, that means our fate is fixed. There's nothing we can do about it. Do you really want your life to be like a vinyl record some heavenly needle drops onto when you're born, and the same events come out of the speaker in the same way, over and over again, no matter how many times it's played? What would be the point of living if we're all just following the grooves of a recording?"

"Take a left up ahead, where that cow path veers off. I don't know what the point of life would be. We can ask him."

"I think I'll stay in the car."

Our headlights swept across the front porch, briefly illuminating an enormous, hairless man clad in custom-made overalls and nothing more. He sat in a hand-carved rocker that would've accommodated Rienzi and me sitting beside each other with room to spare, but it barely contained Posey.

CHAPTER 33

DARLENE PEERED OUT THE WINDOW AT THE FORTUNETELLER. "Can he even get out of that chair?"

"He must, to use the outhouse and such, but I've never seen him stand. His bald head would probably punch a hole in the porch roof if he wasn't careful."

Rienzi shut off the engine and tapped the whiskey cask under my elbow. "He probably drinks this much every night. Will he buy the three that are left?"

"Papa only ever sold him one a month." I opened my door and backed out, lugging the barrel. "Come up and say hey. He likes meeting folks. Please? Do it in the name of science."

"Oh, okay, why not."

The three of us approached the porch steps. I set down the nearly fifty pounds of liquor. "Hey, Mr. Posey. It's been a long time—do you remember me?"

He was big all over: at least seven feet tall and as wide as two men shoulder to shoulder. The overalls he always wore were supposedly handmade by a tailor who came down from Columbus twice a year to outfit him. In the moonlight, his hairless skin appeared as metallic as the coins in our money box. His irises were amber; he didn't have eyelashes or brows. Because Papa had always done bootlegging runs on the night of a new moon, I'd only ever seen Posey in the dim glow of a kerosene lantern he kept nearby, which had cast him in shades of gold. I wondered how he'd look in the daytime.

Stacked beside him was a column of thick, leatherbound books, which he supposedly read all day and night when he wasn't receiving customers. The writing on some of the spines wasn't in English. Rumor had it that such volumes were delivered to him regularly and swapped for the pile he'd finished. Posey never kept any of them.

The rocker creaked as he leaned forward and planted his huge, bare feet. He said in a deep voice I felt in my bones as much as heard, "Roger MacLeod. You outgrew 'Bud,' yes? My condolences about your father. It has been a long time since anybody remembered to bring ole Posey some Asher whiskey." He touched his long, thick fingers to his mouth. "I almost forgot what it tastes like—except I never forget anything." His blocky face tilted to my left. "You know what that is like, Rienzi Shepherd, yes? Never forgetting anything?"

She nodded and whispered, "It's terrible."

"What?" Darlene asked. "Y'all can't forget nothing?"

Posey rumbled, "It *is* terrible. Learning is good, but there is all the rest, too. Every bite of every meal. Every piss and crap and sneeze and burp. Every boring moment that nobody else would want to recall if they could. But we can—and we do."

"You never told me that," I said and took Rienzi's hand.

"I was afraid it would make you self-conscious, knowing I can't forget anything you've ever said or done." She pulled her hand away, and her attention snapped back to Posey. "Wait, you know my name and my…affliction. How?"

He pointed at his heart and then hers. "With mind reading, you might think of anything, including a lie even you thought was true, and I would pick that up and not know the difference. But ole Posey always knows the truth somehow. I do not have a proper name for what happens, so I call it soul reading."

"This is impossible." She plopped into the dust, skirt bunching under her.

"So much of life seems that way, and yet—" he held his arms out, spanning the length of a car "—I am."

My sister said, "Do you know me?"

"Darlene MacLeod, the oldest child of Mance and Reva. Many marriages, much heartbreak, more misery with men in store. But this is the interesting part: a self-appointed new bootlegger. No woman has ever done that around here."

"Yup, and the going price for Asher whiskey is twelve dollars a gallon, but I'll discount it to fifty-five for the whole of it." She propped her foot on the barrel. "Whaddya have?"

He laughed, which must've been what an earthquake sounded like. "The part of you that speaks with no voice tells me the price is fifty for a barrel, but I like your moxie. I will pay you fifty but let each of you ask one question, which I now usually charge two dollars apiece for. This can be about your future, the location of a lost item." He glanced at me with his amber gaze. "Some truth about the dearly departed."

Darlene said, "Okay, it's a deal. Here's my question: Will my bootlegging go good?"

"It will succeed in ways you have not anticipated and cannot imagine."

"What does that mean?"

"Exactly as I said."

I jumped in. "If you ask a vague question, you get a vague answer."

"You coulda warned me. When you and Papa sold him the usual, y'all must've played this game."

"It's not a game. Papa never would ask a question, and needless to say, he'd never pay for me to ask one. He said it made a man weak and took the surprises out of life."

"Well, he certainly got a surprise in the end. Why don't you ask about that?"

"I don't want to waste my question on him. Anyway, it's Rienzi's turn."

"I'll pass," she said, peering up at Posey as if trying to unlock the secret to a puzzle.

He asked, "Are you afraid to skip ahead on your record? Remember, the needle can be moved in two directions."

She shook her head. "I can't figure out how you're doing this."

"Ole Posey does not know either."

"All right, here's something my father's been vague about. I've always wanted to know about my mother's final moments, such as whether she at least had a chance to hold me before she died."

"Your mother held you many times before she died, and she did not suffer at the end. She made sure it was a very tall building she jumped from."

"That's ridiculous," she shouted, voice cracking. "You're wrong about everything. She died just after giving birth to me."

"No, she died by suicide a year after you were born."

"That's a lie—and you're a monster." Tears dripped from her face.

"I do not know what I am, only that I must speak the truth. Sometimes the truth is monstrous."

She drew her knees up, pressed her face into them, and rocked forward and back.

I squatted beside her and placed a hand on her shoulder. "Can I help somehow?"

Face still buried in her skirt, she said, "My earliest memories are of a young woman holding me and singing in Japanese. Several times, she was crying. Years later, when I asked my father about her, he said he'd hired a wet nurse to feed and care for me. I felt such a strong connection to her, even stronger than to him. He said it was probably because she nourished me from her body. But maybe she did more than that."

Shuddering, she looked up at Posey. "Can you tell me why she killed herself?"

"I only ever answer one question per visit for each person."

"Then I'll use mine," I said, "Why did she jump?"

"*Why* questions are hard for ole Posey when the subject is not here." He gazed at the porch ceiling, his pulse visible in a neck as thick and gray as an old tree trunk. "Sakura was blue during her pregnancy and after giving birth, as many mothers are. She also bore the curse of remembering all: every tragedy and sorrow, the pain and discomfort of pregnancy, the agony of birthing Rienzi. Despite her love for her daughter and husband, she no longer wanted to be in this world. This does not answer why Sakura jumped but others choose to live. I only know that she was boundlessly sad despite every kind of support. She had drifted too far beyond the long reach of love."

After a moment, during which everybody seemed to hold their breath, Rienzi murmured, "Thank you."

"You are welcome, fellow keeper of memory. There is much to do before your journey to Texas." He raised a hand to us. "Judicious violence need not always be applied directly to people."

"I don't know what that means either," Darlene said, "but you still owe us fifty bucks."

CHAPTER 34

RIENZI APPEARED DAZED AS WE WALKED BACK TO THE CAR, so I offered to drive the rest of the way to my sister's home. The Hudson had a different feel than Mama's Chevy truck, and I managed to stall it twice while Posey looked on.

Darlene said, "Maybe your question to him shoulda been how to work that there clutch." She snickered and deposited the fortuneteller's money in the box.

"And maybe you shouldn't try to cheat a loyal customer. Especially someone who can look into your soul."

"If'n he looked, he knows I didn't mean nothing by it."

I finally got us back on the road. Rienzi still hadn't said anything since she handed me her key. She merely stared out the windshield as the yellowish beams of the headlights cut through the night. I let a few more minutes pass and then nudged her. "Do you want to talk about it?"

She spoke as if in a trance. "My entire life, I thought I could remember everything since I was a baby except the person who brought me into this world. But it turns out, I'd been recalling my mother's face and voice, her touch and smell, and even the taste of her milk all along. She was with me the whole time, even though she chose to abandon us."

"I reckon people take their lives for all sorts of different reasons. She was so blue she couldn't rise above it. My real father was heartbroken over his crazy wife poisoning their baby and out of his mind with drink. Hugh Bradley felt humiliated enough by Chet that he couldn't stand himself. Seems like being hopeless is a powerful symptom."

She grabbed my sleeve. "If you ever start feeling that way, swear you'll tell me."

"I swannee."

"That's right," she said, a hint of amusement returning to her voice, "you told me once that using the word *swear* is a sin."

"It is," Darlene said. "Mama and Papa drilled that into us."

I mused, "Funny how two people who could cuss the bark off a tree and regularly competed to see which of them could be more unfaithful considered *that* a sin."

My sister said, "You better stop talking bad about Mama. She's been through a lot."

"And she's still peeved that I saved her life back at the Cottontail Café. See if she doesn't bring it up when she finds out about her house and all her things turning to ashes. She'll go on about how I coulda spared her seeing that if only I'd let Papa shoot her in the face."

"Mama never claimed to be a saint. She's got feelings is all I'm saying."

"I don't recall seeing any feelings on display when she gave us boys away. Except maybe relief."

"She's just got her own way of showing them, private-like."

Rienzi asked, "How are you going to keep your bootlegging private?"

"I don't plan to."

"But won't your mother tell the revenue agent? She doesn't strike me as being discreet."

"Now you're gigging her too? I swan, you and Bud are like two peas in a pod. And what did that Posey feller mean about my plan working out strangely?"

"That's not what he said," I reminded her.

Rienzi, of course, quoted him precisely: "*It will succeed in ways you have not anticipated and cannot imagine.*"

"Yeah, that means strangely."

I said, "I think it means things will turn out differently than you planned, but still good."

"Why didn't he just say that then?" She harumphed behind us and then asked, "How huge do you reckon his pecker is? Judging from that bulge in his overalls, I'm guessing it's as long and big around as my arm when he's feeling lovey-dovey."

And so went the conversation, ricocheting between the somber and the profane, as I drove on through the night.

When we reached Darlene's house, the Roman numerals on the dashboard-mounted windup clock showed that it was nearly two in the morning.

The only car parked there was Wyatt's Plymouth. When we went inside, we found the house empty. I'd figured Mama would've returned home, discovered the wreckage, and told Bascom drop her off here. Maybe they'd decided to spend the night in Columbus, where he was no doubt still demonstrating what a perfect gentleman he was.

Cradling her box of cash and coins under one arm and Papa's old rifle in the other, Darlene said, "I'm tuckered out. Rienzi, you want to sleep in the guest bed? Bud can make hisself a pallet in the front room."

"Actually, I have a lot on my mind and want to drive a little. Care to join me, Roger?" Her question sounded innocent, but she gave me a look I'd never seen before: serious eyes that usually meant she wanted my undivided attention but a slight smile, too, which she might've described as *enigmatic*.

Maybe I was in trouble again.

"Um, sure." I turned to Darlene, rubbing my hands together as a cool breeze promised falling temperatures. "We'll be real quiet coming back inside so we won't wake you."

Back in the car, with Rienzi at the wheel, I asked, "Where do you want to drive to?"

"Let's see if the housefire's out." She started the car and navigated back to the highway flawlessly, as if she'd driven the route one hundred times rather than once.

"Are you feeling a little better?"

"I don't know about better—but certainly resolved."

"To do what?"

"Stop looking back so much. When you remember everything, it's hard not to waste your time doing only that. Meanwhile, I haven't been making new memories worth reliving. All I've done for the past few years is study. Even after you came to San Antonio."

"We've had some nice times."

She gave my hand a squeeze. "Randy farm boy jokes aside, you've been sweet, decent, and patient, even when I acted like I'd rather open another textbook than stay up with you."

"Well, it's the middle of the night, and here we are, staying up together."

"I love it—and I love you."

"Love you back. Are you really curious about Mama's place?"

"In part." She hummed to herself, so I decided to be quiet rather than spoil the mood.

Chapter 35

The ruin of my childhood home still glowed orange, and billows of smoke stretched toward the bright moon. Occasional flames danced as the fire found something fresh to devour.

Rienzi pointed out the broken power line still sparking on the ground. "Be careful not to get close to that. Electrocution is a bad way to go. Some prisoners in electric chairs have been incinerated during their executions."

So much for wanting to preserve the romantic mood. I decided I'd misread her signals.

"Um, so the house will probably smolder until this time tomorrow. Is there anything else you wanted to see?"

"There is." She parked and switched off the engine.

I joined her in the weedy yard, coughing a little in the haze and shivering as the temperature continued to drop. She pulled out her hard-shelled suitcase and my coat and knapsack from the floor of the backseat. We'd moved them there to make room in the trunk for whiskey barrels.

I took my gear. "What do you have in mind?"

"Camping." She led me on a wide loop around the wreckage. Despite the new chill in the air, my side facing the fire began to sweat.

Behind the house, where Ed Bascom had flipped a silver dollar in my direction not long ago, the stovepipe jutted from unrecognizable remains of the back porch, roof, and walls. I said, "At the old home place, my grandma had a detached kitchen to spare the home in case of a cooking fire. I wish we'd had that—maybe the Bradleys would've just torched the main house, and we could still have a spot indoors."

"How about the barn?" Before I could answer, she headed there.

No animals had been penned inside for long time, so the cold air only smelled of moldering hay and the smoke seeping between the boards. Enough moonlight shined through the door she'd opened that I could locate a kerosene lantern. I didn't have a flint or matchbook, but with the house ablaze, getting the wick going wasn't a problem—though I nearly roasted my hand touching a long piece of straw to a flaming remnant of my old home.

I found Rienzi in the tack room where we used to keep the gear for Papa's huge warhorse, Dan.

She said, "We could stay here or go up in the loft. Heat rises, so it'll be warmer up there."

"I know a cozier spot."

"Where?"

"I'm standing over it." I swept my shoe across the dirt, pushing some aside to reveal a bit of wood. "It's a trapdoor. Papa kept the moonshine he didn't manage to sell down there, and one time I hid in there, too, when he was fixing to wear out a switch on me. With the lamp on and the hatch mostly closed, you'll be warmer than up here."

Years of soil and dust had compacted atop it, so it took a while to locate the edges and scrape off enough dirt to slide away a repurposed barn door Papa had used for this particular hidey-hole.

Out of habit, I lowered the lantern a foot into the hole and swung it like a pendulum. This illuminated a space about six feet deep, five feet wide, and seven feet long, with wood reinforcing the floor and sides. When Lonnie first showed me the secret place, I'd done this to make sure Papa didn't keep a monster penned down there. As I grew older and wanted some privacy, it was to see whether a family of rats or other critters had taken up residence.

On the side closest to me, a ladder had been nailed into the wood, to make it easy for him to climb in and out carrying a cask of whiskey under one arm. I explained all this as Rienzi joined me at the edge.

She took my hand in hers. "Seems like he went to a lot of effort just to cover up a few barrels."

"Sometimes it was half a truckload or more. You never forget anything, right?"

"I can't, even when I want to."

"Well, recollect how tough times were back in the thirties. Papa might spend all our money from a harvest on liquor but then find out a lot of his usual customers couldn't pay. Posey always had enough because poor folks will fork over what little they have to know their future, but many others couldn't afford it. So he'd store the barrels in here and spend the next month trying to find new customers—and then start all over again."

"Darlene's going to need something like this, right?"

"Maybe Mama will rent her the space."

"Rent?"

"Yeah, I don't expect she'll just give it to her."

"You come from hard people." She grabbed the greatcoat from atop my knapsack and clambered down the ladder. After spreading the coat on the floorboards like a makeshift pallet, she looked up at me and grinned.

I handed her the light so I could descend one-handed while sliding the door across the hole, leaving enough of a gap for air to circulate. We stood toe to toe. In the lantern shine, she'd never looked lovelier. I stammered, "J-j-just got to be careful not to kick the lamp over."

"No sudden movements, I promise." She leaned in and kissed me. Her lips were wet and soft against mine. "Good thing you're not claustrophobic."

"What's that?"

She began to unbutton my shirt. "The fear of confined spaces."

I was afraid of a dozen things at that moment—foremost not living up to Rienzi's expectations—but being with her in a coffin built for two was not among them.

She pulled the shirttails from my pants and ran her warm hands over my chest and back, as if memorizing the contours. Which I supposed she was forced to do anyway because of how her brain was made, but from her smile she seemed to be enjoying it.

"Mmm, farm work, sawmilling, and the Army PT regimen have agreed with you."

It was difficult not to touch her the same way, but I kept my hands down by my sides, sensing that my turn would come if I was patient. "Back at Foster's Drain, when Papa and my real father were first teaching me to swim, I remember how you stared at me while you were holding my clothes."

"'For a little boy you have a lot of muscles,' is what I said. You have even more now." She pressed against me, cradled the back of my head in her hands, and gave me the longest kiss we'd ever shared.

Tilting her face back, she asked, "Are you afraid to touch me?"

"I'm waiting for permission."

"Granted."

Chapter 36

After an ecstatic hour, we dressed to ward off the cold, blew out the lamp, and curled up together, lying on our sides. I spooned against Rienzi's back and rump, with my arm draped around her. "Lordy, you sure did know what you were doing."

"I've read a lot about it—librarians would be shocked to discover the smutty treasures hidden in the pages of innocuous memoirs and anthropology studies. Or maybe it's a secret they keep for themselves but few others know about. Either way, putting knowledge into practice is never as straightforward as I think it's going to be."

The question I was dreading to ask tumbled out unbidden: "Did I, uh, do okay?"

"I don't have any basis for comparison, but I thought you did great. How was I?"

"Very…expressive. I'm used to you being calm and kind of restrained."

"Was I too loud?"

"No, you were enthusiastic. Big difference," I pressed my face into her sweaty hair and nuzzled the crown of her head. "The whole thing was nothing like I expected."

"In a good or bad way?"

"Much better than how the bird Papa called That Goddamn Rooster would pounce on a hen."

She laughed. "That's procreation versus passion."

"But there's no chance we, um, procreated by accident?"

"No, I just started my menses."

"Definition? Please and thank you."

"Menstruation...flow...bleeding down there."

"Oh, right. I overheard Darlene talking to Mama about that one time."

"Well, fortunately, I'm a light bleeder, so we didn't make a mess."

"Which means we could do it again soon?"

She yawned. "Let's get some sleep first, Casanova."

"I've got all these ideas now about things I wanna try. And I'll bet Jay and Chet have done it lots of times and can give me some suggestions."

She went rigid against me. "You can't tell them about this. They'll look down on me if they know, and they'll pressure you to find another girl."

"Why?"

"Boys are weird about what we just did. They all want to copulate like your rooster, but they think nice girls shouldn't. Which means the only girls they think can make their dreams come true are so-called bad girls they have contempt for and wouldn't want their little brother dating."

"Not everybody thinks that way." I gave her a hug. "All the romancing makes me love you more than ever."

"Still, you can't tell them. Do you swannee?"

"Yes, ma'am."

She kissed the back of my hand. "I'm glad you have a happy memory of this."

"I surely do. You?"

"I'll enjoy reliving this one again and again."

WHEN I AWOKE, OUR LOVE nest was no longer dark. Morning light seeped into the tack room of the barn and made it down to us.

Rienzi slept quietly behind me now, her cheek against my back. Sometime during the night, we'd reversed positions.

I needed to pee, so I eased away and covered her with the half of my coat not under her. Creeping up the ladder to the surface, I eased back the trapdoor enough to squeeze through into much colder air. Thoughts of the loving Rienzi and I had shared warmed me as I did my business outside the barn.

The house wreckage continued to smolder and smoke, looking cool on the outside but glowing orange within. I checked the henhouse for eggs, but Mama must've fried the last of the chickens. Fortunately the smokehouse still had hams and sausages dangling from metal hooks in the soupy air, offering the possibility of breakfast. Mama's cast-iron skillet was somewhere under a ton of blazing hot debris and probably was one of the few things she'd be able to salvage, but that didn't help us now.

I searched the barn for something I could cook with and made an entirely different discovery. At some point, Mama or someone else had piled Jay's completed and semi-built inventions into a jumble in one corner. I recognized parts to a still he'd been trying to fashion by hand when we were kids; a bottle-capping machine he repaired and tried to put to use with explosive, geyser-like results; a cigarette-rolling device he'd tinkered with long before he'd taken up the habit; and a dozen other projects that had captivated him. Against one wall, cobwebs cloaked a nine-foot-long wood and wire bow.

Rienzi ascended the ladder, yawning as she went. She wore my greatcoat, which hung on her like a monk's robe and made climbing a chore. I moved in to kiss her, but she turned her face away, saying, "My breath's terrible."

"I don't care."

"So is yours."

"Oh. How about a hug, then?"

She allowed me to embrace her. I talked over her shoulder so my breath wouldn't offend her. "Thanks again for earlier."

"I woke up thinking about it."

"No regrets?"

"Only that we didn't start trying things months ago. If that makes me one of those bad girls, then so be it."

"Want to be bad again right now?"

She backed away. "No, too much chance your mother and her boyfriend will finally show up. What's all that behind you?"

"Jay's inventions and experiments." I pointed out his various projects and told her stories about the wildly varied results he'd achieved. "My favorite was always the big bow and arrow."

She looked closer. "What's it made from?"

"He took a twelve-foot heart pine fence rail, cut it down to nine feet, and then split it to give him just enough wood to work with."

"Why nine?"

"We reckoned the bows the Indians used in the Western picture shows were about three feet long, and Jay wanted to make one that could shoot three times as far, so he figured he should make a nine-foot bow."

"That's logical, but he'd need to be about twice that tall to use it."

"That was the big surprise—hang on. He used a drawing knife to scrape away a bunch of layers until he had the shape he wanted. Meanwhile, he sent me and Chet into the woods to find the perfect arrows. Elderberry bushes can put out branches that are straight and strong, and we gathered a makeshift quiver of them that were roughly six feet long. We had to do all this after we finished our chores—which were almost endless, thanks to Papa—so it took months before we could try it out."

She peered at the weapon. "What kind of bowstring is that?"

"Baling wire. We used it for everything on the farm, from bundling crops to latching doors. It about killed Jay to flex the wood enough to loop the wire into those notches he put at either end."

"Which is my point—he'd need to be a colossus to shoot an arrow like the Indians did in those movies."

"Right, which is why he didn't." I grinned at her, knowing she'd come up with the answer.

She frowned at me, considered Jay's invention again, and snapped her fingers. "He learned about the Battle of Agincourt in school, didn't he? This is the country boy's version of the English longbow."

"Yup. We had no idea what he had in mind either until the day we carried it into the field. He flopped onto his back, put his feet against the bow, and pushed against it as he tugged the wire with both hands. Chet followed his order to load one of our elderberry arrows, which I'd sharpened, notched, and fletched with chicken feathers. Then he pointed his feet straight up and let 'er rip with a loud twang."

"I'm guessing it didn't pierce the heavens."

"Probably not, but the arrow did go clean out of sight. We honestly thought we'd never see it again. Of course, it came back down—and seemed to be heading straight for us." I laughed. "Talk about a mad scramble. It ended up burying itself in the dirt some twenty feet away. After that, we shot arrows down the lane toward Hardscrabble Road when we knew nobody was about, which was a lot safer."

"I want to try it."

"Neither of us is strong enough to flex the wood and pull that wire back very far."

"But we could do it together, either side by side or with you nestled behind me." She winked. "Think of it as a warm-up for tonight."

CHAPTER 37

WE HAD TO MOVE MOST OF JAY'S OTHER COBWEBBED contraptions aside to get to his version of the English longbow. Retrieving it took even longer because Rienzi kept stopping to examine one project after another, sometimes noting areas for improvement, other times expressing admiration for his handiwork.

I couldn't help wondering whether she and Jay would've made the better couple. They seemed well suited as fellow tinkerers. And he was a lot more worldly than me and no doubt had much more experience with girls. As soon as she realized all this, would she dump me? Or would she at least be thinking about him whenever she was with me?

Jay had always carried a torch for Geneva Turner, and they'd made out the other night, but what if he decided Rienzi was a superior fit overall? He'd told me Rienzi was my future, but maybe it would be like Hermann and Cecilia all over again, where the German POW tried to play Cupid for us, and they ended up falling in love instead.

If it came down to fighting Jay for her, I decided I'd do it. He'd destroy me the way Chet used to do, but I would have to try.

"What's the matter?" she asked.

"Nothing." I kicked aside yet another gadget he'd cobbled from other things, all metal teeth and bent tines, its purpose unfathomable but threatening.

"I asked you a question a minute ago, and you only grunted like an ape."

"Hey, everybody knows you're a lot smarter, but you don't have to compare me to a monkey."

"I didn't; I merely likened your grunt to that of a primate. Why are you suddenly so moody?"

Using a scrap of flour sack nearby, I attacked the dusty webs cloaking the giant bow. "How much do you think about Jay?"

"Jay? Hardly at all."

"Aha—hardly ain't nothing." I scraped the wire bowstring clean.

"Looking at these things he assembled, I was thinking he's clever but undisciplined. He seemed to abandon many projects halfway through."

"We didn't have any money. He had to make do with whatever he could find. Lots of times, things needed to be set aside until somebody threw out the right piece of junk. He did the best with what he had."

"You were sounding jealous before and now you're defending him." She took hold of my arm, stilling my cleanup work. "Do you honestly think I have feelings for him or Chet or anybody but you?"

I couldn't meet her stare. "It just seems like everyone else has so much more to offer you."

Her questions came rapid-fire. "Was the confidence and bravado you put on display yesterday just a ruse to get what you wanted? Are you having second thoughts about me now that I'm no longer pure? Or do you see me as a bad girl and want to discard me like the trash Jay used to rifle through?"

"None of those things." I let the soiled cloth fall to my feet and slumped against the barn wall with my knees drawn up. "I'm afraid."

"Of what?"

"Losing everything now that I finally have it. A beautiful, brilliant girl in love with me, a life with prospects far away from this dusty ole speck of land on a dead-end road. I can't bear the thought of starting from scratch again. Alone."

"But see how you're making that a self-fulfilling prophecy? Acting jealous and insecure will drive me away. Risking everything to save people who never asked to be rescued—and won't appreciate it—will cost you that life and those prospects far from here."

I sighed. "Maybe that's what us MacLeods do: sabotage ourselves so we can't keep something we're afraid we'll lose anyway."

"Even if that's how your family has always been, it doesn't mean you need to follow the same pattern. A brave person wouldn't do that."

"What if I'm not really brave?"

"Telling me you're afraid makes you brave—and smart. Only foolish people claim to have no fear."

I dared to look into her dark, shining eyes. "Sorry for making a fuss. Did I ruin what we have between us?"

"No, but if you really think so little of your worth, then I made a huge mistake giving myself to you. It's an error I don't intend to repeat."

"W-w-wait—" I stammered, but her look told me I better not beg. "Okay," I said, "I read you loud and clear." I rose, pushing against the splintery wall for support, angry that I'd tarnished her opinion of me. Maybe not irreversibly but certainly for a long time to come. How could I have been so stupid? I deserved the needlelike slivers of wood that pierced my back and shoulders. Or maybe I ought to have my hand shoved into Jay's evil-looking contraption.

She indicated the longbow. "Do you still want to try this, or would you rather mope around all day?"

"Good God Almighty, you're relentless."

"I remember you telling me about the way drill sergeants push everybody to do more than they think they can achieve. All of us can use a kick in the pants sometimes."

"You don't seem to need that." Over one arm, I slung a burlap sack from which six-foot elderberry shafts protruded, fletched with dusty chicken feathers in mottled grays, browns, and reds. I gripped one end of the bow and dragged it along the path we'd cleared.

Rienzi hefted the other end, lightening my load. "Posey lit a fire under me. Like I told you yesterday, he made me realize I was spending all my time storing away knowledge like a miser and looking back at my history instead of making good new memories."

I wasn't helping in the creation of a new memory she could recollect fondly, so I told myself to straighten up and fly right, like the song advised.

We lugged the huge weapon outside. I nodded at the still-smoldering wreckage of the house. "If you want to shoot at a target, this will be easy to hit."

"No, I want to see how far we can make it go."

We tromped around the side of Mama's ruined home. "How about here?" she asked. "I parked far enough into the yard that we won't hit the car. The arrow should go straight down the lane."

"Okay. We can lie on my coat, so our clothes won't get dirty."

Rienzi set down her end, shrugged out of the greatcoat, and draped it on the ground. After she sat on it, I positioned the inside of the upper half of the bow against the soles of her low-heeled shoes and sat beside her with the bottoms of my own footwear pressed against the lower half. As much as I wanted to try the other position she'd mentioned, with her spooned in front of me, she surely didn't want me pressed tight against her backside after I'd disappointed her with my childishness.

I removed an elderberry shaft from the bag and placed it between us. "Once we pull the wire toward us a little, I'll try to keep it taut while you center the arrow. Then we'll both yank it while pushing with our feet to bend the bow, rock back and lift our legs a bit to give the arrow some height—and, on three, let it fly."

The beauty of heart pine was that the wood was so dense with pine oil it resisted rot, which was why it had been used for centuries to make fence rails, floorboards, and so much else that it had been logged out of existence. Unless someone set fire to the bow, it would last another hundred years or more. The downside was that the density made it even harder to flex than a regular piece of pine.

We grunted and strained. The wire dug into our fingers as we tried to pull it toward our chests. Finally the bow began to curve a little, and the punishing bowstring eased back a few inches. Rienzi fitted the arrow while I groaned through gritted teeth. She resumed pulling, and the bow cooperated some more, but nowhere near the deflection Jay had achieved. I was years older than he'd been when he created this weapon, but somehow I wasn't as strong yet as he'd been way back then.

On a count of three, we lifted our legs about thirty degrees. My stomach muscles knotted as we held the position for another three-count.

We shot the arrow between our feet. The wire twanged and snapped against our shoe tops, stinging my toes.

As the arrow blasted away like a rocket, a car turned from Hardscrabble Road and drove our way. We dropped our legs and sat up, the breath catching in my throat. I couldn't tell the make of the vehicle yet. It was just a dark shape spitting a plume of dust behind as it clattered over the uneven surface. The arrow bore down on it. I hoped our little bit of fun wasn't going to get someone killed.

Our shot plunged into the dirt, and a moment later the tires on the right side of the car rolled over the elderberry shaft, crushing it into the sandy dirt.

Shaking blood back into my fingers, I asked, "Did you think we were going to hit the car?"

"For a second, until I estimated the velocities of both objects, holding their accelerations constant." She rubbed at the red lines that creased her hands and glanced at me. "What? It's a textbook physics problem."

I returned to staring at the car. If the Bradleys were back to gloat—or seek additional revenge—we could at least fire some more arrows at them. Maybe the sheriff and Brooks were finally coming to check out reports of a possible housefire. Or Ed Bascom and Mama had returned at last from their Columbus trip. Their arrival would mean she could start to deal with the destruction of everything she owned and figure out where to resettle and what to do next.

The car, it turned out, was a black Oldsmobile touring sedan, at least ten years old. I didn't know anybody who owned one. It stopped with a squeak of its brakes a few dozen yards away. A man and woman sat in the front, each framed in a separate rectangle of windshield, with a vertical bar dividing the two pieces of glass. Curiosity seekers, no doubt. Possibly they'd seen the smoke and decided it was more than what a chimney would put out.

Rienzi and I got to our feet. She asked, "Anyone you know?"

"No, but since I grew up here, I reckon I represent the family." I approached the newcomers. The couple watched me for a moment, trading comments, before they both climbed out and shut their doors. They looked like townies.

The thin, dark-haired man had a neatly trimmed Van Dyke and was dressed in a starched white shirt with a checkered suit jacket; a wide, loose tie; pleated pants; and wingtip shoes. His companion, who was just as skinny but looked a few years younger, wore her brown hair up, with curly strands falling over her ears. She had on an unbuttoned white cardigan over a dress with little flowers on it. A cream-colored purse hung from one shoulder, and her feet were tucked into high button shoes. Their thin-lipped smiles looked more automatic than friendly.

"Hey," I said. "How y'all?"

"Fair to middlin'," the man said in a deep voice that sounded familiar. "By the looks of that there house, you're having a right bad day."

"Yes, sir. Do you live around here?"

The woman spoke up, her voice soft and musical. "Near enough. We saw the smoke from the highway. Kitchen fire?"

"I don't know, ma'am. We got here after it'd started."

She peered past my shoulder. "That your girlfriend yonder?"

"Yes, ma'am." I glanced back. Rienzi had draped my now-dusty greatcoat around her shoulders and was walking toward the Hudson.

"Her car has a Texas plate. Did she drive all that way to see you?"

"Um, she did, but how did you know?"

"What a pretty little thing. Is she a Chinese, like the Dragon Lady in *Terry and the Pirates*?"

"Half-Japanese."

"No fooling," the man said. "A Nip?"

I squirmed, struggling between politeness and anger. "I don't care for that term—sir."

"No offense meant." He leaned against his door and folded his arms. "After all, it don't look like she coulda bombed Pearl Harbor or nothing."

The woman said, "You must be Bud."

"Roger, ma'am. Do you know my people?"

"We *are* your people. This here's your Uncle Harvey, and I'm your Aunt Rutha."

CHAPTER 38

IT WAS LIKE ROUNDING A CORNER AND STUMBLING INTO A PAIR of demons. Too bad we hadn't put that elderberry shaft right through the windshield and into one of their hearts. I took a step back, wishing Rienzi and I were still side by side on the ground with our shoes pressed on the bow and another arrow notched. "You're Papa's brother and sister."

"Big as life," Harvey said, holding his arms out, "and twice as spiffy."

Rutha said, "You're exactly how he described you, birthmark and all, but he didn't say how growed up you are."

I wanted to run to Rienzi and beg her to drive us back to Texas that instant. Something held me in place though, a question that had burned in my mind since my sister showed up at the kitchen door on New Year's Day, bruised and bloody. "Why are you doing all this to your family?"

Rutha looked at the back of her fingers, as if inspecting the nails. "Sorry I got rough with your sister, but an example had to be made. Reva just wasn't listening to reason."

"So why take it out on poor Darlene?"

"Because she wasn't carrying the gun that killed our brother, the way Reva does. That hussy waved it around the first time we came calling like she was fixing to shoot us too. But your sister was unarmed."

"That was your niece you stomped."

"I know—I feel terrible about it." She examined her other hand and rubbed at a knuckle.

"You're both evil, just like Papa."

Harvey said, "You best mind that tone, bucko. Remember you're talking to your elders. And betters."

"Why do y'all think Mama has any of Papa's money?"

He replied, "Mance told us a big payday was a-coming and he'd share it with us. A grand for me and another for your aunt here."

"That's a fortune."

"He was always good that way, taking care of family."

I snorted. "Taking care of you two, maybe. He didn't give a flip about me or my family."

A gust of wind blew smoke over us. Rutha inhaled as if smelling roses and smoothed her dress. "He had a lot of mouths to feed."

"Yeah, I've met two half-brothers so far. How many more are there?"

Harvey shrugged. "The ladies always did take a shine to him, but we never asked, and he didn't say. What he did talk about was that payday. His widow-lady let us go through his office and tromp through their house, but we didn't find any big pile of cash. Reva must've taken it when she killed him."

"You're lying already. Bonny Peterson said she's never seen you."

"No, she's the liar. Maybe Mance's two widows are in cahoots."

I decided to try a lie of my own. "Okay, I'll level with you. Mama did have the money, but she put it in a hiding place Papa made under the kitchen floor." I pointed back at the fiery remains of the house. "And now it's a big pile of ash, not cash—along with everything else there—so you might as well leave us alone. Leo Bradley and his sons set the fire. If you want to take it out on somebody, go after them."

"For your sake," Harvey said, "I hope that ain't so."

"What's that mean?"

Rutha took a gleaming chrome revolver from her purse and pointed it at me with a steady aim. Her expression was blank, like

I was nothing to her but a means to an end. At least Seth Asher and the Bradleys had looked angry behind their guns; I understood that. She seemed bored, which was a whole lot scarier.

As my bravado failed me, my guts turned into a gully full of ice water. I began to tremble. All I could think of was that I had to stay alive for Rienzi. Remembering every detail of my murder, she would be haunted forever. Assuming Rutha didn't shoot her too.

Harvey said, "Since you're probably Reva's favorite—not being Mance's and all—she might finally do what's right and either produce his money or come up with somebody else's. Because we'll tell her you're the one who'll get what-for otherwise."

No way would Jerry happen by and save me this time. There was no sign of Chet on the horizon with the truck full of rifles, and Jay was probably with Geneva. I glanced back at Rienzi, who now watched us from beside her dad's car. Maybe she planned on giving chase if they abducted me.

"What happens now?" I asked.

Rutha said, "You take us to wherever your mama's at."

"She was here earlier," I lied. "Her boyfriend's a federal officer, you know, and her cousin, the High Sheriff, could be on the way now because of the arson she told me she was going to report."

If they were alarmed by her connections to various lawmen, they didn't show it. Rutha waved the gun toward their car, beckoning me. "Come on then. Let's go look for her."

"Tell your Oriental gal we'll take her too," Harvey said. With a snicker, he added, "Don't want her to get no fancy ideas about running us off the road and rescuing you or nothing."

I did an about-face and walked toward the Hudson. Various escape scenarios raced through my mind, but each one ended with the car bogging down in sand, snapping an axle, or Rienzi or me—or both of us—getting shot.

Harvey called, "That's far enough. Tell her to ride with us."

I cupped my hands around my mouth to holler, but she said, "I could hear everything." She walked up beside me, my greatcoat fairly swallowing her, as we went back toward my aunt and uncle.

"Sorry to get you into this," I murmured.

"We're together," she whispered back. "Nothing else matters. Though I wish I had my purse with Dad's gun inside. I left it in the barn." She stared at Harvey and Rutha like she was sizing them up.

We stopped near the horizontal chrome bands of the Oldsmobile grille. I asked, "Where do you want us?"

Harvey said, "You ride up front with me, and the ladies'll sit in the back."

"No," Rutha said. "I don't like how the Nip is watching me. See how she's standing with her weight just so, ready to spring? She's a fighter. If we're gonna take this one, I want her in the trunk."

"No!" I shouted. "Put me in the trunk instead. Then you can keep your eyes on her."

She cocked the revolver. "I could just plug her and leave her for the razorbacks."

"The trunk's fine," Rienzi told them, sounding calm even if she wasn't. She kissed my mouth, fast and cool. "I love you."

"I love you too."

"Awww," Harvey said, "that's sweet, ain't it, sis?"

"Sweet as a gumdrop, for sure. And probably will last about as long."

The red haze returned to my vision. I wanted to lunge at Rutha, who trained her gun on Rienzi, but she wouldn't hesitate to shoot us both. Instead I stayed put, helpless, tears stinging my eyes as Harvey led the love of my life to the rear of their car and opened the trunk with a key.

I remembered Buck Bradley threatening to break my arms and legs to make sure I'd fit in the Nash's trunk. Fortunately Rienzi was smaller and more flexible than me.

Rutha didn't relax until Rienzi had folded herself inside the trunk and my uncle slammed the lid, trapping her in darkness, maybe with precious little air. My aunt lowered the hammer on her gun and smirked at me. "Come on, out with the threats. 'If you harm one hair on her head…if you this…if you that.' Tell you what, if she done stayed in Texas where she belongs, she'd be safe and sound. Ain't life funny that way?"

CHAPTER 39

IMAGINING A BUNCH OF POSSIBILITIES—SNATCHING AT RUTHA'S gun, trying to make Harvey a shield as I'd done with Nadine, running for the giant bow or even farther for the purse Rienzi had left in the barn to grab her dad's gun—all led to the same likely outcome: they'd kill me and then Rienzi. The only option left was keeping us both alive and waiting for a chance to escape or get the upper hand. Still, the red that was tinting my vision told me, deep down, I wanted to destroy them.

I asked, "What do I need to do to get her out of there?"

Rutha told me, "Take us to your mother."

"Okay, she's probably still at the sheriff's office. Y'all can turn yourselves in and make things easier for everybody."

"Pass," Harvey said with a laugh. "Where can we find her after that?"

"Dunno."

Rutha glanced at her shiny revolver. "We're wasting time. Get in the car."

"Ride up front," Harvey said. "Shotgun. And don't you wish you had one of them now?" He snickered again.

"No. I've seen and held a lot of guns this week. None of them solved a thing."

"But not having one puts you in a pickle too. Like your aunt done said, life's funny that way."

Rutha opened the front passenger door and stepped back, gun hanging casually at her side. It infuriated me that she didn't think I was a threat—and it also made me feel small and weak.

Once I'd seated myself on the frayed, stained cloth seat, where ticking was visible between loose threads, she slammed the door and got into the back directly behind me. The interior smelled as dusty as every other vehicle I'd ever been in except for the Shepherds' Hudson, a product of driving along dirt roads with the windows down. But there was something else too: rot. The seats had gotten wet at some point, and mold had set in. Underfoot, the floorboard felt spongy.

"How do I know Rienzi will be okay?"

"You don't," they both said in an eerie chorus.

"She's gonna get bounced around something fierce. It's not fair. She didn't do anything to y'all."

Harvey started the Oldsmobile. It backfired once before the engine caught and settled into a rumble. The loud bang must've sounded to Rienzi like a bomb going off beneath her.

He said, "It ain't fair that Reva killed our brother and took the money he promised us. That's what started all this—so blame her."

After putting the car in gear with the floor-mounted shifter, he made a sharp U-turn that caused the car to slide sideways and reminded me of Chet's exit. What could have happened if my brothers had stuck around? We would've had three rifles against one or maybe two handguns. No contest at all.

I stopped myself before imagining the slaughter. Would it have really settled anything? For all I knew, Papa's siblings had a dozen cousins who'd swear revenge, and they all probably would've had families, too, demanding blood if we somehow came out on top a second time. And on and on, with us always looking over our shoulders and forever worried about Mama and Darlene. And bodies stacked up to the sky. Somehow, I had to end this with these two but not touch off an even bigger war.

"Hey," Harvey said, looking at me more than he watched the road as we jounced over the rough surface, undoubtedly putting

Rienzi through hell. "I think we got off on the wrong foot. Let's start over again."

"You mean without my girlfriend in the trunk and Aunt Rutha not pointing a gun at me through the seat?"

He sighed. "Okay, tough guy. You know, you got a lot of Mance in you."

"Comparing me to him isn't gonna get you on my good side either."

"What, 'cause he tore you up a few times? I guaran-damn-tee that me and him had it worse when our old man was still around. No matter what he did to you and your brothers, y'all got off easy."

The red in my vision now pulsed in time with my heartbeat. I thought about Wanda's advice again, about not giving anyone my power by letting them get to me. After taking a few deep breaths while counting to ten, I said, "Holding us prisoner isn't going to get you anywhere. Mama doesn't have anything she can sell anymore. For sure she doesn't have any money."

"So she says," Rutha piped up behind me. "She also says she didn't shoot Mance, which makes her word more'n a mite suspect-like."

Harvey braked at the intersection with the highway and jiggled the scarred black ball at the top of the gearshift. "Right or left?"

I thought about Nadine and Seth Asher, and Brindle. They had a store of guns and a willingness to use them. Hopefully they'd remember their feelings for us at the end of our encounter rather than at the beginning. "Go left."

He looked both ways and then followed my advice. "Lookee there, you do know where she's going."

"I've got my suspicions, is all. Did Papa tell you about his old bootlegging days?"

"Sure. He always gave us a cut."

Another reason why we'd lived so poor. "Well, she told me that, after she got done with the High Sheriff, she was going to take her truck and head to Florida to strike a deal with the ones who make the whiskey. She's decided to follow in Papa's footsteps to earn the money you're demanding."

"A lady bootlegger?" Rutha cried. "Not in my lifetime. This boy's spouting nonsense, Harve. Let's put them in a ditch on the side of the road and take a little target practice."

He didn't reply immediately, but he did ease off the accelerator. My latest lie had just doomed us. I opened my mouth to protest, but then my uncle sped up and said, "No, he's our only lead on finding Reva. Think of him as bait."

"But we can't use him as bait if'n she don't know we got him. Stop the car, and I'll make like Annie Oakley on his Jap gal until he tells us where Reva's really holing up."

"I don't want you shooting up the trunk. This car's got enough wear and tear. Besides, she'll bleed all over the place. It'll stink for weeks."

Rutha shouted, "Then we'll yank her out of the trunk first and she can bleed on the ground, for Chrissake."

"Stop it, both of you," I yelled even louder than them. "You don't need to shoot anybody." In a quieter voice, I said, "She's not heading to Florida until later anyway. If you don't wanna go down there, we can wait for her at the one other spot I know she'll be."

"Where's that?" Rutha asked.

"The Bradley place. She wants to go after Leo and his sons. You can be ready when she gets there." It was the only other location I could think of where the denizens bristled with guns and were spring-loaded to use them. My lies were piling up as I tried to conjure a decent trap I could snare them with. Of course, Rienzi and I would have to escape being massacred, too, but one problem at a time.

Harvey said, "How do we know she ain't been there already?"

"Because she said she was going to see the High Sheriff first."

He tapped the three spokes connecting the steering wheel to its post, apparently considering my story. "All righty then, where do the firebugs live?"

"West of Colquitt, out near Mayhaw."

He nodded, and we headed toward Colquitt at a faster clip.

"I don't like it," Rutha said. "How do we know this ain't another snipe hunt?"

"We don't, so how about this: if we come up empty there, you gut-shoot the Nip, and we leave her behind." He glanced at me. "You good with that, bucko? Huh? That Bradley place still the most likely spot we'll run into her?"

Praying harder than I ever had before, I muttered, "It's the best notion I got."

CHAPTER 40

As we drew closer to Colquitt, with Mayhaw due west of there, I tried to picture where the Bradley farm was. When I was a kid and Buck Bradley was my nemesis, my brothers and I sometimes talked about taking the fight to him on his home turf. I hoped I could recall a landmark or something else that would lead to the correct turn. Of course, if they had moved to another farm sometime in the last decade, my gambit would doom Rienzi for sure.

There had to be a way to lower the tension with my aunt and uncle. If they saw us as mere teenagers—and not just any youths but their nephew and his innocent girlfriend—it was possible they'd ease up. To make that happen, though, perhaps I first needed to see them as people too.

Taking a closer look at Harvey, I noticed how his clothes bagged on him. He wasn't just thin, he was emaciated, like he had some kind of wasting disease. Or possibly he felt the need to keep up the appearance of a successful man but had only a little money left over for food. I knew what it did to the body and mind, going to bed hungry and waking up even hungrier.

His fingers trembled a bit against the wheel, and his wrists poked out of shirt cuffs that were frayed and gray with grime. He and his clothes were like the car he drove: their best days were long ago. And he smelled even worse than me, as if he hadn't bathed in weeks.

I risked a glance behind me. Rutha also showed signs of poverty with her gaunt face and sunken eyes. Her bony shoulders were obvious through a sweater that looked moth-eaten.

Hard times made for hard, desperate people. I knew from experience that the scars went clear to the core. And some folks going through such misery stopped seeing those around them as fellow victims. Instead they became obstacles or opportunities, nothing more.

If Papa had indeed looked after them, he'd done a terrible job. Possibly he strung them along with the promise of a big payday for a good long time, while he enjoyed being married to the lovely sawmill heiress and pretended to be a saved soul instead of the tyrant who'd ruined my childhood and that of my brothers.

Rutha scowled. "You looking back here in hopes the Great Speckled Bird done carried me away? Or maybe I got myself raptured?"

"No, ma'am," I said, sliding more into the accent of my youth so I'd sound like them. "I just wanted to see you better, is all. I never met any of Papa's people, so I was looking for resemblances."

"We're the only ones you'll ever lay eyes on—the last of the whole sorry bunch."

"That's a real shame."

"Yeah, I can tell how broken up that makes you. Now turn your face back around. That there birthmark ain't doing you any favors."

I'd heard much worse as a kid, but her insult still stung. I pivoted away, hoping she didn't see me flinch. "Um, Uncle Harvey, how do y'all usually spend your days? I don't guess this is what you'd wanna be doing if you had your druthers."

He snorted. "You're mighty right. We go from town to town, putting our fingers in a bunch of pies. Sometimes we pull out a ripe plum, and other times it's more like a tough ole muscadine."

"I'm guessing it's mostly muscadines lately?"

"Could be, but we'll turn it around—your mama's the key."

A truck overtook us, crossing the double-yellow line to zip past. It swung back into our lane to avoid a collision with a honking Studebaker in the northbound lane.

The noise of the car horn faded away, and Rutha said, "Speed up. We'll miss our chance with Reva—if we don't get run down first."

Harvey complied, which produced another backfire from the tailpipe beneath poor Rienzi. "Bud, why you wanna know so much about us?"

I thought for a moment about what he might like to hear. "I only grew up around Mama's people. It never occurred to me there was another whole side of my family I could meet."

Rutha hissed in a voice full of hurt, "You mean to say Mance never talked about us?"

I wasn't about to tell her that Papa had never mentioned either of them—she was liable to shoot me in a blind rage. Instead I said, "No, ma'am, he talked about y'all a lot, but to hear him tell it, you and Uncle Harvey were always off galivanting somewheres far away."

"Like where?"

"Uh, it's hard to remember." I crossed my fingers. "Savannah?"

"We wasn't ever there, liar. You wouldn't know the truth if it walked up and bit you on the ass."

Harvey said, "Well now, we did run that grift at the hotel on Jekyll Island, near enough to Savannah."

Relieved, I said, "That must be what I was recalling. I probably asked him where the island was and only recollected the part about Savannah."

"Bullfeathers," Rutha spat. "Never try to con a pro, kid. I ain't believed a single word you've said and won't trust none to come."

"Lay off him, sis. You wasn't never much of a conversationalist nohow, so let the men chat, and you clean your gun or something."

"*Or something*. It only needs cleaning if I get to shoot it. Bud's Jap honeypie is gonna be first in line if he don't get his facts straight and lead us to Reva."

We cruised through Colquitt, the town even sleepier than usual midmorning on a Saturday. Not a police officer in sight, and I didn't spot either the sheriff or Brooks. I wasn't sure how I would've signaled someone anyway, but I'd hoped to catch a break.

"How far are we away?" Harvey asked.

"Not much farther," I guessed. "They're off Mayhaw Road."

"Just about everything is, that part of the county. Gimme some particulars."

My armpits became slick with sweat. "I'm trying to remember. It's been awhile. I know it's roughly halfway between here and Mayhaw."

The sun had warmed the interior enough that we cracked the windows a few inches. It felt good to smell earth and dewy grass instead of the decay inside the car. The scents and the rippling sound of the wind made me wonder what Rienzi was able to hear and smell. And wonder how much longer she'd have to endure the torture she must've been going through—something she wouldn't be able to forget if she tried.

We turned onto Mayhaw Road. I scanned ahead, searching the dirt tracks on either side for something familiar and silently cursing the vertical bar that bisected the windshield and blocked some of my view.

After a few miles, I spied a narrow lane off to the left with a car on its side in a ditch. Not an uncommon sight where poor roads, dim headlights, and drunks at the wheel often led to midnight mishaps. But as we drew closer, I thought I recognized the front of the brown car. The bulbous hood reminded me of the Bradleys' Nash 600.

I pointed it out. "I think the farmhouse yonder is theirs."

"If that jalopy is, too, then they're having as bad a day as you and your mama and Tokyo Rose are." He swung onto the dirt road, giving us a better view of the tipped-over Nash with its two driver's side tires in the air. Bullet holes punctured the grille and glass.

A figure slumped near the undercarriage, face in hands, shoulders shaking. It was a woman with long black hair going gray, which had come loose from a kerchief.

Harvey asked me, "You reckon your mama did that?"

I did a quick count of the bullet holes, not as fast or accurately as Chet would've, but it told me enough. "Too much damage for Papa's Colt to do, even if she somehow reloaded."

He stopped a dozen paces from the wreckage. The woman wiped her tears and looked up at us. "What're y'all staring at?" Her shout sounded hoarse. "Ain't it enough my man and boys got hauled away—now there's looky-loos gawking at what's left? Go on and git."

"What should we do?" Harvey glanced back at Rutha.

"Ignore the old biddy."

"Go on, I said." Leo Bradley's wife stood, hands on her hips. Her face was the color of raw beef from her weeping. She stared harder into our car and met my gaze.

"You," she shrieked. "Ain't your goddamn family done enough to us already?" She stooped, reaching behind her. As she straightened, she swung the stock of a hunting rifle against her shoulder and took aim.

"Back up," Rutha hollered.

Harvey cursed as he jammed the car into reverse and stomped the accelerator.

The woman started firing.

I doubled over, nose to knees, holding my breath. My trap had worked—now Rienzi and I just needed to survive and escape.

The first shot tore through the split windshield—whether Harvey's side or mine I couldn't tell. All I knew was that a startled cry followed, high-pitched but muffled. It came from Rienzi in the trunk.

CHAPTER 41

More rounds struck the car. I stayed doubled over as we raced backward on the dirt road.

God forgive me, I'd just gotten Rienzi killed. It should've been me. It should've been *me*.

"Dammit," Harvey muttered repeatedly. He was trying to hunch down while looking through the rear window, his right arm thrown across the top of the front seat.

A horn blared and tires skidded moments before he bounced the Oldsmobile onto the pavement and braked to a halt. If Mrs. Bradley didn't end us, some motorist would.

From behind me, a window squeaked as Rutha lowered it. The noise of Leo's wife shooting at us became clearer, but that sound and all others were soon drowned out by Rutha opening up with her revolver. All six shots in quick succession.

Hard enough to hit someone ten feet away while standing still. She was crazy to think she could shoot that woman.

Over the *snap snap* of her dry-firing on spent cases, Rutha cursed a blue streak, using terms I'd never even heard in the service. As if her nasty words would reach their target any better than her bullets.

Harvey wrestled the car into a forward gear, and we raced away from the scene, leaving smoking rubber on the highway. I risked a look ahead. We were roaring back toward Colquitt. Air keened through the windshield on Harvey's side, the glass there pierced by the first rifle round.

I could follow its trajectory as if it were drawn through the car interior with a dotted line. Near Harvey's shoulder, the front seat bore a hole, as did the back seat. The slug had then torn into the trunk...and through Rienzi.

She'd only cried out once. I had to hope she died quickly.

All my fault.

Rutha snarled, "Goddammit," sounding exactly like Papa at the height of his fury, and threw her empty gun against the opposite door. Then she turned on me. "You sonofabitch, you led us into a fucking ambush."

"How could I know the sheriff arrested her husband and sons, and she'd be there?"

"Still no Reva," Harvey muttered. "And our car's shot to pieces." He gestured ahead, where steam escaped from holes punched through the hood.

Rutha cranked up her window. "That ain't the only thing what's shot." She fingered the ragged circle where the round had tunneled through the back seat. "Leastwise, the old bat took care of our Jap problem. You hear her scream, nephew? Sounded like a little girl."

Tears carved furrows in my cheeks. "It should've been me."

"No, you still might be useful. She was dead weight. Now literal-like." She cackled and peered through the hole. "There's daylight coming in through the trunk lid, so that slug must've went all the way through her. I bet I can make her out."

Rutha pressed the right side of her face against the seat, her eye positioned over the gap. "Harve, you might need to go west again to get the morning sun to shine through there. That way, I can tell Bud where all she got hit."

"There ain't no call for tormenting the boy."

"You mean like he's—" She screeched and tumbled backward into the footwell. Her hands pressed her right eye. Blood welled between her fingers. She squirmed in the narrow space, wailing.

The now-crimson tip of an elderberry arrow, which I'd sharpened as a boy, slid back through the hole in the seat and disappeared. Rienzi must've smuggled it in the sleeve of my greatcoat.

I didn't know whether it was a sign of life or her dying act. My spirits lifted and then crashed as I bounced from hope to grief—and back again. In one bold move, she'd shown more sand than I had during this whole misadventure. I needed to make sure it wasn't in vain.

As Rutha thrashed and caterwauled, Harvey yelled questions about what happened, hardly glancing at the road. The white sweater sleeve she now pressed to her face was soon soaked through with gore.

I leaned over the seat and snatched her revolver and purse. After dropping back in place, I commenced a frantic search for spare bullets.

"Gimme that." Harvey reached for the gun but swerved off the road and nearly rolled the Oldsmobile. He wrestled with the wheel. Finally regaining control, he put us back onto pavement.

The jostling caused Rutha to howl even more.

I groped in the purse left-handed while I held the weapon far from him in my right. Tissues and bobby pins, narrow boxes and tubes—I felt every other damned shape but the one I wanted.

He tried to elbow me in the face, but I blocked him with the purse, using it like a boxing glove. That gave me an idea. I threw a left jab at his ear, not hard enough to bounce his head off the side window or stun him, but I did redden it. Hopefully he'd think twice before trying again.

During the skirmish, items from the purse tumbled out. Typical stuff most women carried but no ammunition.

I took another gamble. "Gotcha," I announced over Rutha's sounds of agony. Blocking Harvey's view with my half-turned body, I thumbed open the cylinder of the revolver, shook out the spent cases, and pretended to load a round from the purse. With my fake shot lined up, I cocked the hammer and touched the barrel to his battered ear.

"Pull over," I ordered.

"Go to hell." He increased our speed, which made something clatter under the hood.

I knew if I did have the ability to shoot, it would be suicide to pull the trigger. His grim smile told me he knew this too.

Then I realized his smile was for another reason. He'd eased his left hand off the wheel and inside his suit jacket, a bit of which now poked toward me, as if he aimed a gun my way. "We got us Mexican standoff, bucko. We could shoot each other, and nobody comes out on top. Or I could shoot you first."

"Show me your gun."

"Sure—if you show me your bullet."

Rutha moaned, "I'm blind, Harve."

"That what happened? What got in your eyes?" Despite a gun to his head and his threat of one aimed at my heart, he sounded like he was just passing the time of day with her.

"One got poked out."

"So, you're just blind in one eye, is all."

"Goddammit, are you arguing with me?"

"Just getting the lay of the land."

"Soon as I get my hands on that yellow bitch, her losing both eyes is only the start." With a groan, she sat up, still pressing the sleeve of the once-white sweater to whatever remained of her right eye. Her face, hands, and clothes were a clotted mess. She fixed her left eye on me as I held the gun to her brother's head. "There ain't no more bullets."

"I found one." My hand started to tremble.

"Horseshit."

"Sorry, nephew," Harvey said. "Looks like our side is still with the Mexicans. But this ain't a standoff—it's the Alamo." His left hand reappeared from beneath his suit jacket wielding a pearl-handled, two-shot derringer. "I'll thank you not to clean my ear with that there barrel no more. The wax might clog it."

Options came to mind, none of them good. All of them resulted in me getting shot. In case Rienzi was still alive, I needed to stay whole and give her a fighting chance.

I slumped back against the passenger door and tossed the gun onto the purse at my feet. Any stored-up energy drained out of me.

"What should we do with the two of them, sis?"

"Let's go back to Reva's bonfire and roast us a couple of piggies."

CHAPTER 42

BY THE TIME WE MADE IT BACK TO COLQUITT, GEYSERS OF STEAM jetted from the bullet holes in the hood. I prayed we'd break down, but no such luck. The Oldsmobile might've been a goner, but it wasn't dead yet.

Harvey passed the derringer to Rutha, who pressed the over-under barrels to my head. "Put everything back in my purse the way you found it, and stick my *empty* gun in there too."

She didn't fuss when I stuffed the items in higgledy-piggledy, but she did point out the stray bobby pin and pencil stub I'd overlooked on the seat. Her left eye obviously worked just fine.

A few more people roamed the town square, and traffic had increased. Everybody gave us curious glances, but no Good Samaritans waved us over to offer help with our car troubles. Of course, one look at Rutha and they would've torn out screaming.

We made it back to Highway 27 with more clatter from the engine. Harvey kept his speed down and piloted us back to Hardscrabble Road.

The engine finally seized up a hundred yards from what remained of Mama's homestead. Someone was there—a dark-colored vehicle was parked near the Hudson, and at least one person stood in the yard.

Harvey put his car in neutral, and we coasted to a stop along the right side of the dirt lane. "Reckon we're taking shank's mare the rest of the way. How you wanna play this, sis?"

"Bud's finally gonna be useful—as a hostage if things turn ugly." She set the derringer aside long enough to tear off the least-gory sleeve from her white sweater and tie it around her head at an angle so that it covered the wound while leaving her other eye unhindered. Then she aimed at me again.

"And the girl?"

"Leave her in there. We only got two bullets. If this goes our way, I still want to roast that little bitch and this one in the embers yonder."

He removed his key from the ignition and tucked it in his pocket. "Okay, Bud, march. And no funny business. Even with one eye, your aunt's a crack shot."

They made me lead the way. As I walked, I increased my stride bit by bit, counting on Rutha's injury and their general unhealthiness to hamper them. The Army Air Forces had made me even fitter than I'd been already. I could've outpaced them in a few steps, but I made the increments subtle.

The scene ahead became clear: the car parked beside the Hudson was the oxblood Chrysler Royal sedan. Papa's old car—now Bascom's. He and Mama had finally rejoined us from Columbus. Naturally, their timing couldn't have been worse.

She wore a knee-length ruby-red dress and matching shoes and stalked from what used to be one end of the housefront to the other, hands on her hips, head down. I imagined her muttering, "Aye God..."

The revenuer was in the side yard poking at the smoldering debris with one end of Jay's giant bow. He'd rolled up the sleeves of his white dress shirt, tie flapping in the slight breeze. A gray fedora shaded his face.

I listened for Harvey and Rutha's shoes crunching the grit behind me and judged I was nearly out of derringer range, regardless of how good she was at shooting. If Rienzi could take big risks to give us an edge, so could I.

With my next step forward, I broke into a sprint, counting on them to follow. They were about thirty yards from the house—no way would they turn around and race twice that distance just to get back to a dead car. Much more sensible to try to catch their fleeing hostage and regain control of the situation.

Sure enough, Harvey panted and sounded like he stumbled trying to catch up as he said, "Get back here, dammit."

Rutha yelled, "You're dead now," but she held her fire. Just my luck she didn't waste her bullets again.

"Mama," I shouted, "run for it." I dashed past Bascom's Chrysler and the Shepherds' Hudson and headed for her, intending to take her with me around the side yard. If we could get to the barn where Rienzi's purse was, we'd have the six bullets in her father's revolver versus their two shots.

She turned and seemed to need a moment to understand what she was seeing. Instead of fleeing Papa's siblings, though, she kicked off her shoes and charged them, snarling, "You leave my boy alone."

I tried to block her, but she shouldered me aside. My instincts told me to still make for the barn. But I couldn't abandon her now that she was hurrying toward danger to defend me.

As my aunt and uncle reached the cars, they split up. Rutha took the path between the autos, while Harvey went along the driver's side of Bascom's sedan. My aunt flung open the Chrysler passenger door with her free hand and emerged a moment later with Mama's purse. Like a veteran basketball player hurling a no-look pass to a longtime teammate, she chucked it without a glance over the car roof into Harvey's outstretched hands.

Mama came to a skidding halt, the open car door between her and Rutha, with the over-under barrels of the derringer pointed at her face. My aunt thumbed down the hammer. Mama raised her hands in surrender.

I flashed back to Papa in the Cottontail Café nearly touching Mama's gasping mouth with his Colt and saying, "Bye-bye, baby." It was as if his haint had taken possession of his younger sister's body and was fixing to avenge himself.

This time, though, I was too far away to save her.

"Don't!" Ed Bascom cried. He had plunged the tip of Jay's longbow into the embers, setting fire to it, and now charged Papa's siblings, the weapon converted into a flaming, nine-foot spear. Harvey was the closest target, his hand inside the purse, mirroring me earlier as he blindly groped for something to give him an edge. He backed away as Bascom drew nearer.

Mama's boyfriend moved between Harvey and the car, jabbing with the fireball, and forced my uncle to retreat even more. I saw what the revenue agent had in mind. Harvey was reversing course toward the coil of still-energized power line that had torn loose from the house. One more backward step, and it would electrocute him.

Harvey tossed the purse aside and brandished Papa's old snub-nosed Colt. "Drop it."

Bascom hesitated but then let go of the flaming longbow. The fire continued to dance on the tip, even against the sandy soil. With all the oil encased in the heart pine, it could burn for days.

My heart sank. If I'd been in his shoes, I would've heaved it at Harvey, forcing him to step back to avoid it—the last action that man would have taken in this world, except to die.

Then I noticed the line between him and my mother. If Harvey fired and missed the agent, he could've hit Mama. Bascom was making sure that didn't happen.

It was the agent's turn to retreat now, hands in the air. He sidestepped as he did so. Now if Harvey's aim was off, he could hit Rutha instead.

I stayed frozen in place, afraid that going to anyone's aid would get that person killed.

My aunt said, “Give us our money.” Her derringer hadn’t wavered from Mama’s face, and neither had Mama given any ground.

“I told you all along, I don’t have anything of Mance’s except his gun. Harvey’s got it now, so y’all have cleaned me slap out.” She gestured behind her at the ruin of the house. “Look there. That was the sum total of all I had in this world.”

“But you killed Mance. Now you gotta pay with his money or your life.”

“Like I keep saying, I didn’t do it. Did I want to after he shot me? Hell yeah, about a hundred times over. But him being hauled away from the café by the police was the last time I ever saw that pig fucker.”

“Don’t.” She shoved the gun closer to Mama’s face. “Don’t you lie to me, and don’t you drag his name through the mud. He was the only one that ever cared about us.”

“Count yourself lucky. The only time he cared about me was when his stomach was empty. Or he wanted to empty his pecker. And he had plenty of other gals for those things too.”

Rutha’s blood-streaked face became stone. The knuckles of her right hand tensed as her finger tightened on the trigger.

It was like Mama had a death wish. I braced for the shot that would end her.

“Please,” Ed Bascom moaned. Tears dripped off his jaw. “Please don’t kill my wife.”

CHAPTER 43

"WIFE?" I CRIED.

Then I noticed the gleam of a gold wedding ring on her raised left hand. She said over her shoulder, "Yeah, we saw a justice of the peace in Columbus yesterday. Sorry y'all didn't get to be there."

I glanced at the man who I now had to think of as my stepfather. He was also holding his hands up, and he, too, wore a wedding band I'd overlooked in all the chaos.

Harvey said, "Well, ain't that sweet. Reva's not just sleeping with the enemy—she done married him."

"That don't change nothing." Rutha touched the makeshift bandage over her right eye and snarled at Mama, "Gimme one reason why I shouldn't put you down like a rabid dog."

I needed to stay alive so I could rescue Rienzi, but first I needed to save my mother and Ed. "Money," I answered for her.

Ruth's good eye flicked from Mama to me. "Go on."

"We don't have enough to cover the big payday Papa promised y'all, but we can make a down payment. See, we do have a woman bootlegger in the family." I told them about the three hundred dollars in cash and coins Darlene collected overnight from our sales of the moonshine.

Mama said, "My girl's done gone into business for herself? Imagine that." She sounded impressed and oddly unworried about the gun in her face.

I added, "And the two barrels of whiskey in the Hudson will fetch another hundred."

"You still got some Asher liquor?" Harvey rubbed his mouth with his free hand. "Ain't had any of that since Mance was in business with them."

Rutha spat, "It's another of his lies."

"Look in the back seat of the car to your right."

"No, you're trying to trap us again, you sneaky sonofabitch."

Mama said, "Yeah, he is my son, and I'm the grandest bitch of all. You wanna be just like me, but you don't measure up." She glanced back at me. "Go fetch out those barrels and show them."

I eased around the passenger side of the Hudson.

Rutha said, "If you come up with a gun, the last thing I'll do is send your mother to hell ahead of me."

"There's just moonshine back here." I opened the suicide door and hauled out one of the nearly fifty-pound barrels. "Where do you want me to put it?"

Harvey said, "Lookee there, sis. The kid spoke the gospel truth after all. We'll haul it away in this here Chrysler. It was Mance's, so it's only fitting that we take it."

Ed asked, "Can we at least get our luggage from the trunk?"

"We're taking that too—call it a penalty for y'all coming up short. No telling what we'll find in there from y'all's honeymoon." Grinning, he shifted his gaze to me as I cradled the cask in my arms. "Bud, put them on the backseat."

I lugged the barrel over to the Chrysler, moving behind Ed, and followed Harvey's instructions. Though I wanted to say something encouraging to my new stepfather, I couldn't think of anything except, "Sorry."

He continued to face my uncle with his hands in the air. His voice sounded like a whisper meant only for me. "You've got nothing to apologize for. You're doing great."

Rutha pressed at the gory sweater sleeve again, as if the pain had worsened. "But that's nowhere near the two thousand Mance promised. I want everything owed to us right now."

Mama shrugged. "You don't deserve nothing, so you'll have to take it piecemeal. We'll come up with the rest by and by."

"Then hand over your rings and any cash. We'll put it toward your tab."

While I collected the other barrel and placed it beside the first one on the backseat, Mama and Ed pulled off their rings. Rutha slipped Mama's onto her right hand, while Harvey pocketed Ed's ring and the cash from his wallet.

The petty stealing twisted the knife more than their other thefts. Disgusted, I slammed the Chrysler door, but all the windows were down, so I didn't get the satisfying noise I wanted.

"Just one second," Harvey said. "Open that again, Bud, and pry off one of them lids. I wanna toast our new partnership."

I did as he ordered and stepped back.

Harvey spun Ed around, knocking off the gray fedora, and grabbed the back of his collar. Bending him double, Harvey forced his face down into the open barrel of whiskey. With his gun hand, he pressed the Colt against my stepfather's spine.

"Eddie!" Mama screamed. "Aye God, leave him alone!"

My stepfather squirmed and thrashed as Harvey held him in place, drowning the poor man as moonshine sloshed all over the fabric seat. Finally, Harvey pulled Ed out and pitched him onto the ground sputtering.

Alcohol plastered the hair to his scalp, soaked through his dress shirt, and dripped from his skewed tie. He sobbed as he pawed at his eyes. His whole face must've felt like it was on fire.

Harvey banged the barrel lid in place and said, "That's for dogging my brother all them years. It's only fitting that Asher whiskey did the punishing."

"Now what?" Rutha asked. She kept the derringer on Mama, whose arms were starting to droop.

"We pay a call on Darlene and collect that three hundred Bud mentioned. And then we come back again and again and take whatever they got until they done paid their debt."

"When we get back here one day soon," Rutha told Mama, "you better have the rest of it."

Mama replied, "We'll see what happens, won't we? Though I reckon you'll only see half of what we do. Best keep an eye out."

Rutha sneered and made to backhand Mama with her gun, but instead she swung into the passenger seat and slammed her door.

Harvey pressed the Colt against the top of Ed's head. "The car keys, please."

My stepfather stopped wiping at his eyes long enough to dig a keyring from his pocket and hand it over.

Harvey slid behind the wheel and cranked the engine. He saluted me, reversed the Chrysler a dozen feet to get past the Hudson, and put it into first gear. They eased away at a stately pace, as if they wanted the evidence of their victory to linger in our sight—and keep the knife corkscrewing even deeper in our guts.

I'd never had any intention of letting them take Darlene's money. I made a move toward the burning longbow, but Mama had beaten me to it.

She struggled to lift the nine feet of dense wood and looked at me with pleading in her eyes.

I took a portion closer to the fiery tip, and together we charged the departing Chrysler.

"Now," she said.

We heaved the ungainly spear through the open back window on Rutha's side. It struck the back of the seat near her, setting it alight. Then the flames found the spilled whiskey.

The Chrysler interior became an inferno. Screaming, Papa's siblings tumbled out of the stalled car with fire spreading over their clothes and hair. The stench and their shrieking made for a godawful combination.

As evil as they were, I couldn't just stand there and watch them burn alive. "Hurry!" I shouted at Mama as I took off running.

"Nope. They're getting a taste of hell."

"They'll suffer even longer if they live," I hollered as I reached Harvey.

"Aye God, fine." She stormed over to Rutha.

We rolled them on the sandy soil. Harvey whimpered and seemed to speak in tongues even after I smothered the blaze. Patches of his clothes fell away in charred tatters, revealing skin underneath that looked as roasted as a well-done sausage. His face was spared, but much of his hair had turned crispy. While I tumbled him along the ground, the snub-nosed Colt that once belonged to Papa and had been used by Mama to murder him fell from Harvey's waistband. I chucked the gun back into the torched automobile, which had rolled to a stop nearby. I hated Papa's old revolver even more than his sedan. It was fitting they would be destroyed together.

On the other side of the burning car, Rutha wailed louder than when Rienzi had skewered her right eye. Mama cursed as she extinguished the last of the flames.

The conflagration now engulfed every bit of the Chrysler. I was just sorry we couldn't rescue Mama and Ed's luggage from the trunk. Whatever things she had taken with her on their trip to Columbus—and inadvertently saved from one fire—were being consumed by another. She truly would be starting from scratch.

I called to her, "The gas tank might explode, and any bullets surely will. We need to drag them away from here."

Harvey's wrists were so thin, they felt childlike as I clamped on. He and Rutha cried even more pitifully as we pulled them along the ground, no doubt aggravating their burns.

It wasn't until I started going through his scorched pockets, gathering the keys to the Oldsmobile and Ed's ring and lightly toasted cash, that I noticed how much my hands hurt. Oval blisters sprouted in a dozen places where the fire had seared me. No good deed went unpunished.

I stumbled down the road toward Harvey and Rutha's shot-up wreck of a car, praying I would find Rienzi alive.

CHAPTER 44

I KEPT TELLING MYSELF IT WAS OVER. MY NEW STEPFATHER WOULD arrest Harvey and Rutha for assaulting a government agent, kidnapping, and possessing illegal alcohol. There would be a trial and separate federal prisons for them somewhere far away. Maybe it would be the first time in their lives they would be apart. After each of them eventually got out, revenge might be the first thing on their minds, but it wouldn't be the first or even the twenty-first thing they'd have to deal with. And if they did eventually come for Mama again, she wouldn't be alone in facing them down. That would have to be enough.

Those thoughts gave me the second wind I needed to hurry the rest of the way to the Oldsmobile. I called Rienzi's name and rapped twice on the trunk. "Hey, are you still okay? It's just me. Harvey and Rutha are done for."

Her voice came through the hole punched through the lid by Mrs. Bradley's rifle slug. "How do I know this isn't a trap? They could be forcing you to say that, to keep me from jabbing them with my arrow again."

Hours crammed in there and being nearly shot for her troubles hadn't dulled her logical mind any. I thought a moment and replied, "There's nothing I could say to convince you, so I'm going to unlock the trunk and step back. You can stab to your heart's content."

I did, and then she did. She lay curled on her back, knees pointed upward. Shielding her eyes from the morning glare with one hand, she flailed away with the broken-off section of sharpened elderberry cane she'd smuggled in my coat. The thick wool provided a pallet for her, just as it had in the barn. I was sure, though, that her memories inside this small space would be the stuff of nightmares instead of sweet dreams.

Sweat glued the black hair to her scalp as much as the whiskey had soaked Ed's. Judging from the hole in the barrier separating the trunk from the back seat, the slug had passed only a few inches above her chest.

After another moment of needless self-defense, she lowered her weapon, squinted at me, and whispered, "Are we really alone?"

"Yep. Can I help you out?"

"You're going to have to. Other than my hands, I don't think I can move anything."

I reached under my greatcoat, which she'd soaked through with sweat, and scooped her up with it. She felt clammy in my arms and smelled of body odor and engine exhaust. Though she didn't weigh much, the blisters on my palms and fingers seem to explode with fire against the coarse fabric of my coat.

She'd given me the happiest moments of my life mere hours before, but never had I been more grateful and in love than when I lifted Rienzi Shepherd from that trunk and held her to me.

Resting her face against my chest, she said, "Tell me everything."

"It's a long story, but it's also a long walk. Are you going to keep that piece of arrow?"

"Forever."

I started carrying her back along the dirt lane. "Why'd you decide to blind Rutha's eye with it? Weren't you afraid she'd shoot you or worse?"

"It was obvious that, as with all bullies, she'd never really been hurt before. I made her afraid of me. Deep down, she knew I'd spared her—I could've shoved this into her brain if I'd wanted to."

"And why didn't you?"

"I was afraid that if I killed her, Harvey would kill you in retaliation. Also, remember my philosophy about violence judiciously applied? I thought that realizing how vulnerable she was would make her less dangerous. It wasn't necessary to kill her—taking her eye would defang her, so to speak."

"Well, it worked. She was still scary as all get-out, but in the end, she lost her nerve."

Her neck creaked and popped when she turned her head to face forward as we drew closer to the burning Chrysler. "But you sure didn't lose yours. Are you responsible for that car fire?"

"Me and Mama. I was following Posey's advice about applying that judicious violence to something other than people. Mama just wanted to make them pay anyway she could."

"Whose car is it?"

"My new stepfather, but we're getting ahead of ourselves."

Cradling the love of my life, I made a wide loop around the conflagration, in case something did explode, as I described the ordeal Rienzi had missed but in which she still managed to play a huge role.

By the time we reached my childhood homestead, my arms felt like old rubber bands, the blisters on my fingers had begun to pop, and my throat was dry from talking.

The flames consuming fuel in the Chrysler's gas tank leaped much higher than the scattered fires still eating away at Mama's house. She had recovered the two-shot derringer from Rutha but kept the gun at her feet as she tended to Ed. My aunt and uncle sprawled where we'd left them in the dirt, whimpering and writhing and no more of a threat than turtles with crushed shells.

"Want me to set you on the ground, or should I prop you next to your dad's car?"

"The latter. I need to straighten my legs before they freeze in a fetal position."

I eased her down, making sure her shoes were flat on the dirt and steady before leaning her against the side of the Hudson. She winced as she stretched and flexed. I stood by, ready to catch her, but she seemed to recover more of her strength with every passing moment.

"Will you be okay while I check on everybody else?"

"Yes, but could you help me take off your coat? The wet wool smells even worse than I do."

I did as she asked and tossed it onto the back seat of the Hudson. Then I kissed her cool mouth. "Love you. Back in a jiffy."

From the side yard, Mama had brought the dented hubcap we once used as a water dish for the chickens. She'd filled it from the handpump and now pressed soaked tissues to Ed's eyes as he continued to sit in the spot where Harvey had dropped him. On her left hand glinted the wedding ring she'd recovered from Rutha, making me wonder whether she'd yanked off the woman's burnt finger with it.

As I approached, my stepfather tipped up the gray fedora Mama had returned to his head and peered at me. His narrowed eyes were so bloodshot they looked crimson, but hopefully there wouldn't be lasting damage.

I handed over his wedding ring and scorched cash. "Sorry about your car."

"It once belonged to Mance, so maybe it was cursed anyhow." His voice was raw, which I expected after a near-drowning, but something else was wrong with it too. He sounded like he was half-asleep, with the *s*'s coming out as *sh*'s.

"I couldn't think of another way to stop them."

"Me neither," Mama said. "Thank you for helping me." While I gawped at her, replaying words I'd never heard her utter before, she said, "Them hands have seen better days. Bring them closer."

She took hold of my wrists, brought my fingers close to her mouth, and began to murmur. An unearthly coolness touched all ten digits and spread to my palms. I felt the heat rise to the surface and then lift away like steam.

In a manner of minutes, the blisters had vanished. She'd talked the fire out of me. I'd heard her mother had been able to do that, but I had no idea she could. Though a ring of angry red sores now surrounded her mouth, she didn't seem to pay them any mind.

I examined my hands and rubbed my fingers together. The skin was warm and smooth, as fresh and new as on the day I was born. "Good God Almighty, Mama, thank you. They feel so much better."

"That weren't nothing. All the gals in my family got the gift. Comes in handy in the kitchen and doing the wash over a bonfire."

Ed shook his head. Then his chin sunk to his chest, as if the effort had exhausted him. "Reva, my love, you continue to amaze me. You do. What were you shaying—saying—to make the burns go 'way?"

"I don't rightly know. The spirit just sort of comes over me, and I commence to speak."

I asked, "Should you talk the fire out of Harvey and Rutha too?"

"Unh-uh. Matter of fact, I got half a mind to pick up that busted wire thing with them blue sparkings and give them a jab or two, but I ain't sure how long it'll reach."

"Mama, if you touched it, you wouldn't have half a mind anymore. You'd be left with no mind at all—and no heartbeat. The electricity would kill you slap dead."

"See there? That's the trouble with highfalutin gadgetry. Fire's a lot easier to reckon with."

Ed touched her hand. "It was right Christian of y'all to shave them. I mean save them."

I shrugged. "I'm not sure Jesus would've slung a nine-foot flaming spear at his wayward aunt and uncle."

"Why not? He gave those money changers in the temple holy hell. She…see…there're times it's the only way to get folks' attention."

I asked him, "Did Harvey hit you on the head? You're slurring your words."

He gave us a lopsided grin. "Kinda ironic that I ended up gulping more illegal whiskey than I inhaled. Even with the pain I'm in, I'm pretty well lit. Though not as lit as my car."

I had to laugh as I helped him to his feet. He steadied himself with his hands on my shoulders and then patted my back, as if to say, "Attaboy." It felt good and right. I decided I was going to like having him as my stepdad. Then I remembered how I'd rejected his gift of a silver dollar when we met and indeed wanted to kick myself for that show of defiance—just for different reasons than I'd imagined back then.

Seeing as how he was the happy kind of drunk, I decided to keep things light, saying, "You know, Papa lied to me years ago. He said you can always tell quality moonshine because it burns blue." I pointed at the Chrysler. "There's only red and orange, even though I know the Ashers make good whiskey."

"You're telling me." His laughter soon turned to hiccups, and he needed steadying again.

"Mama, come say hey to Rienzi. I wanna introduce her to Mr. Bascom."

"Call me Eddie. Everybody else I care about does." He draped an arm around my shoulders and the other around Mama's waist, and we led him to the Hudson.

Rienzi was doing some knee bends and seemed to be feeling much better. Once the initial chitchat with Mama and Eddie was out of the way, she asked him, "What will happen to Roger's aunt and uncle now?"

Still slurring his words, he said, "I put them under arresht… arrest…for every federal crime I can think of. And Reva's cousin's gonna wanna press local charges. Roger, I'm in no condition to drive. Would you kindly go to Sheriff Reeder's office and ask him to send a car? Those two can get a little patching up in his jail." He fumbled in his pockets for his wallet and finally managed to pull out a business card. "Call thish number while you're there. Tell them what happened—just that I'm hurt, not drunk, or I'll never live it down—and they'll shend…send…a marshal to take Bonnie and Clyde there into federal custody."

"I'll bet Reeder won't like you claiming first dibs."

"We're all family now. Maybe he'll turn the other cheek as a wedding present."

Mama said, "If he don't, he knows he'll get what-for from me."

"Rienzi?" I said. "You wanna stay here and rest or go with me?"

"I've been forced to rest all day—except for getting to half-blind a bully. I need some more action."

"Okay, but keep that arrow in the Hudson. Lawmen don't take kindly to stabbings."

We promised to return soon with the posse. Rienzi let me drive.

As I turned the car around, it struck me how much my childhood home now resembled a war zone. The house lay in ruins, one car continued to burn, and another had been shot all to hell. Two seriously wounded people lay curled up on the ground, and Mama tended to the other casualty. Unsurprisingly, she was the last one standing.

My mother was many things, but first and foremost, she was a survivor. Maybe I should've recognized that quality in her from the start and left well enough alone. Or maybe everything had to happen just as it did.

CHAPTER 45

AS WE CRUISED ALONG HIGHWAY 27, I SAID, "I'VE GOT ANOTHER wonder your science books can't explain."

I displayed one hand to her as I steered with the other and described the blisters that had been there from saving Harvey's life and how Mama healed me.

She kissed my palm and held it to her cheek. "I saw the sores around your mother's mouth. Combined with how thin she's become, I thought she was sick."

"Those sores weren't there until she talked the fire out of me. How's science going to explain that?"

She scooted closer, and I draped my arm around her shoulders. Though she smelled bad from her confinement, she felt great against me. "I'm not going to try to find a logical explanation," she said. "No hypotheses or theories. I'll just marvel along with you."

"Hey, really? This is news. Did I pull the right girl out of the trunk?"

"I had a lot of time to think in there. About how I feel about you, about myself."

Before Harvey and Rutha showed up, we'd squabbled because of my insecurities. Cold sweat now dampened my face. I stammered, "Um, have I ruined everything between us?"

"Absolutely not." She kissed my cheek. "I only wish we'd furthered our relationship sooner, in all kinds of ways. I realize I was holding us back. Now, we need to make up for lost time."

Relief swept through me like a cool wind in August. "You told me Posey opened your eyes about having happy new experiences instead of reliving your past and keeping your nose in a book. Is that it?"

"It's more than that. I want to spend my days documenting wonders and marvels instead of trying to explain them away with neat, sterile theories. Remember in *Hamlet*, when he has a conversation with his father's ghost?"

I made my voice extra twangy. "Who exactly is this Piglet fella you're going on about?"

She jabbed me in the ribs, probably harder than she intended. Probably. "Go ahead and play the bumpkin for everybody else, but I know the real you."

"You're mighty right, ma'am. I reckon Mrs. Gladney done learned me a peck of Shakespeare after all." I cleared my throat and recited in my best classroom voice, "'This above all—to thine own self be true, and it must follow, as the night the day, thou canst not then be false to any man.'"

"That's my other favorite *Hamlet* quote. What I had in mind was when his friend Horatio calls the conversation with the ghost 'wondrous strange,' and Hamlet replies, 'And therefore as a stranger give it welcome. There are more things in heaven and earth, Horatio, than are dreamt of in your philosophy.' I want to welcome the wondrously strange. This place keeps reminding me that my philosophy has been too confining to see anything but a sliver of life. I want to experience every bit of the strange and wonderful that I can."

"There's less of that around here than when I was growing up, but there are some mighty peculiar things still to be had." I turned off the highway, and we approached Colquitt. "Um, what happens when somebody thinks he's being true to himself, but he needs to change if he wants things to get better?"

"Are you thinking about everything that happened this week, with you trying to help people even when they didn't see it that way?"

"Yeah, playing God, deciding what's best for everybody. It's an easy trap to fall into when the people around you seem to be making such a mess of things."

"Overall, would you say people are better off because you and your brothers came back here?"

"Well, the Bradleys are in jail, and Harvey and Rutha will be joining them, so bad people are getting their just desserts. But we chased Darlene's husband away, and she turned to bootlegging to make ends meet. Plus, we touched off a feud that cost Mama everything she had in this world. On the whole, maybe we came out even or only a skosh to the good?"

"I think you're selling yourself short, but you always do that. It's a forgivable character flaw." She bussed my cheek again, this time with a loud smacking sound. "Speaking of forgivable, do you think you'll see Jay and Chet again before we have to leave, so you can watch them kiss and make up?"

"We're gonna see one of them real soon." I pointed ahead, where Mama's pickup sat across from the sheriff's office.

I parked behind it, noting the huge dent Jerry had put in the back when he rescued us. That seemed like a month ago. There was new damage, though: two bullet holes in the tailgate.

As we approached the front door, the worries conjured by those holes evaporated like the fire from my hands. I knew by the sounds of jeering and the laughter booming from the interior that I was in fact about to reunite with both of them.

I opened the door on a scene of mayhem. Chet hunkered behind Brooks's desk, his back to us, and Jay lurked in the doorway of Sheriff Reeder's office, looking our way. Both were armed with rubber bands as their slingshots and bent-open paperclips like elongated letter *s*'s for their ammunition. About two dozen of those clips littered the floor. With all we'd gone through, and as grown-up as they looked, it was easy to forget we were all still kids at heart.

Chet jumped up and fired his missile, which ricocheted off the metal jamb to Jay's left. Simultaneously Jay launched five clips at once from a complex weave of rubber bands stretched between his fingers. Two of them nailed Chet in the chest. The other three sailed past him and popped me—a couple in the gut and one in the groin, stinging a bit.

"Sorry, Roger," Jay said, as Chet laughed and cursed our older brother's latest invention.

I shook my head. "After having so many guns pointed at me all week, I finally got shot—by my own kin."

Chet fired his rubber band at Jay—as close to admitting defeat as he was likely to come—and turned to me. "I'll bet y'all just laid around and mooned over each other since yesterday. Listen to what real men have been up to in that time."

He told us about coming to see Brooks and the sheriff to report that the Bradleys torched Mama's home and how he and the lawmen schemed to flush Leo and his sons from their farmhouse. Then Jay came along to bury the hatchet with Chet. After listening to their strategy, he offered up a new idea: He and Chet would drive by the Bradley place in Mama's truck, which they'd know on sight, and make enough noise to draw them out. Then my brothers would race past where the sheriff and Brooks would be waiting behind their patrol car, rifles at the ready just in case.

Jay lit a cigarette. "The High Sheriff even deputized us." With his free hand, he pointed at three paperclips twisted together to make a six-pointed star, which hung from his shirt pocket. "They didn't have any more real ones, so I fashioned these for Chet here and me. Anyway, we executed the plan this morning. It worked pretty well, but the old Chevy's gearbox picked that moment to get finicky. By the time I jammed it into first, they'd climbed in their Nash and were coming for us, hell-bent for leather, with Buck and Mike leaning out their windows and firing away with revolvers. Mama's truck took two in the rear. It was like being in the war again."

"How'd you manage to escape?" Rienzi asked.

Chet jumped in. "Reeder wasn't kidding about Brooks being a crack shot. He killed their car with just a few well-placed rounds—I mean graveyard dead. The sheriff scored some hits, too, but after the fact. The Nash went into a ditch, and Leo and his boys got pretty busted up." He jabbed his thumb over his shoulder. "They're moaning and groaning back there in the jail cells."

I said, "Did y'all ever solve the mystery of how much Reeder knew about the hidey-hole Brooks uncovered in Mama's kitchen—well, what used to be her kitchen?"

"Yeah," Jay replied as smoke drifted from his mouth. "The sheriff wasn't hiding nothing. Brooks shared his plan with him beforehand—they're as thick as thieves, but on the right side of the law."

"Y'all had most of yesterday to spring that trap. Why'd you wait until this morning to do it?"

Chet shuffled his feet while Jay grinned. "Reeder had business at the courthouse on Friday afternoon, and he wanted to flush the Bradleys out in good light. So me and Chet spent the day together, and last night we talked our girls into going on a double date."

Rienzi said, "Chet, you have a girlfriend?"

"I wouldn't go that far. Let's do more paperclip wars." He cast about Brooks's desk, apparently searching for office supplies.

Between puffs, Jay said, "Trudy is a colored girl who works at her mama's diner. She and Chet get on like a house afire—and we all know just how hot that is."

Chet popped him in the ear with a new rubber band. "I'm warning you..."

"Needless to say, this double date wasn't a public affair, and Geneva took some persuading—she's not as broad-minded as I'd thought. Trudy brought Dora's famous burgers and those amazing fries. One taste helped Geneva come around. We finally all loaded up in the truck, real cozy-like, and went to Spring Creek."

I said, "Did y'all, um, make any progress?"

"Well, it was too cold to skinny dip, so we each took our girl to the opposite side of the campfire and swapped slobbers until it was time to get them back home, and then we slept in the truck near Geneva's house since we didn't wanna wake Darlene."

Little did he know, Darlene was still making deals on moonshine long after he and Chet huddled down to sleep in Mama's Chevy. I nudged Chet, always a dangerous thing. "So, how was it?"

"How about I sock that kisser of yours so it doesn't work for a month?"

Jay chuckled. "Just second-base stuff, nothing too risqué for Chet's maiden voyage." A rubber band knocked the cigarette from his fingers. He recovered his bent Lucky Strike from the floor and started smoking it again.

Of the three MacLeod boys' late-night romantic forays, only I had managed a home run. That made me all manner of proud, but I remembered Rienzi's warning and didn't gloat. Instead I looked at the mess they'd created around the office and asked, "Where are Reeder and Brooks anyway?"

"A guy stopped in an hour ago to say some crazy lady is shooting at passing cars on Mayhaw like they're tin ducks at a carnival. They went to pick her up."

"Will they have room for two more in the cells?"

"Why?" Chet asked. "Y'all come to turn yourselves in as prisoners of love?"

Rienzi pushed his chest while sweeping out his legs. He sat hard on Brooks's desk, eyes wide with startlement. She pointed Jay to the deputy's chair. "Be quiet for a minute, and you'll hear a real story of derring-do. Roger, the floor is yours."

CHAPTER 46

SOUNDING DULY IMPRESSED, JAY AND CHET PEPPERED US WITH questions as we helped them clean up. We all agreed to meet up at Darlene's later, and then my freshly deputized brothers left to arrest Harvey and Rutha and load them in the bed of the Chevy for transporting back to the station.

While Rienzi used the washroom to freshen up, I placed a collect call to the number on the card Eddie had given me and reported the story he wanted me to tell. As he'd predicted, a US marshal would arrive on Monday to take Papa's siblings into federal custody. My second call was a local one to the rural electric company to have them de-energize the power line to Mama's place before she accidentally killed herself.

As we were walking to the Hudson, Reeder and Brooks pulled up with Mrs. Bradley cuffed and glowering in the back seat. Thirty minutes later, with the highlights of our story retold, we were finally on our way.

It was past noon, so I took Rienzi to Dora's for a cheeseburger, fries, and an RC Cola. As soon as we entered the diner, her face lit up. The King Cole Trio singing "Route 66" on the jukebox competed with animated discussions at every table and barstool as colored men and women chatted, laughed, and smoked while savoring their food and drink.

The only white patron—my old friend Jerry Flynn—shook hands with a Negro man in a three-piece business suit and slid off his stool. I hustled Rienzi over to it, so she'd have a place to sit.

"Hey, Jerry, this is my girlfriend, Rienzi."

"The one from Texas? You came a long way for a short stay."

"It was well worth it." She put her arm around my waist.

Having her so close, after all we'd been through, was the best feeling in the world. I wanted it to last forever. Only one way to make that happen…

Jerry asked, "Yer problems getting any smaller, Roger?"

"Shrunk down to nothing," I replied. "And we didn't even have to rob a bank or steal from moonshiners."

"Best news I heard all day. My boss was pretty sore about the dent I put in the front of his truck—I'm glad I won't have to run nobody over for y'all."

"We couldn't have come out on top without your help. Thank you."

"I'd do it all over again in a heartbeat." He indicated the man in the suit. "Say hey to my friend Reverend Brightharp."

We shook hands. As I was introducing him to Rienzi, I blurted out, "Actually, she's not my girlfriend—um, she's my fiancée."

The clergyman and Jerry, as well as Rienzi, all said in unison, "Oh?"

"At least, I hope she will be. May I?" I took the empty cola bottle beside the reverend's plate and fished an errant paperclip from my pocket, absently put there while we'd tidied the sheriff's office. Twisting the metal around the narrow glass neck, I fashioned an engagement ring that was more octagonal than circular. The two ends jutted out in a V-shape but were devoid of anything precious on their prongs.

I lowered myself to one knee and took Rienzi's hand.

The joint, which had sounded so raucous before, quieted. Dora, Trudy, and the waitresses stopped their work. Even the King Cole Trio cooperated, transitioning to the ballad "For Sentimental Reasons."

A man farther down the counter said, "What's that white boy up to?"

His female companion smacked his arm. "What you shoulda done years ago, lunkhead. Now hush up and let me hear this."

I cleared my throat, as I was apparently not only proposing to my girl but performing for a crowd. "Rienzi Shepherd, I can only afford to give you wires shaped liked rings and rocks as big as diamonds, but I promise to always see you, hear you, and be your wondrously strange fella for the rest of my life. Will you marry me?"

She gave my hand a squeeze as her eyes glistened. "Yes, Roger MacLeod, I will be your wondrously strange wife. Together we'll create so many happy memories that even I won't be able to remember them all."

Rienzi beamed at me despite the absurd makeshift band I pushed onto her finger.

Long ago, Mrs. Gladney had predicted that when I proposed to my best girl, it would be my happiest day ever. As with so much else, she was right, but it still surprised me how weightless I felt, as if I didn't have a care in the world.

I rose, took Rienzi in my arms, and kissed her. In that moment, the only three people in the room seemed to be me, the love of my life, and Nat King Cole crooning about giving his heart away. I knew exactly how he felt.

Everybody in the diner erupted with cheers and applause. Reverend Brightharp and other men pounded my back and shook my hand, and women embraced Rienzi like she was family.

Trudy plunked two uncapped RCs on the counter for us and declared, "Y'all's lunch is on the house."

Jerry pumped my arm, congratulated Rienzi, and then scribbled an address on the back of a receipt he took from his pocket. "Write and let me know when and where yer wedding is, you hear? I'll drive that bread truck to Texas if I have to." He and his friend exited together, talking and laughing about something. Probably my absurd proposal.

We dropped onto their vacated stools and accepted more handshakes and hugs from patrons until the spotlight on us dimmed at last and we had a moment to ourselves.

Rienzi took my hand. "I knew you wanted to ask me since early this morning when we were in our secret spot underground. I'm glad you waited until now, so it wasn't just a noble gesture you felt like you needed to make afterward."

Trudy set two plates of cheeseburgers and fries before us. "After what?" She gave us a devilish grin.

Rienzi answered, "After he saved my life." She recounted the events of the day, making me sound much more heroic than I'd been.

Trudy rang up a customer and bumped the till closed with a hip. "Mm-mm-mm, sounds like something Chet woulda done."

I swallowed my bite of hot, succulent cheeseburger, wiped the juice from my chin, and said, "Did he promise to write after he goes back to his base?"

"Not just that, he gave me the specific number of letters I can expect in any given month. Your brother really likes to count things." She beckoned us to lean in until our foreheads almost touched hers. "Forty-four kisses he gave me last night. He says he likes double digits, even numbers, repeating numbers, and ones you can divide by four, so he was a very happy boy."

Rienzi said, "I'll bet he was. Will you be able to keep things confidential? This isn't exactly a cosmopolitan town. I'm sure there are people in your own community who'd look askance at a relationship with him."

Trudy cut her eyes at me. "Does she always talk like she's reading from a dictionary?"

"Yep, but if you hang in there long enough, you get the gist."

She took care of another customer's payment and then told my fiancée in a low tone, "I know when I'm safe and when to mind my p's and q's—just like I'm sure you do."

"That's good. I just don't want some bigot starting a race war over a *Romeo and Juliet* type of situation."

"I only went through the seventh grade because there's no colored high school around here, so help a girl out. What are you saying exactly?"

"You and Chet are star-crossed lovers, battling against the odds to make a life together."

"*Star-crossed.* Sounds kinda romantic when you put it that way. Speaking of which, when are you two lovebirds getting hitched?"

I took Rienzi's hand. "I sprung the engagement on you, so you decide when we jump the broom."

"Maybe you, me, and my dad will come back here in the spring and get Reverend Brightharp to marry us on this very spot."

Trudy shook her head. "Talk about starting a race war." She gave us a wink and returned to serving customers.

We finished the meal, thanked our hostesses, and accepted a final round of congratulations as we made our way to the door. I opened it for Rienzi, who stepped outside and burst out laughing.

Someone—probably Jerry and his friend—had soaped the windows of the Hudson with the message, "Just engaged and wonderfully strange."

CHAPTER 47

SATURDAY AFTERNOON, WE MET MY BROTHERS, MAMA, AND Eddie in Darlene's kitchen. Mama still wore the soot-stained, ruby-red outfit—the only clothing she now owned—despite Darlene's repeated offers of one of her few dresses. Eddie had dried and dusted off his clothes; eyes clear, he looked dapper again with his tie knotted, hair combed, and gray fedora in hand. Meanwhile, Rienzi, my brothers, and I had all changed from our grubby duds into clean ones we'd packed: a plaid skirt and blouse for my fiancée and short-sleeved dress shirts and khakis for the MacLeod boys. No surprise, all three of us continued to have the same taste in clothes, except Jay's fit him better, as usual.

There were only the three mismatched chairs and a stool, so all the women sat, and the men pressured me to take the fourth seat as the "baby of the family." Jay, Chet, and Eddie leaned against the counter.

Darlene touched Mama's ring hand. "It's so exciting about you and Eddie getting hitched."

"Good thing for you he's part of the family now," she replied, "seeing as how you became a bootlegger overnight." She narrowed her eyes at our stepfather. "I might've took his name, but I'm real good at *withholding* things too. He'll look the other way if he knows what's good for him."

"Reva, I know exactly what's good for me." He sounded stone-cold sober again.

Darlene said, "Now, Mama, selling the Ashers' liquor will keep a roof over my head and food in the larder. I ain't gonna thank Roger and them for scaring off Wyatt, but I kinda like being on my own, with no man making me do this, that, and the other." She turned her attention my way. "Speaking of you, everybody tells me y'all had an even busier morning than Jay and Chet."

I took Rienzi's left hand, careful not to impale my palm on her jagged ring. "Yeah, and on top of everything else, we just got engaged."

Everybody started talking at once, and it took a few minutes to provide enough details to satisfy them. Darlene kissed Rienzi's cheek, Eddie shook our hands, and Jay and Chet teased us and ruffled my hair.

Mama stayed silent until we settled down. Her stare bore into me like Mrs. Bradley's rifle slug punching through the Oldsmobile seat cushions. "In all my livelong days, I never thought one of my children would go and marry a foreigner."

Rienzi rolled her eyes. Before she could speak, though, Eddie jumped in. "Now, Reva, she's as American as you are, born right here in the US of A. So what if her mother was Japanese?"

"But ain't Orientals just yellow nig—"

"Mama," I said, getting to my feet, a warning in my voice. "Didn't you once tell us your great-grandfather on your papa's side was a full-blooded Creek Indian?"

"I mighta done." She traced her thumbnail in the grain of the tabletop.

"So how'd you like somebody calling you names?"

"Hmm…well, I reckon we're all mutts of one kind or another. Lemme see that." She pulled Rienzi's left hand closer, studied the twisted paperclip, and shook her head at me. "Boy, I still say I done raised you better than this. You oughta know not to propose to a girl without a proper ring. I best not catch your brothers cheaping out like such. Here—" She tugged off her gold wedding band and held it out. "This ain't decent for getting engaged neither, but we sorta skipped that step."

I asked, "Did Rutha's finger come off with it?"

"Just some burnt skin. It cleaned up real nice. Y'all can return it after you give the girl something fitting."

Rienzi said, "Thank you, Mrs. Bascom, but I think I'll wear Roger's present. You won't find another one of these in the world—just like him."

She huffed and pushed her band back on. "You got you a strange one for sure, Roger."

"So I've heard. Speaking of Rutha and strange behavior, I've been meaning to ask: Why'd you keep goading her when she held that gun on you?"

"She was scared of me, and I wanted to make her even scareder. You could see it in her eyes. Well, her one good eye, thanks to your odd duck."

Rienzi touched my arm. "That's why she made Harvey lock me in the trunk, remember? Bullies recognize and fear strength."

"But the gun still coulda gone off by accident, Mama. It's like you have a death wish or something."

She shrugged. "We're all gonna die sooner or later."

"Come on, Reva," Eddie said. "No point keeping them in the dark any longer."

Mama peered at the tabletop. "Well, it could be that I'm going sooner instead of later."

Darlene squeaked, "What's that supposed to mean?"

"I'm dying, honey."

My sister started to cry, and my eyes teared up too. I'd pegged scarecrow-thin Harvey as having a wasting disease and worried about Mrs. Gladney's health as well. It had never occurred to me that Mama's scrawniness was anything but the result of the kind of poverty I scammed my way into the military to escape.

Whenever I talked about Mama or thought of her, she was fixed in my mind as a survivor, the last one standing, somehow eternal as she connived and clawed her way from one day to the next like a character from a Greek myth who staggered through an endless series of catastrophes but always overcame, forevermore: the Hardscrabble Goddess.

I could cheerfully go for a year without seeing her, but I always figured she would be there when scorn gave way to sentiment and I found myself missing her tenacity and gumption. But apparently grit wouldn't be enough to save her this time.

We all talked over each other again until Mama shouted, "Aye God, shut up." Once we quieted, she said, "We went to Columbus to see this doctor, a specialty type of sawbones. He said I got a cancer in my gut."

Rienzi asked, "Can't he operate?"

"Sure, he'd love to cut me open like a hog after first frost. But something about where it's at makes it hard to stop me from bleeding out while he's chopping away. Plus, it's already the size of a baseball—which is a good one on me 'cause Mance played the game. No matter what I do, I can't get shed of him."

I asked Eddie, mostly to make someone else hurt because, surprisingly, I hurt so much. "Did you marry her before or after the doctor gave her the news? What was it, love or pity?"

His steady gaze bore no malice. "Afterward, but I intended to regardless of the diagnosis. It's always been about love."

Shamefaced, I looked away. "Sorry, I was out of line."

"It's okay. I went through the same shock you're feeling. It's natural to lash out."

Darlene continued to weep, rocking in her chair. Mama rubbed her back. "It's gonna be okay, baby. I might got years left in me. The doc said so."

My sister wiped her eyes and sniffled. "You wanna do the bootlegging with me while you still got some vim and vigor?"

Mama nodded and smiled as the idea seemed to take hold. "Sure, honey. I'd love that. You and me, right up until the end." She looked at Eddie and asked, "You got anything to say against it, Mr. G-man?"

"I can see y'all now," he replied, "taking to the backroads on a moonless night, outrunning, outgunning, and outsmarting the goddamn revenuers."

They laughed together.

I hadn't heard Mama do that in years. It sounded natural, like Eddie made her laugh all the time. And maybe this was how Darlene's bootlegging venture would succeed as Posey had predicted: in ways she hadn't anticipated and couldn't previously imagine.

Chet clapped his hands once to get our attention. "I still got a question. Mama, you said you can't get shed of Papa no matter what you do. But didn't killing the sonofabitch make him go away for good?"

"No, since I didn't shoot him. Why won't anybody believe me?"

Eddie said, "I've always believed you."

"I don't mean somebody sweet on me. I mean my boys—who're supposed to love me just because. Why can't y'all trust my word?"

Jay blinked his wet eyes through a stream of cigarette smoke. "We were sorta glad to think you did—like you were getting revenge for the whole family. I especially thought you did it for yourself and me, seeing as how he tried to kill us both."

"Well, I'm sorry to disappoint you. Your mama ain't a murderer."

Rienzi said, "I'm sure it's nothing personal, Mrs. Bascom. In stories, the culprit is always the one with means, motive, and opportunity. You had all three, so Occam's razor applies."

Chet said, "I don't know who this Occam fella is, but a razor's more my style. She used a gun."

"Aye God, I didn't use anything on anybody."

Everybody started talking yet again except me.

What if those we thought were lying had been telling us the truth, and vice versa? And if Mama really didn't kill Papa, then who did? Jay's comment reminded me about his life insurance story and the big payday Harvey and Rutha were counting on. Maybe Papa had tried that scam again, and it literally backfired.

During a lull in the conversations around me, I said, "Mama, I'm not sure I can clear your name, but I might be able to at least get you something for your troubles." I glanced at Rienzi and then back to her. "If you want my help, that is."

"You helped plenty stopping those two peckerwoods—I couldn't have done it without you. Whatchu got in mind?"

"I need to question someone, and I'd like you and the rest of the family to come with me. All y'all got roles to play."

Eddie asked, "Who are we going to see?"

"Bonny Peterson at the sawmill store."

CHAPTER 48

IN THE SMALL GRAVEL LOT IN FRONT OF BONNY'S GROCERY, Jay and Chet parked the truck on one side of me and Rienzi. Darlene braked the Plymouth nearby with Mama and Eddie in the back seat.

The seven of us went in, single file and ladies first. Eddie closed the door behind us and planted himself there to block the exit and prevent others from entering. We fanned out, with Rienzi beside me, Jay and Mama to our right, and Chet and Darlene on our left. To my knowledge, Mama had never seen Bonny before. She brushed at the soot and grime that stained her ruby dress, squared her shoulders, and finger-combed her graying hair.

Bonny wasn't behind the cash register this time; she was rearranging cans on a nearby shelf. Dressed to the nines as before, this time she wore a silky pink-and-white number, with a skirt that ended above her knees, and two-inch heels. Gardenias once again perfumed her, and the waves and curls in her blonde bob looked like she'd spent all morning getting them just so.

"Hey there," she said. "Looks like you boys brought company this time. How can I help y'all?"

This was my idea, so I took the lead. "Ma'am, we promised to stop by again before our leave was up. We have a few more questions for you."

"Well, fire away, soldiers." She moved behind the counter, where she kept her cut-down shotgun.

"Papa's brother and sister, Harvey and Rutha, are in custody for a bunch of crimes."

"That's good news. From what you said, they weren't nice people."

"This is my sister, Darlene. They hurt her something awful, as you can see from the bruises on her face."

"Oh hon, that's terrible what they did to you. Can I get you some aspirin or something?"

"No thank you, ma'am." Darlene lifted her chin and looked down her nose at Bonny, the same proud way Nadine Asher had carried herself.

I took Rienzi's hand. "And this is my fiancée, Rienzi. They stuffed her in the trunk of a car and nearly got her shot."

Bonny made more sounds of distress and offered condolences.

"At the door is federal agent Ed Bascom. They almost blinded and drowned him in alcohol."

"That's just terrible."

"And to my right is my mother. She was threatened and terrorized repeatedly by those two, and her name has been dragged through the mud since Papa was murdered. Harvey and Rutha and everybody else blame her, but she didn't do it."

"I'm glad to hear that, but I still haven't heard any questions, Roger."

"Why did you lie about Papa not having two nickels to rub together when you met him?"

She placed a hand over her chest. "That wasn't a lie. I don't believe he did."

"He had a 1942 Chrysler Royal sedan, bought just after he was released from prison. He drove past me and Chet back then while we were near freezing to death. Papa was wearing a coat and gloves when he tooted his horn and waved at us."

"He told me he won the car on a bet about who could hit a baseball the longest."

Chet snapped, "But how'd he pay for gas—or the fancy duds?"

"I honestly don't know."

Jay said, "Speaking of honesty, Harvey and Rutha bragged to Roger here that you let them prowl both the office where Papa was murdered and y'all's house to convince them there were no piles of cash lying around. But you told us you'd never seen them."

"They did all those terrible things Roger just named, so I can't imagine why you're willing to take their word over mine."

I hollered, "Who did you get to dig up Papa's body?"

Chet pointed at her. "What did they do with it?"

Jay and the others began shouting charges at her. Darlene's cry of "Why do you hate us?" echoed above the rest and seemed to rattle the windowpanes.

Bonny could've kept lying her way out of our barrage—after all, we didn't have any proof—but the crossfire of questions and the weight of our accusations seemed to get to her. She brought out the shotgun from under the counter and tracked it back and forth. As I feared would happen, I was staring down the wrong end of yet another firearm.

Breaking from our script, Rienzi stepped forward. "You can't shoot your way out of *this* problem, ma'am. There are too many of us, spread too far apart."

"But you're willing to be the first to die?"

My fiancée shrugged. "A few of us will reach you before you can reload, and what follows will be drawn out and very painful for you. It can only end one way."

Bonny shook her head. "I'm not confessing to a thing—not that I've done anything to confess to. Now y'all get out."

Eddie cleared his throat. "Actually, you're not only threating me, a federal lawman, but Jay and Chet were deputized by Sheriff Reeder, so you've got local trouble too."

“Go ahead and take me to jail. I have a lawyer. Y’all don’t frighten me.”

I’d expected that if our flood of accusations didn’t break her, the notion of being arrested would, but she was as tough in her way as Papa had been. We were on the verge of having to admit defeat. Unless I came up with something, we’d leave with no answers and nothing to help Mama.

I tried to imagine what would actually scare the woman. It turned my stomach that I knew the answer. With so much pain inflicted on me in my childhood, I understood what kind of threats cut to the bone. “The thing is,” I told her, “you won’t be going to jail. We don’t have time for a trial and such. You’re just gonna disappear.” I snapped my fingers as Rienzi stared at me. “You’ll never see your son again. No chance to say goodbye to him. The MacLeod boys will be the last ones you’ll ever set eyes on.”

“That’s right,” Chet said, not missing a beat as I changed what we’d rehearsed. He cracked his knuckles and gave her a bloodthirsty leer, while Jay remained silent but set his jaw in a grim line, a soldier ready to charge.

Though they were poised for action, I could tell they waited for me to give the command. Somehow I’d gone from being the baby of the family, always the lowest rank, to the one issuing orders.

Was I capable of carrying them out myself? I realized I could if I had to. Without hesitation. Maybe I took after Papa more than I still wanted to admit.

The barrel of her shotgun wavered as trembling wracked her body. “You’re goddamn savages,” she cried. “All of you.”

Eyes wide, Rienzi looked like she agreed. I reached for her, but she backed away.

That broke the spell. I was even sorrier for scaring her than Bonny. Ashamed by what I was capable of.

Addressing both of them, I softened my voice, coming all the way back to myself. "We don't wanna be savages, but time's almost up, and my brothers and I can't leave our family in a lurch."

Jay and Chet blinked at me and each other, maybe realizing how close they'd also been to becoming the thing we'd spent our whole lives trying to escape.

I held my hands out to Bonny. "You didn't wanna kill him, but you had to, right?"

She rested the shotgun on the counter and whispered, "Yes."

"What's done is done. All we wanna know is why. Did he take out an insurance policy on you, so shooting him was self-defense?"

Bonny frowned. "What? I don't know a thing about any insurance."

Mama said, "Enough of this. He gave me plenty of reasons to end him, but I didn't. What reason did he give you?"

Bonny considered us fanned out in a wide semicircle and sighed. She returned her weapon to its hiding place under the counter. "The sawmill, my lumber company. When I married Mance, I had to sign it over to him. Then I discovered that he planned to sell it and skedaddle with the proceeds. He was going to cheat me and my son out of everything my first husband and I built together. I couldn't let him get away with it."

Mama folded her arms. "So you shot him and started the rumor I done it."

"I didn't have to gossip—everybody assumed it was you. Like you said, you had plenty of reasons, and folks around here seem to know them all."

Chet said, "We went to visit his grave in Eldorendo and found it dug up and his coffin missing. Who did that?"

"A couple of hired hands. Not too bright but as loyal as the day is long. They were supposed to fill the grave back in so nobody would be the wiser." She shook her head. "Something must've spooked them, and they left the job half-done."

"But why steal his body in the first place?" Darlene asked.

"He didn't deserve to lie in consecrated ground, hon. My men burned him up in his casket and scattered the bones and all in the woods, just like he bragged about doing to his father and uncle."

I couldn't say I objected to that. It was easy to imagine Jay, Chet, and me doing the same to the sonofabitch. "We wanna do a deal."

Bonny's gaze shifted from me to my brothers and back. "What kind of deal?"

"Harvey and Rutha said that Papa planned to give them two thousand dollars—I reckon from the sale of your company. You saved it by killing him, so two thousand seems like a fair starting point."

She frowned. "'Starting point.' Which means there's more?"

"You put us all through hell because you didn't fess up. And there's a price to be paid for that, especially if you're going to let folks continue to think our mother did the deed."

"So, you're not only savages but common blackmailers, same as Harvey and Rutha."

Eddie said, "No, we're accessories to murder after the fact, seeing as how we're going to let you skate instead of watch you hang—or make you vanish. Surely that's worth something to you."

"How much?"

I turned to Mama, curious about whether she'd go with the hundred-dollar-per-month figure she cited when we were hatching the scheme I was trying to get back on track or if she'd feel sorry for another woman Papa wronged. "Name your price. It's your reputation being sullied."

"*Sullied?* You're starting to sound fancy, like that fiancée of yours. My price is two hundred dollars a month for the rest of my life."

"You mean to say that if I pass away before you," Bonny said, "you're going after my son's inheritance?"

"It'll be really bad luck if something happens to you before my cancer gets me. You might only have to pay out a few hundred. At most a few thousand. A bargain either way to keep from getting dead."

Bonny chewed her lip and clicked her pink-painted nails on the counter. "What guarantee do I have that the sheriff or some federal marshal won't show up after all?"

I said, "Like Eddie just told you, we're now accessories to your crime. You can rat us out if we tattle, but that won't happen. You're worth much more alive—and free."

She glared at us one by one, ending with me, the spokesman. "I don't suppose you'll take a check?"

"Cash on the barrelhead, please and thank you. Two thousand plus Mama's first two hundred."

"What if I told you the same as I told Mance's loathsome brother and sister: I don't have any piles of cash lying around."

"Then I'd say you're not as good at business as you claim to be. A go-getter like you would have something set aside for a rainy day."

As she appeared to hesitate, I decided she needed one more push. "Take the deal and you'll have lots of time to make plenty more money and leave your son a tidy fortune. But if you disappear today, think of everything *he'll* lose."

She gave each of us another glance and then nodded. "At my house, there's a library with money tucked inside most of the books. When Harvey and Rutha went in there, they looked for secret doors and hidden safes but didn't crack a single cover. Dumb people always discount the value of reading."

Hanging her head, she said, "I'll call for my car."

CHAPTER 49

DURING THE DRIVE BACK TO DARLENE'S, RIENZI AND I BROUGHT up the rear of the MacLeod convoy. She cut her eyes at me as she steered. "Those threats you came up with—killing Bonny and hiding her body somewhere—was that just an improvisation, or did you intend to do that to her?"

"You were the one who told her that the folks she didn't shoot would tear her to pieces. Did you mean what you said?"

"I was merely giving her my hypothesis, predicting the likely outcome from her intended course of action. And you're changing the subject."

"But if she started shooting and you survived, would you have attacked her?"

"I would've disarmed her."

"And, just for the sake of hypothesis-ing, what if you saw that one of her shots killed me?"

She tapped the steering wheel with her thumbs. "I'll allow it's within the realm of possibility that I would've avenged you. Now let's address your threatening remarks."

"The truth is, I wanna think I was just trying to sway her, but I also know how desperate I felt. Willing to do whatever I had to."

"Killing her wouldn't have fixed anything."

"It wouldn't have gotten Mama and Darlene any money, but, to use your words, it would've avenged them at least." I hung my head as Bonny had. "It's awful to think I'm capable of doing everything Papa and Harvey and Rutha did. Or even worse."

"Capable of violence maybe, but the Roger I know would never hurt innocent people."

"It broke my heart, frightening you back there when I was trying to put the scare into Bonny."

She squeezed my hand. "It's a credit to you that you noticed—that you care."

"But I still feel like I need to make this up to you in a big way."

"Maybe I'll let you."

We all enjoyed a rare moment of celebration on Saturday evening. Rienzi and I raided Mama's smokehouse; Darlene, Jay, and Chet dug sweet potatoes and cut collard greens from her winter garden; and Mama directed Eddie about what to pull from Darlene's icebox while she commandeered the stove and skillet.

Despite our festive mood, we rushed through our meal. My brothers had taken turns using Wyatt's razor beforehand and kept finger-combing their hair while they stood and ate at the counter. Meanwhile, Mama and Eddie repeatedly eyed each other and smiled, and Rienzi and I played footsie the whole time. I suspected that everybody but Darlene had romance on their minds.

Out front, we split up with a promise to gather again on Sunday morning before the longer-lasting separation that would take us to different parts of the nation. And with three of us in the military, maybe around the world. Chet said he'd drop Jay off at the Turner home, where Geneva was waiting, before driving into Colquitt to pitch in at Dora's. No doubt, he hoped to make time with Trudy afterward, away from prying eyes.

Mama hijacked Darlene's Plymouth so she and Eddie could go to his house in Baker County. The newlyweds talked about getting a nice new car and taking some road trips now that money wasn't the issue—but the relentless march of time was. After that, she would help Darlene run moonshine and have a grand old final adventure. Perhaps go out in a blaze of glory.

After everyone else drove off, I leaned against the Hudson with Rienzi, saying to my sister, "Thanks again for sharing your windfall with everybody."

"If it weren't for all y'all, I wouldn't have a cent to my name or any kind of a future."

"But you *would* have a husband. I can't say sorry enough about that."

"We both know my marriage was doomed. If you boys hadn't run Wyatt off, I woulda done it sometime or other. Anyway, I'm through with men…though that Seth Asher is awful dashing."

I grinned at her, wondering when she'd claim Husband Number Six. "Whatchu gonna do with your night?"

"Figure out hiding places for my money. That Bonny had a book for every dollar to her name, but I ain't got a single one in the house. I'm fixing to build a new place with a library."

Rienzi said, "Well, we're going to tool around, maybe stop off somewhere for a late-night snack. Don't wait up." She opened the driver's door and slid behind the steering wheel.

"Okay, you two lovebirds. I had my fill of all that and then some, but y'all go get it outta your system."

We wished her a good night and made a beeline for Mama's barn.

CHAPTER 50

On Sunday morning, I woke earlier than Rienzi, as before, and left the barn to take in the crisp winter air and the flat green and brown landscape under a wide, robin's-egg sky. I'd spent so much of my life trying to escape this little piece of Georgia, but now I knew I would miss it. The best memories from my childhood carried with them the coppery smell of the creeks, the coolness of the forest floor under my bare feet, the bright sweetness of a ripe sugarcane stalk.

Thinking about those details distracted me from how much this place had changed and how many more changes were to come. In time, it would be all but unrecognizable, and the special people I grew up around, from Wanda to Posey, would be gone.

Except for another brief reunion for Mama's inevitable funeral, my brothers weren't likely to return again except to spend time with their girlfriends. And maybe to whisk them away one day—though where Chet and Trudy could go and not create a scandal was a mystery. Maybe someplace like Paris? Imagining Chet at an outdoor café, nibbling a croissant with a beret perched on his head, made me laugh out loud.

"What's so funny?" Rienzi came up from behind and wrapped her arms around me.

I described the picture in my mind. We continued to build on the imagery: Trudy playing an accordion and quoting Jean-Paul Sartre while Chet did a mime act with their performing monkey. The idea left us lying helpless in a giggling heap on the tack room floor.

Staring at the rafters and underside of the tin roof, I caught my breath and said, "I'm gonna miss Colquitt something awful. With all that happened to me growing up, I never expected to feel like this. But the best times of my life have been here too—mostly with my brothers and with you."

She tapped my forehead. "Whenever you want to go home, you can just think about it, and you'll be back here."

"But what if I can't remember the way things smelled and sounded and tasted and all?"

"Then you'll make up the details, and they'll become just as real as the forgotten facts."

"Will you mind if I sometimes ask you to describe things and people exactly as they were, instead of some cobbled-together version in my head?"

"I'll be happy to. In return, if I'm trapped in a bad memory and can't stop thinking about it, will you help me make a beautiful new one?"

"Of course. Do you wanna practice, my bride-to-be?"

"I do."

We arrived at Darlene's after everybody else. They teased us about getting an early start on our marriage, but mercifully without any of the ugly scorn Rienzi had feared. Maybe with the week we'd endured, even a family as rambunctious as mine was willing to cut us some slack.

As we chatted with each other, I pretended my brain was a movie camera filming my family before events, illness, and the simple passage of time stole all of them from me. I'd never be able to match Rienzi's recall, but maybe I could capture some key images.

Darlene, with her face still healing but smiling broadly enough to show the gaps where two teeth should've been. Now she had the money to give herself a beautiful smile again and an unexpected business that would present her with danger, adventure, and challenge in equal measures.

Jay, the war veteran, inventor, and lover of life, smoking a Lucky Strike as he described five different ways for our sister to conceal money in a shoe, each new idea more ingenious than the last. Unable to fix our shattered childhoods, he now managed to create something special wherever he went.

Chet, a berserker but also a fighter for freedom—including the freedom to love who he wanted to, traditions and cultures be damned. If his pent-up rage could find a productive outlet, the world would never be the same.

Eddie, Papa's dogged pursuer who fell for his opponent's ex-wife. His commitment to show our mother the time of her life in the short span she had left made me wish I'd treated this worthy man with respect rather than suspicion from the get-go.

And Mama, the last one standing on the field of battle and the first of us destined to depart that field. In a few months or a few years, the woman who had given me and my brothers away when we were younger would bring us all back together one last time—though she would only be there in spirit.

Watch the film of this day, I told myself. *Do it often so you don't forget how happy and sad you are.*

"What are you thinking?" Rienzi asked.

"I'm thinking you're right. Home is only a memory away."

Before Rienzi and I gave my brothers a lift to the bus station, we said our farewells to Darlene and Eddie. Then, Chet and I followed Jay's lead, in birth order, as each of us gave Mama a kiss on the cheek and held her for a long moment.

Forgiveness, regret, and love filled me as she and I rocked in place together: the proper way for a son to say goodbye to his mother.

Author's Note

Reviews, as much as sales, are the lifeblood of books: five-star reviews from readers create instant credibility and give those unfamiliar with an author's work the confidence that they're investing their money in a sure thing. The new fan might then post a favorable review, too, which could encourage someone else to buy the book, and so it goes. If you would be willing to post an honest review of *Return to Hardscrabble Road* wherever you shop for books online—or on Goodreads—and send a screenshot of your review (or the link to it) to me at GeorgeWeinstein@gmail.com, I will send you a brand-new *Hardscrabble* short story featuring Roger MacLeod and some of the characters who made these books so satisfying to write.

Speaking of sequels: though I'm a big fan of them when I read for pleasure (spending time with Longmire, Millhone, Reacher, Plum, Bosch, and many others), I once swore I'd never write one, despite many fans of *Hardscrabble Road* wanting to know what happened after the final page. Did Mama really shoot Papa? Do Roger and Rienzi grow even closer? What happened to Jay, Chet, Darlene, Nat, Wanda, and the others?

During book club talks, I would tell the stories behind the story—the real people who inspired much of the cast of *Hardscrabble Road*—and separate the facts from the fiction. However, it was the characters who populated my novel, not the actual folk, who captured readers' imaginations. They wanted more of their adventures, regardless of whether those exploits were made up.

Still, my mind was elsewhere. After having success with my small-town murder mystery *Aftermath* and the kidnapping thriller *Watch What You Say*, I wanted to turn my attention back to the historical fiction of my earlier novels (*Hardscrabble* and *The Five Destinies of Carlos Moreno*) but go in a new direction. I delved into some research about post-Revolutionary War America and the declining age of piracy and started a vague outline of a novel.

As I was doing that, though, emails continued to come in from fans who loved *Hardscrabble Road* and wanted to know if there would be a sequel. Royalty checks from my publisher further confirmed that the book remains popular: it continues to outsell all my other ones combined and probably will always do so. Plus, I really did miss Roger, Rienzi, and the other characters who made *Hardscrabble Road* memorable. I decided to set aside the post-colonial historical novel and honor the choice of many of my readers.

I'd like to tell you my *Hardscrabble* sequel came forth effortlessly as a fully formed and complete work over the course of a few weeks. Instead, I'd barely made a start of it when my first wife, Kate (to whom I'd dedicated all my books up to that point), decided she was no longer the person she'd been all her life. Gender, presentation, and finally even whether she wanted to exist anymore were up in the air. Being supportive wasn't enough to keep us together…or keep her alive. Amidst all that, writing suddenly held no allure. Precious little did.

But I'm here to testify that new love in middle age can be sweeter, mellower, and even more fulfilling. I've been friends with Kim Conrey for a dozen years thanks to the Atlanta Writers Club. When our marriages were dissolving simultaneously, we found even more to talk about than usual and discovered we had more in common than either of us could've imagined. Falling in love with this wickedly smart and funny, gorgeous woman—who is a dazzling good writer to boot (check out her science fiction romance debut *Stealing Ares*)—was the easiest thing I've ever done.

Kim not only inspired me to love again but also got me to return to writing in earnest. I paced *Return to Hardscrabble Road* like a thriller, with a physical or an emotional cliffhanger at the end of nearly every chapter. The tight prose and harrowing situations were balanced with more humor than I managed in the first book. While it's not intended to be a comic novel, many early readers have told me how much they found witty and joyous in these pages versus the doom and gloom of much of the first book. I also didn't strive as hard to achieve beautifully crafted phrases, clever metaphors, and other literary hallmarks at every turn, preferring instead to focus on emotional honesty, visceral details, and muscular verbs to put you in every scene and hold you there like the safety bar on a roller coaster.

While *Hardscrabble Road* was about 80 percent true and 20 percent made-up, I decided the sequel would need to have the opposite ratio, because the real-life people who inspired many of the characters went on to lead mercifully ordinary lives all around the South. They didn't all come together for more hell-raising escapades, but that's the joy of writing novels instead of biographies. I'll be happy to sort fact from fiction again for the book clubs to which I hope to be invited for an in-person or virtual talk (please write to me via GeorgeWeinstein@gmail.com with your invitation).

To turn this book from a postponed fantasy into a published work, I owe my biggest thanks to Kim, who used inspiration and persuasion in equal measure and removed obstacles so I could write and rewrite. The reason we're friends in the first place is that she's also part of the best critique group around, at Scooter's in Roswell, Georgia: a group of writers whose mission is to take any manuscript and make it better. They do, and I'm thusly grateful to Chuck, Kathy, Patrick, Gaby, Dan, and the rest. Thanks also goes to my publisher, SFK Press, for creating the beautiful books I'm proud to display and promote.

Will there be a sequel to my sequel? I know now to never say never. I enjoyed writing about established characters so much more than I thought that I am now pursuing an *Aftermath/ Watch What You Say* sequel. I'll be teaming Janet Wright with Bo Riccardi and sending them on a *Thelma and Louise* sort of adventure. And who knows? Maybe Roger will make a cameo in it. He would be in his early nineties if he does show up, but I know some energetic nonagenarians who'd make excellent role models. Ed, I'm thinking about you!

—George Weinstein
Marietta, Georgia
July 2022

About the Author

George Weinstein is the author of the beloved Southern Gothic historical novel *Hardscrabble Road*; its sequel, *Return to Hardscrabble Road*; a novel of forgotten US history, *The Five Destinies of Carlos Moreno*; women's fiction about reinvention titled *The Caretaker*; the sassy, small-town, amateur-sleuth murder mystery *Aftermath*; and a kidnapping thriller with a dude in distress and a chromesthetic damsel riding to his rescue, *Watch What You Say*, among other works. His website is GeorgeWeinstein.com, and he can be found on Facebook (@george.weinstein.5), Instagram (@georgeweinsteinga), and TikTok (@georgeweinstein).

George is also the executive director of the Atlanta Writers Club (AtlantaWritersClub.org) and has helped thousands of writers on their quest for publication through the club and its twice-yearly Atlanta Writers Conference (AtlantaWritersConference.com), which he has managed since its creation in 2008.

Share Your Thoughts

Want to help make *Return to Hardscrabble Road* a bestselling novel? Consider leaving an honest review of this book on Goodreads, on your personal author website or blog, and anywhere else readers go for recommendations. It's our priority at SFK Press to publish books for readers to enjoy, and our authors appreciate and value your feedback.

Our Southern Fried Guarantee

If you wouldn't enthusiastically recommend one of our books with a 4- or 5-star rating to a friend, then the next story is on us. We believe that much in the stories we're telling. Simply email us at pr@sfkmultimedia.com.

CPSIA information can be obtained
at www.ICGtesting.com
Printed in the USA
BVHW070728061022
648779BV00002B/13